# MURDER ON
# TRINITY PLACE

Center Point
Large Print

Also by Victoria Thompson and available from
Center Point Large Print:

*City of Lies*
*Murder in Murray Hill*
*Murder in Morningside Heights*
*Murder in the Bowery*
*Murder on Amsterdam Avenue*
*Murder on St. Nicholas Avenue*

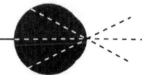

**This Large Print Book carries the
Seal of Approval of N.A.V.H.**

# MURDER
## ON TRINITY PLACE

### A Gaslight Mystery

Victoria Thompson

CENTER POINT LARGE PRINT
THORNDIKE, MAINE

This Center Point Large Print edition
is published in the year 2019 by arrangement with
Berkley, an imprint of Penguin Publishing Group,
a division of Penguin Random House LLC.

The text of this Large Print edition is unabridged.
In other aspects, this book may vary
from the original edition.
Printed in the United States of America
on permanent paper.
Set in 16-point Times New Roman type.

ISBN: 978-1-64358-232-0

Library of Congress Cataloging-in-Publication Data

Names: Thompson, Victoria (Victoria E.) author.
Title: Murder on trinity place / Victoria Thompson.
Description: Center Point Large Print edition. | Thorndike, Maine :
    Center Point Large Print, 2019. | Series: A gaslight mystery
Identifiers: LCCN 2019012498 | ISBN 9781643582320
    (hardcover : alk. paper)
Subjects: LCSH: Large type books.
Classification: LCC PS3570.H6442 M8787 2019 | DDC 813/.54—dc23
LC record available at https://lccn.loc.gov/2019012498

To my dear friend and fellow author, Susanna Calkins, for giving me the idea for this book.

# I

"All he ever talks about is milk."

"Milk?" Sarah Malloy echoed. "Oh, because he owns a dairy, I suppose."

Mrs. Ellsworth nodded. Sarah's neighbor had dropped in on the day after Christmas to invite Sarah and her husband, Frank, to dine with the Ellsworth family and her son's new in-laws. But she had also felt compelled to warn them about the new bride's father, Clarence Pritchard, and his tendency to talk about his work.

"I suppose that's only natural," Sarah said. "He's rather successful, isn't he?"

"Oh yes, which I'm sure he'll mention. Oh my, I hope I haven't talked you out of coming. I'm anxious for you to know Mrs. Pritchard better. She's such a lovely person, which is probably why Theda is such a delightful girl. But Mr. Pritchard can be a bit of a bore, I'm afraid."

"I'm sure we'll manage. Malloy can always launch into a tale about his adventures in the police department if it's truly an emergency."

"Or perhaps he could tell us about his new life as a private detective. I would be forever grateful. And Mrs. Malloy is also invited, although when I spoke to her about it yesterday, she said she'd

7

be needed to watch the children if I also invited Maeve."

Sarah smiled at that. Mrs. Malloy and Mrs. Ellsworth had become good friends, as unlikely as Sarah had thought it when her mother-in-law had come to live here. But Mother Malloy would never feel comfortable at a formal dinner party, even at her friend's house. "Were you going to invite Maeve?"

"I was considering it. I've invited Harvey, too, and I thought he might like having a pretty girl to talk to."

Sarah's nanny was certainly a pretty girl. "Harvey? That's Theda's brother, isn't it?"

"Yes, I'm sure you met him last month at the wedding."

Ah yes, the sullen young man who had drunk too much and passed out. "I'm sure Maeve will be thrilled to be included, but won't the Pritchards think it odd you invited our nanny to a social event?"

"I'll tell them she's Catherine's governess."

"Do people still have governesses?" Sarah asked in amusement.

"I'm sure they do somewhere. The Pritchards won't know, and they'll be too polite to ask."

They chatted for a few minutes about the arrangements. Then Mrs. Ellsworth said, "I don't suppose Mr. Malloy would be willing to do our first step this New Year's."

"You mean to be the first man to step over your threshold after midnight to bring you luck?" Mrs. Ellsworth was notoriously superstitious. "Doesn't Nelson usually do it?"

"Yes, but I thought it would be fun to have someone else do it this time. We just need a dark-haired man to come in with a lump of coal and a few coins right after midnight to ensure us a prosperous 1900."

"I'm sure Malloy would love to do it," Sarah lied, easily picturing how he'd roll his eyes if asked to participate in one of Mrs. Ellsworth's superstitions, "but we'll be going down to Trinity Church to hear the bells ring in the New Year, and I'm not sure when we'll get back."

Mrs. Ellsworth brightened at that. "I suppose you'll be driving down in your new motorcar."

"Yes. Gino will drive it, of course. He's got it running perfectly, which I understand is quite a challenge." Malloy's partner had taken quite an active interest in the motorcar and its inner workings, which was fortunate because Malloy had no interest whatever.

"Oh yes, those machines are quite unreliable or so I've heard. I don't know why anyone would bother with them if they could have a horse. But if Mr. Donatelli is with you, I guess he won't be available to do the first step either."

"Could Mr. Pritchard do it? Or Harvey?"

"Oh no. They're both too fair, even if they'd

agree. The first stepper must have dark hair, and I have a feeling neither of them would take it seriously in any case, especially Harvey."

Sarah had to agree, but she chose tact instead. "Young men often don't take much of anything seriously."

"Yes, and Harvey is a bit spoiled, I fear. As for Mr. Pritchard, just between us, he isn't the easiest man to tolerate, either. When he gets started on the subject of milk, well, you can just see from her expression that Mrs. Pritchard would like to murder him."

"I would only do this for Mrs. Ellsworth," Malloy said as he crossed the street with Maeve and Sarah to their neighbor's house that Friday evening. Sarah laid her head on his shoulder in silent thanks as they walked arm in arm.

"I'm sure Mrs. Ellsworth would be gratified by your devotion," Maeve said with a smirk. She'd dressed with particular care this evening, but Sarah couldn't imagine she wanted to impress Harvey Pritchard. No, Maeve would have a deeper plan.

"I'm just repaying a few debts," Malloy insisted. "Mrs. Ellsworth has helped us with a case or two."

"And she saved my life once, which I'll never forget," Sarah said. "So that explains why Malloy and I are here, but why are you going, Maeve?"

"Just to be neighborly." Maeve smiled as if

butter wouldn't melt in her mouth, but Sarah wasn't fooled.

"You don't have your cap set for Harvey Pritchard, do you?" Sarah asked in mock horror.

"Not likely." Maeve had attended the wedding, too.

Sarah needed another minute to finally figure it out. "You told Gino you'd been invited, didn't you?" Sarah and Malloy had often discussed his partner's infatuation with Maeve and her apparent enjoyment in tormenting him.

"I may have mentioned it."

"Poor Gino," Malloy muttered. Sarah had to agree. She had an idea that Maeve's account of the coming evening would include marked attentions to her from Harvey Pritchard, whether such attentions actually occurred or were even welcome.

They had reached the Ellsworths' house, and Maeve preceded them up the porch steps to ring the bell.

Nelson Ellsworth answered the door and welcomed them. The Ellsworths didn't have live-in servants, just a daily maid who was probably busy helping Mrs. Ellsworth with the dinner. "Mother and Theda are finishing up in the kitchen," he said when he'd taken their coats. He escorted them to the parlor, where the other guests were gathered. "I believe you know my in-laws, Mr. and Mrs. Pritchard, and their son, Harvey." The Pritchards were seated on the sofa,

11

and Harvey lounged beside the fireplace, his arm draped in what he probably imagined was a debonair pose on the mantelpiece. "And Mr. Donatelli, of course."

Mr. Pritchard was slow to rise at the entrance of the ladies, but Gino jumped up immediately, smiling a little too smugly. Sarah glanced over just in time to catch Maeve's astonished expression before she recovered herself.

"Gino," Sarah said quickly. "How nice to see you." *And what a surprise,* although she didn't say that.

"Yes," Maeve said through almost-gritted teeth. "You didn't mention you would be here."

Gino shrugged inside the tailor-made suit Malloy had insisted he get when they started their detective agency. "I hadn't been invited yet."

"Mr. and Mrs. Malloy," Mrs. Ellsworth greeted them as she entered the room. She was still smoothing her black bombazine gown, probably having just removed her apron. "How good of you to come. And Maeve, so nice to see you."

When they'd greeted her in return, she turned back to Maeve. "When Mr. Donatelli called on us the other day, Theda and I were telling him about giving our first dinner party. When he asked who was going to be my dinner partner, I realized I had an odd number of guests and invited him to join us. Nelson, get our guests some sherry to warm them up."

Gino smiled with apparent innocence at Maeve, who wasn't fooled for a moment.

Sarah and Malloy left them to it and went over to greet the Pritchards. Mrs. Pritchard was an attractive woman who had certainly been a beauty twenty years ago and now, at forty, would still turn a few heads. She smiled and returned Sarah's greeting, although the smile didn't quite reach her eyes. She seemed rather tense, too, which was odd since she was attending what amounted to a family dinner. "Clarence, you remember Mr. and Mrs. Malloy," Mrs. Pritchard said to her husband in a tone that reminded Sarah of the way she spoke to her children when reminding them of their manners.

"Of course I do," he snapped. "Met you at the wedding, I think." He was a tall, angular man who reminded Sarah of a stork, with his beaklike nose and gangly limbs. He shook Malloy's hand and nodded to Sarah. He didn't meet her eye, though, and she didn't think he'd looked directly at Malloy either. If Mrs. Pritchard seemed tense, Mr. Pritchard was downright rigid, and his gaze kept darting around the room, as if he expected something untoward to appear.

When they'd all seated themselves and Nelson had served them some sherry, Sarah tried to make small talk with the Pritchards while still keeping an eye on Maeve and Gino, who had joined Harvey at the fireplace. Maeve appeared determined to make the best of the situation and at least get Harvey to speak to her, while Gino seemed content merely to admire her efforts. Completely oblivious, Harvey drained his sherry glass and signaled Nelson for more.

Mrs. Pritchard dutifully answered Sarah's questions about her health and how nice their Christmas celebration had been, but she kept glancing at her husband anxiously. Was she afraid? Yes, that was fear in her eyes, but why should she be afraid?

Before Sarah could figure it out, Theda appeared and greeted her guests. She was a sweet girl who had inherited only a hint of her mother's good looks, but Nelson was smart enough to see her inner beauty. The adoring look he gave her said that marriage had only deepened his feelings for her.

After the obligatory welcome, Theda invited everyone to come to the dining room. The table had been set with Mrs. Ellsworth's best china and silver and a centerpiece of holly and pinecones. Everything sparkled in the gaslight.

Theda directed everyone to their places. Nelson sat at the head of the table and Mrs. Ellsworth had given her daughter-in-law the place of honor at the foot. Theda's mother sat at Nelson's right and Sarah at his left. Theda's father sat at Theda's right and Malloy at her left. Mrs. Ellsworth was beside Malloy, with Gino between her and Mrs.

14

Pritchard. Harvey was between Sarah and Maeve on the other side of the table. If Gino resented being seated between two older females, he gave no sign of it. Instead, he set himself to being as charming as possible to both of them. If only Harvey had exerted himself half as much, Maeve could have succeeded in her plan to make Gino jealous, but he concentrated on eating and emptying his wineglass as often as possible. The poor maid could hardly keep up, between serving each course and refilling his glass.

They were waiting for dessert to be served when Sarah realized Mr. Pritchard hadn't mentioned milk once the entire evening. In fact, he had hardly spoken at all. Theda had tried to include him in her conversation with Malloy, but he'd been almost as single-minded about his dinner as his son, responding only sporadically.

Mrs. Ellsworth had been smiling at one of Gino's remarks when she suddenly said, "You are such a delightfully dark young man. If only you weren't going to Trinity Church on New Year's Eve, you could be our first stepper."

Mr. Pritchard's head jerked up. "Trinity Church, you say? I don't suppose they're holding a proper celebration there."

For some reason this made Mrs. Pritchard gasp and Harvey mutter something that might have been a curse, but Sarah appeared to be the only one who noticed their reactions.

15

"They're holding the same celebration they've been doing for the past fifty years, I believe," Malloy said across the table. "They have a church service and play a few songs on the bells. They've got quite a set of them there, as I'm sure you know. Ring out the old and ring in the new, as they say."

"But nothing special? Nothing to acknowledge the new century?" Pritchard demanded.

"Oh dear," Mrs. Pritchard murmured.

"I believe we're celebrating the start of the twentieth century *next* year," Malloy said, a little puzzled. "At least that's what I read in the newspapers."

"Newspapers? Bah, what do they know?"

"Yes, what do they know?" Theda agreed too quickly and too cheerfully. "Mother Ellsworth has made the most scrumptious apple tart for dessert. I can't think why it's taking so long to bring it in."

"Can you imagine saying the twentieth century doesn't start with the year 1900?" Pritchard said, clearly angry about this for some reason. "Our years have started with an eighteen for the entire nineteenth century. Any fool can see that when it changes to a nineteen, it's the start of the new century."

"That's certainly reasonable," Theda said with a desperate glance in Nelson's direction.

"Yes, it is," he said quickly, if a little uncertainly.

16

"But time didn't start with the year zero," Maeve said.

Everyone turned to her in surprise, especially Mr. Pritchard.

"Well, it didn't," she said defensively. "Time must have started with the year one."

"What does that have to do with anything?" Gino asked, clearly amused.

She glared at him. "If the first year was one and a century is one hundred years, the century ends at the end of year one hundred, not year ninety-nine."

Which was the argument Sarah had been reading about in the newspapers for months as the end of 1899 approached.

"Very logical, young lady," Pritchard said scornfully, "but there is no logic to when time began. The Gregorian calendar, which we use today and by which we determine that this is the year of our Lord 1899, didn't come into use until 1582, not *year one*. There never was a year one, not even with the Julian calendar, which came into use in our year 46 BC. Before that, the Romans didn't measure time by our calendars or even recognize the concept of BC, so to them it was the year 708 *ab urbe condita*, which is a year-numbering system used by some ancient Roman historians, although it was never actually used by the Romans themselves, who didn't number their years at all but referred to them by the names of the rulers in power at the time."

Pritchard let his very satisfied gaze touch everyone around the table, and for a long moment, no one could think of a single thing to say in response to his lecture.

Finally, Malloy said, "So there was no year one?"

"Never. Not ever. So we can count time the way it should be counted, and the year of 1900 should be the first year of the twentieth century."

"Clarence, let's remember we are guests here," Mrs. Pritchard said a little sharply.

"Nonsense. Theda is our daughter. Besides, I'm sure these people are glad to know the truth instead of that garbage the newspapers are publishing. Something must be done. We only have two days left."

"What do you propose we do?" Gino asked with apparent seriousness that didn't fool Sarah at all.

Sarah glared at him this time, and Mrs. Pritchard made a small sound of distress, but he ignored them both.

"We must spread the word," Pritchard said. "We must tell everyone. This is an outrage. The new century must be welcomed with ceremony."

Theda had gone pale, Mrs. Pritchard looked as if she really might want to murder her husband, and Harvey had once again drained his wineglass. Before anyone could speak, however, the maid carried in the tray of desserts.

"The tarts are here," Theda cried with relief. "Mother Ellsworth made them. Did I tell you? They're so delicious."

As the maid served the tarts, Mrs. Ellsworth managed to catch Sarah's eye and send her a silent plea for help. Sarah wasn't certain what she could do, but after racking her brain, she took advantage of the momentary distraction of the sweet treat to say, "Mr. Pritchard, do you pasteurize the milk at your dairy?"

Harvey's expression when he turned to her was pure astonishment, and she could feel the wave of dismay from the others, but Pritchard leaned forward so he could see her past Maeve and Harvey. "Of course I do. Do you know that bad milk has killed thousands of children in this city alone?"

"Yes, I do," Sarah said. "I know that only a few years ago half of the children in New York died before their fifth birthdays."

"Because of swill milk," Pritchard confirmed, nodding vigorously. "Some died from the milk itself and some from consumption and other diseases that took them because they were weakened by the bad milk. I call my company Pure Milk so people know that's what I sell."

"Do you deliver in this neighborhood?" Sarah asked. "I have two children, you see, and I'd like to be sure they're drinking the very best milk I can find." She caught a glimpse of Malloy, who was staring at her in wonder.

"Yes, we do," Pritchard said, but he got no further.

"These tarts are delicious, Mrs. Ellsworth," Gino said. "But then, I've never tasted anything you made that wasn't delicious."

"Mrs. Ellsworth taught me to cook," Maeve reported, obviously having joined Gino's blatant effort to change the subject.

"She's teaching me all her recipes," Theda said. "I just hope I can learn how to do them as well as she does."

"You're all too kind," Mrs. Ellsworth said. "I'm sure Mrs. Pritchard is an excellent cook as well."

And so, by the simple method of not giving him another moment of silence to fill, they managed to keep Mr. Pritchard from causing any further disturbances during dessert. When they were finished, Theda suggested the ladies withdraw so the men could enjoy cigars and brandy, and all the women gladly did so.

As soon as they were safely in the parlor again, Mrs. Pritchard took Mrs. Ellsworth's hands. "Oh, Edna, I'm so sorry about Clarence. I don't know what's come over him. These past few weeks he's talked of nothing except the new century, and he won't listen to reason at all."

"That's all right, Ilsa. I know how men get. My late husband had his own hobbyhorses. He used to have opinions about all sorts of ridiculous things, and as much as he annoyed me then, I'd

20

give anything to hear him spouting off about them now."

Mrs. Pritchard smiled wanly at that, but she didn't look as if she'd miss Mr. Pritchard in quite the same way. "And Theda, dear, I'm afraid he ruined your first party."

"Not at all. I'm sure we'll look back and laugh someday," Theda said with forced cheerfulness. "Let's sit down and forget all about it."

But they couldn't forget about it for long because they soon heard Mr. Pritchard shouting.

"Oh dear," his wife said, rising to her feet and wringing her hands helplessly. "I never should have let him come."

The parlor door flew open and Pritchard was there, his face alarmingly red and his eyes wild. "Come along, Ilsa. We're leaving."

"But Father, we were going to play charades and—" Theda tried.

"Ilsa, get your coat!" Pritchard thundered, ignoring his daughter completely.

Theda's face crumbled and Nelson, who had come in behind his father-in-law, hurried to her side.

"Really, Mr. Pritchard," Gino was saying, "we agree with you completely." He and Malloy had followed their host from the dining room.

But Pritchard wasn't listening. He was throwing coats off the hall tree until he found his own and his wife's.

"I'm so sorry," Mrs. Pritchard whispered to Mrs. Ellsworth before taking her coat from him and allowing him to hustle her outside.

Pritchard stopped in the doorway and turned back. "Are you coming, Harvey?"

"No, I'll make my own way home."

Satisfied, Pritchard pulled the door closed behind him and his wife.

For a long moment the others were all too stunned to even move, and then Theda burst into tears. As Nelson tried to comfort her, Mrs. Ellsworth fetched a small glass of brandy and made her drink it.

"I don't know what could have come over him," Theda said between sobs.

"He's always been a strange bird," Harvey said, "but lately, he's been stranger than usual."

"Has something happened recently to cause him strain or anxiety?" Sarah asked him.

He gave her a startled glance and said, "Of course not" a little too quickly. Then he turned to his sister. "Little bug, I'm going to scamper. Don't give the old man another thought. He'll probably forget this even happened by tomorrow." Before anyone could stop him, he made his escape.

"I think we should go, too," Sarah said.

"But we were going to play charades," Theda wailed.

"We'll do it another time," Mrs. Ellsworth promised before escorting the last of her guests into the foyer. "I'm so sorry this happened. I have no idea what could have set him off like that."

"You don't need to apologize to us," Sarah assured her. "You're not responsible for any of this, and obviously, Mr. Pritchard is not himself."

"He certainly isn't. The worst thing I've ever seen him do is bore people with the history of milk production in New York City," she said sadly.

Malloy helped Sarah with her coat while Gino picked up his and Maeve's off the floor and assisted her. By mutual agreement, Gino went home with them. Malloy's mother was surprised to see them back so early, and they had to tell her about their strange evening.

"I almost choked when you asked him about pasteurizing his milk, Mrs. Frank," Gino said when they'd finished the tale. By then they were drinking coffee in the parlor.

"I was just trying to distract him, and it was the only thing I could think of."

"It was brilliant," Malloy said, taking her hand and pressing a kiss to the back of it.

"I just want to know which one of you got him all riled up again after the ladies left," Maeve said.

"It was Harvey," Gino said. "Although I can't figure out what he said that made the old man so mad."

"I can't either. I thought he was actually trying to agree with him," Malloy said.

"What did he say exactly?" Sarah asked.

The two men exchanged a glance as they tried to remember. "Something about how he'd bet most people agreed with him about the turn of the century being this year, I think," Malloy said.

"Oh, that's right, and then Pritchard said something about how Harvey would bet on anything, and the next thing you know he's yelling something about his milk trucks and . . ." Gino gestured helplessly.

"It didn't make much sense," Malloy admitted.

"Sounds like he's losing his mind," Mrs. Malloy said. "Mrs. Ellsworth always did think he wasn't quite right."

"She warned us he can be rather boring on the subject of milk," Sarah said, "but this was something else entirely."

"Which reminds me," Maeve said. "What is swill milk?"

"Probably what you were raised on," Mother Malloy said.

"I thought I was raised on cow's milk."

"Cows fed with swill," Sarah said. "That's the leftover mash from breweries. Instead of throwing it away, they'd feed it to cows."

Maeve frowned. "But why? I thought cows ate grass."

"Only if they're on a farm where there's lots of grass," Malloy said. "Years ago, they used to have farms with cows right here where the city is now."

"That's right," Mother Malloy said. "There was a wall on Wall Street to keep them from wandering downtown."

"Really?" Maeve marveled. "A wall?"

"How do you think that street got its name?" Mother Malloy said.

"I don't know. I never thought about it."

"But the city got bigger and they tore down the wall and built houses on the farmland, so there wasn't any place for the cows to graze close by anymore," Malloy continued, "so they started keeping the cows in big warehouses in the city and feeding them swill."

"But I know they keep cows out on the farms upstate and bring the milk in on the trains," Gino said.

"They do now," Sarah said, "but we didn't always have trains and when we did, we didn't have a way to keep the milk cold, so the cows had to be nearby."

"Now they put the milk in big metal cans and cover them with ice," Malloy said. "But we haven't been able to do that until recently."

"And they only started pasteurizing milk in the city a few years ago, so even if the milk was fresh, it might still be contaminated."

"You asked Mr. Pritchard if his company pasteurizes his milk," Gino said. "Does that mean not all of them do?"

"That's exactly what it means. And some companies are still keeping cows in the city and feeding them swill."

"But isn't milk just milk? If it comes from the cow, why does it matter what the cow eats?" Gino asked.

"Swill must not be as nourishing as grass," Sarah said. "Swill milk is thin and kind of bluish, so dairies would mix things like starch or chalk or even plaster into it to make it whiter."

*"Plaster?"* Maeve cried.

"And it would also make babies drunk," Mother Malloy said.

Everyone turned to her in surprise.

"Drunk?" Gino echoed. "Babies got drunk on milk?"

"Of course. Swill is what is left when they make whiskey. Why wouldn't it pass into the milk?"

"How horrible," Maeve said with a shudder.

"As I mentioned at dinner, lots of babies died from drinking bad milk," Sarah said. "I guess I can understand why Mr. Pritchard is a bit *enthusiastic* about the subject."

"But no babies die because of New Year's Eve," Gino said, "although a lot of people do get drunk, so why is he so *enthusiastic* about that?"

No one had any idea.

"At least New Year's Eve will be over in a few days, so Mr. Pritchard can go back to just talking about milk," Malloy said. "Are you really going to start having his milk delivered here?"

Sarah smiled. "We already do. We switched to Pure Milk as soon as Nelson and Theda became engaged."

"It was Edna's idea," Mother Malloy said. "But I didn't see any reason not to."

"Nor did I," Sarah said. "Theda will probably inherit the dairy or at least part of it someday, so we're doing our part to support it."

"Someday might come sooner than she expects if Mr. Pritchard doesn't stop being so obnoxious about the new century," Maeve said. "Did you see the way Mrs. Pritchard looked at him when he started ranting?"

"Fortunately, wives don't murder their husbands just because they're embarrassing," Sarah said.

"If they did, there wouldn't be any husbands left alive," Malloy added with a grin.

Frank braced himself against the leather seat and once again cursed himself for buying a motorcar. Why anyone thought this was an improvement over a horse and carriage, he had no idea. Whizzing along like this, they were all freezing, even though they were completely bundled up, with woolen underwear beneath their clothes and dusters over their heaviest coats and mufflers wrapped up to their hats.

Fortunately, the city streets were still crowded at this late hour as people roamed around, waiting for the stroke of midnight that would mark the beginning of the New Year, and the crowds kept Gino from going much faster than five miles an hour. The motorcar could go up to twenty miles per hour or so Gino had informed him. Frank couldn't imagine why anyone would need to go that fast. Five miles per hour was enough to rip your eyeballs right out of your head, which was why they all had to wear goggles in addition to the cotton dusters that protected their clothes from the dust and dirt of the streets. Someone should really come up with a way to protect them from the wind, at least.

"Get a horse!" some wit hollered from the safety of the sidewalk. Frank glared at him, but Sarah and Maeve waved gaily. Sarah seemed to be enjoying herself, even if her elaborate hat kept threatening to blow off, and Maeve was positively thrilled. She'd claimed the front seat beside Gino, which was fine with Frank. He much preferred sitting in the rear seat—the tonneau—with Sarah, snuggled under the fur lap robe.

At last they reached Trinity Church, or near enough, and found a place to park along Broadway. The grounds around the church had filled long ago, and pedestrians were spilling off the sidewalk and the grassy median into the wide street. The racket was nearly deafening, as seemingly every reveler had purchased a tin horn from the peddlers making their way through the crowds. A few other motorcars had also pulled up along the street.

"Look at that phaeton," Gino said. "Come on, Maeve. Let's get a better look at her."

Without so much as a backward glance, Gino hopped down and assisted Maeve to the ground so the two of them could go off to question the phaeton's owner, who would probably be thrilled to discuss it with them. The decision to select a gasoline-powered vehicle over an electric- or steam-powered model had been a difficult one, and Gino enjoyed arguing their reasons with people who had chosen differently.

"Are you warm enough?" Frank asked Sarah.

"Oh yes, although I imagine riding in the motorcar will be much more pleasant in warmer weather."

Frank wasn't so sure, but he said, "At least we have a place to sit to listen to the bells."

"And almost as good a view of the crowds as if we were in the bell tower," she said.

She was exaggerating, but only a little. The tonneau was at least a foot higher than the front seat of the vehicle, putting them well above street level. The design had something to do with the mechanical structure of the vehicle, although Frank hadn't understood it when Gino explained, and he wasn't really interested in finding out more about it.

They sat for a few moments, watching the people milling about and tooting their horns and taking surreptitious sips from hip flasks. Everyone seemed to be having a good time except one gentleman who was lurching through the crowd and stopping to speak to anyone who would pay him the slightest heed. Whatever he was saying apparently met with no one's approval because, without exception, each person or group of people he addressed turned away from him after a moment or two.

"Is that . . . ?" Sarah asked, peering through the night as the man passed under a streetlamp. "Could that be Mr. Pritchard?"

Frank looked again and realized she was right. He was closer now, and Frank caught the words *new century* being shouted over the din from the crowd and the tin horns. "Oh no. He's trying to convince people they should be welcoming the new century."

As they watched, Pritchard approached three men who were laughing at something one of them had said. After a few moments, their smiles faded and one of them started shouting at Pritchard. More words were exchanged, and one of the men gave Pritchard a shove that sent him staggering.

Frank was half out of his seat before Pritchard got his balance, and Sarah grabbed Frank's arm and pulled him back down. "He won't thank you for coming to his rescue," she said.

She was right, but Pritchard was going to get himself into real trouble if he didn't stop accosting people. "We can't just let him go."

"No, we can't," she said. "But he's coming this way." She started waving. "Mr. Pritchard!"

Frank waved, too, and Pritchard finally noticed. He moved toward them, a puzzled frown on his face, and Frank noticed he seemed a little unsteady on his feet. Had he been drinking? Certainly, most of the crowd had been.

"How nice to see you, Mr. Pritchard," Sarah said. "Is your family here as well?"

Pritchard peered up at them, still frowning uncertainly as if trying to bring them into focus. "Malloy, is it?" he finally said. "Theda's neighbors."

"That's right." Sarah glanced around. "I don't see Mrs. Pritchard. Is she with you?"

"No. Stayed home. I have to do this by myself. It's important."

"I'm sure it is," she said, "but it's getting late. The bells will start ringing pretty soon. Why don't you climb up and sit with us?"

Frank had to bite his tongue to keep from rescinding the invitation. The last thing he wanted to do on New Year's Eve was play nursemaid to a drunken man he didn't even like, but Sarah was right to want to help him. The crowds would get even more unruly when the bells had finished their toll, and Pritchard probably wouldn't get off with just a shove the next time he offended someone. "Yes, climb up, or you can sit in the front, if you prefer. We've got an extra lap robe, too."

"Can't. I've got work to do. There's not much time left." Without another word, he turned and stalked off, back into the crowd.

"Do you think I should go after him?" Frank asked her.

"I don't think he'll come back with you, but we should at least try. He looks almost ill."

He did, too. Drunk or sick, he shouldn't be wandering around alone, annoying strangers. "I hate to leave you here alone."

"Look, Gino and Maeve are coming back."

And they were, talking and laughing like nothing was wrong. "I'll go after Pritchard, then. Make sure Gino stays with you and Maeve, though."

But by the time Frank had climbed down from the tonneau, Pritchard had disappeared into the darkness, swallowed up by the throngs. The streetlamps didn't really help, because if someone wasn't directly under the light, they were in the deep shadows and even harder to see. Pritchard's height should have made him stand out, but either the city was full of tall men tonight or Pritchard had vanished. Frank could see little beyond the people jostling one another around him.

After what seemed an eternity of fruitless searching, the Trinity bells struck the hour and the crowd erupted into celebration. Tin horns bleated and hundreds of people beat on anything that would make noise, creating a deafening din. When the twelfth chime had died away, the bells began to play "Auld Lang Syne," and the crowd joined in, singing the familiar words with much enthusiasm and little harmony. When it was finished, the crowd began to shift and shiver, like a pot of water beginning to boil. Everyone, it seemed, had someplace to go. Many were probably heading to saloons to get even drunker than they already were, while others were heading to parties or other celebrations. The Trinity bells began another song, although Frank didn't listen closely enough to identify it.

Left with little choice, he allowed the surge of the crowd to carry him back to Broadway, where he found the motorcar again. Maeve had climbed into the back with Sarah, where they were huddled under the fur lap robe.

"No luck?" Sarah called when he was close enough to hear her.

He shook his head.

The bells continued to ring. Now it was a hymn, he thought. The Episcopalians had different hymns than the Catholics, and Frank hadn't been in a church since his first wife had died, so he couldn't be positive, but it sounded like a hymn. He climbed into the empty front seat beside Gino. "Maybe we'll see him go by."

But of course they didn't. A good portion of the crowd waited until the bells finished their concert, and Frank and his crew waited until even they were gone, and still no sign of Pritchard. Gino finally got out and turned the crank to start the engine. They were back at home before Frank realized what his fruitless search had cost him.

"I didn't get a kiss at midnight," he informed his wife, who was only too happy to rectify the omission.

"I didn't get a kiss either," Gino tried.

But Maeve said, "I'm sure Mrs. Frank will be happy to kiss you, too."

Frank and Sarah had invited her parents for New Year's Day dinner, and they'd had a lovely day. Mr. and Mrs. Decker thoroughly enjoyed the Malloy children, even though neither child was related to them by blood. Sarah had adopted Frank's son, Brian, and they had both adopted Catherine, the child Sarah had rescued. Such legalities hardly mattered anymore, though. They were a family now.

Mrs. Malloy and Maeve had just taken the yawning children up to bed when the doorbell rang. Their maid, Hattie, answered it and announced that Mrs. Ellsworth had come to call. But when she appeared in the parlor doorway, she plainly hadn't come to call at all. She'd obviously just thrown her coat on without bothering to button it, and she wasn't even wearing a hat.

Her expression could be described only as frantic.

"Oh, Mrs. Frank, I'm so sorry to interrupt, but we've just had the most awful news. Mr. Pritchard's been murdered."

# II

"Murdered?" everyone echoed.

The next few minutes were a blur as Sarah got Mrs. Ellsworth to sit down, and Malloy poured her a splash of brandy, and Sarah's mother went to fetch Mrs. Malloy from the nursery because she and Mrs. Ellsworth were such good friends.

When Mrs. Ellsworth had sipped the brandy and Mrs. Malloy had joined her on the sofa to offer moral support, Frank said, "Now, tell us what happened."

"Nobody knows what happened, not really. All we do know is Mr. Pritchard went out last night by himself."

"Yes, he was at Trinity Church for the bell ringing," Sarah said. "We saw him there."

"You did? What was he doing when you saw him?"

Malloy and Sarah exchanged a glance, not wanting to hurt Mrs. Ellsworth any more than necessary.

"Don't spare my feelings," Mrs. Ellsworth said quickly. "He was probably trying to spread the word about the new century. His wife tried to stop him from going out, because she knew he was very upset that no one was interested, but . . ."

"That's what he was doing when we saw him," Malloy said.

"He didn't look well either, so we asked him to come and sit with us in the motorcar," Sarah added, "but he refused."

"Of course he did," Mrs. Ellsworth said sadly. "He had a mission."

"Malloy went after him," Sarah said, "but lost him in the crowd. We even waited until nearly everyone had gone after the bell concert was over, but we never saw him again."

"It seems he didn't come home at all last night," Mrs. Ellsworth said. "Mrs. Pritchard had gone to bed, and Harvey was out celebrating, of course, so neither of them realized he hadn't come in until this morning. Even then, they weren't too worried. He might have overindulged and decided to stay with a friend, but . . ." Her voice caught, and Mrs. Malloy encouraged her to take another sip of the brandy.

"How did they find out he was . . . dead?" Sarah asked as gently as she could.

"The police came to tell them. Someone found his body this morning on the church grounds. The staff must have been cleaning up. He had some of his calling cards in his pocket, I think. Anyway, it took them most of the day to get someone out to their house, and by then Mrs. Pritchard and Harvey weren't home because they had already come to our house for dinner. They still weren't really worried about him, just annoyed because he was missing a family gathering. Then their maid came to tell them, and Harvey went down to the morgue to identify the . . . the . . . him."

"Poor boy," Sarah's mother said. She'd never met Harvey.

"Is Mrs. Pritchard still at your house?" Sarah asked.

"Yes, and I should go back. I just wanted you to know so you didn't have to read about it in the newspapers. Mrs. Pritchard is bearing up very well, but poor Theda is terribly upset. Nelson has his hands full with her, I'm sure."

"Then I'll go back with you, Edna," Mother Malloy said.

Sarah glanced at her mother, who instantly understood her dilemma.

"Sarah, I'm sure the family could use your support as well. Your father and I can see ourselves out."

"Of course we can," her father said.

"Oh, I couldn't ask you to—" Mrs. Ellsworth began but Sarah cut her off.

"Nonsense. That's what friends are for. How many times have you come to us in our hour of need?"

Mrs. Ellsworth was still protesting when Mother Malloy and Sarah escorted her out the door and across the street. Malloy had whispered that he'd explain everything to Maeve and be along as soon as Sarah's parents were gone. Mrs. Ellsworth hadn't locked the door behind her, so they walked right into her house. They could hear Theda sobbing in the parlor, and Mrs. Ellsworth went straight to her.

When she and Sarah had hung their coats, Mother Malloy went to the kitchen to brew some tea, and Sarah went to see what she could do in the parlor.

Both Nelson and Mrs. Ellsworth were trying to comfort Theda on the sofa, but Mrs. Pritchard was sitting off by herself beside the fireplace, staring blankly at the fire. Sarah went to her.

"I'm so sorry, Mrs. Pritchard. Is there something I can do for you?"

She looked up in surprise, as if she hadn't even noticed Sarah's arrival. "What? Oh no, dear. I'm fine."

She looked far from fine, although she certainly didn't look grief stricken. People reacted in many different ways to shock and loss, however, so Sarah didn't find that odd. Also, the Pritchards hadn't seemed to be a particularly devoted couple, and Mr. Pritchard appeared to be a difficult man, so perhaps Mrs. Pritchard was actually feeling relief and the guilt that would go with such an unseemly reaction.

"Mrs. Ellsworth said that your son has gone to the morgue."

"Yes, he . . . They needed someone to identify

the body. I would have gone, but he said it was no job for a female. Nelson wanted to go with him, but Harvey wouldn't hear of it. I hope . . . He isn't brave, you know. Harvey, that is. He pretends to be, but he's still a boy in so many ways."

"Most men are, I fear," Sarah said, taking a seat beside her. "We saw Mr. Pritchard at the church last night."

That seemed to alarm Mrs. Pritchard. "You did?"

"Yes. He was . . ." No sense in describing what he'd been doing. "We saw him in the crowd. We were in our motorcar, which is rather high off the ground, so we had a good view of everything."

"Did he see you?" That seemed an odd question, but Mrs. Pritchard could be excused for asking an odd question.

"Yes, we waved and he came over to speak to us. We thought he looked . . . Well, he didn't seem quite himself, as if he might not be feeling well. We invited him to join us, but he declined."

"When was this?"

Another odd question she'd expect the police to ask but not the widow. "I'm not exactly sure, but sometime between eleven thirty and midnight."

She nodded as if that somehow satisfied her. "Was he . . . talking about the turn of the century?"

"He may have mentioned it."

Mrs. Pritchard smiled sadly. "Of course he did.

He must have been trying to convince everyone there that they were witnessing a momentous event and not properly acknowledging it."

And had he annoyed the wrong person who had been too drunk or too angry and had used too much force in silencing him?

"Did you say Father didn't look well, Mrs. Malloy?" Theda asked. Nelson and Mrs. Ellsworth had managed to calm her, but she still looked devastated.

"Yes, he . . . I mean . . ." She didn't want to say he looked drunk.

"The police said he was murdered! But perhaps they horrified us for nothing. Who would murder Father, after all? Perhaps he was simply ill and . . . and . . ." The thought of her ill father dying alone was, after all, almost as horrifying as the possibility of his murder, and Theda dissolved into tears again.

Eventually, Mrs. Malloy brought them all tea, and Mrs. Ellsworth and Sarah managed to put Theda to bed, but they had to wait for Harvey's return so he could take Mrs. Pritchard home. Malloy had also arrived after seeing Sarah's parents off. He and Nelson were conferring when Sarah and Mrs. Ellsworth came back downstairs. Nelson would be filling Malloy in on what little they knew so far, and Malloy was probably asking him a lot of questions he wouldn't have any answers for.

Mrs. Malloy went home once Theda was settled, so Sarah and Mrs. Ellsworth did their duty to comfort Mrs. Pritchard until Harvey returned. She was, as Mrs. Ellsworth had said earlier, bearing up very well. As far as Sarah could tell, she had yet to shed a tear.

"They said he was murdered," she said when Sarah sat down beside her again. "I know Theda doesn't want to hear it, but that was the message from the police. I don't suppose they'd say such a thing if it wasn't true."

"It's hard to believe something like that could happen with so many people around," Sarah said. "Maybe they were mistaken."

"Do you really think so?"

Sarah couldn't tell if she welcomed the idea or not.

"They must have seen some evidence of murder," Malloy said. "They wouldn't have said that if there was any chance it was natural causes."

Sarah frowned at his bluntness, but he only shrugged in reply. He probably thought it was cruel to give her false hope, and he was probably right.

"I'm just sorry for Theda," Mrs. Pritchard was saying, apparently not giving in to hope, false or otherwise. "She and her father were very close."

As women have done for centuries, Sarah and Mrs. Ellsworth managed to fill the silence with small talk and keep Mrs. Pritchard distracted for nearly another hour before Harvey finally returned.

His face was ashen and he smelled of liquor. Plainly, he had not come straight back. He stopped dead when he came into the parlor and saw everyone staring at him expectantly.

Malloy said, "You identified him?"

"Yes, it was him, all right. He'd been strangled," he blurted.

Mrs. Ellsworth gave the horrified cry that should have come from the widow, but Mrs. Pritchard only sighed with what sounded oddly like relief.

"They said he wasn't robbed, but his money and his watch were both gone," Harvey reported in outrage.

"Then, that's what happened," Mrs. Pritchard said. "Someone tried to rob him, and he put up a fight."

Sarah glanced at Malloy, who shook his head, silently telling her this wasn't the right time to explain how these things went. Ladies like Mrs. Pritchard couldn't be expected to know that pickpockets didn't murder their victims, and police officers routinely helped themselves to whatever valuables they could find on dead bodies. If they said Pritchard hadn't been robbed, that meant a patrolman had relieved him of his watch and money. Sarah certainly hadn't known those things a few years ago, before she

44

met Frank Malloy and started solving murders.

"We should go, Harvey," Mrs. Pritchard said, rising. "We've imposed on these good people long enough."

"You are welcome to stay here tonight," Mrs. Ellsworth said. "It's so late . . ."

"I've got a cab waiting," Harvey said, and that decided the matter.

When they were gone, Frank and Sarah took their leave as well, reminding Mrs. Ellsworth and Nelson they were happy to help in any way. As they put on their coats, Mrs. Ellsworth said softly, so Nelson didn't hear, "Mrs. Pritchard took the news very well."

"She was probably in shock," Sarah said.

"She wasn't the least bit upset when he didn't come home this morning, and I got the feeling she didn't mind at all that they had to come here without him. Theda was fretting the whole time, wondering what could have become of him, but neither Ilsa nor Harvey was at all concerned."

Which told Sarah more than she really wanted to know about the Pritchard family.

Frank went out the next morning to find what newspapers he could, and he was glad to see most of them hadn't seemed too interested in Clarence Pritchard's death. Those who covered the story gave it only a paragraph or two, and some of them didn't even mention his name, just that a body had been found near Trinity Church on New Year's morning.

Frank and Sarah were in the parlor, poring over the stories, when Gino Donatelli arrived with newspapers of his own. "Did you know Mr. Pritchard was murdered after you saw him the other night?"

"Happy New Year to you, too," Frank said, "and yes, we knew." He told Gino briefly how they had learned about Pritchard's murder the previous evening.

"I knew I should have come here for dinner yesterday," Gino lamented.

"I'm sure your family appreciated having you home for the holiday," Sarah said. "Did you have breakfast? Can I get you some coffee?"

"Do you think my mother would let me leave the house without eating? But coffee would be nice . . . Where's Maeve?" Gino asked when Sarah left to fetch the coffee.

"She's not back from taking Catherine to school. What newspapers have you got there?"

By the time Maeve returned, they'd sorted them out, and Frank had found a few he'd missed in his own search this morning.

"Do they have any idea who killed him?" Gino asked when they'd finished reading all the accounts.

"They didn't last night," Sarah said. "According to Harvey, he was strangled."

"Do they think he was robbed?"

Frank shook his head. "The police say not."

"Then it was probably somebody who got sick of arguing about the turn of the century," Gino said.

"Would somebody really kill him over that?" Sarah asked skeptically.

Frank had been wondering that himself. "It doesn't seem likely, but we did see at least one man get a little rough with him, and most of the men in that crowd were drinking."

"Some of them had been drinking all day," Gino said knowingly.

"All right," Sarah said. "I can understand that someone would have been annoyed with him, and Mr. Pritchard might not have realized he should stop arguing and move on, but he was *strangled*."

"What does that matter?" Gino asked.

"I could see it if somebody punched him or pushed him, and he fell and hit his head. That's what happens when men argue. But it takes a long time to strangle someone, and with so many people around, why didn't anyone stop it?"

"Or why didn't the person doing the strangling come to his senses before it was too late?" Gino said. "You're right, it takes a long time to strangle someone."

"And a lot of effort," Frank said, remembering victims he'd seen who had been strangled. "If somebody was drunk enough to think it was a good idea, they'd probably be too drunk to do a good job of it."

"Which makes Mr. Pritchard's murder seem very suspicious indeed," Sarah said.

"So you think somebody murdered him for a mysterious reason that we don't know?" Gino asked with more delight than Frank thought was appropriate.

But Sarah only shrugged. "I know, it's hard to believe. The man owned a dairy, for heaven's sake. What could he possibly have done to get himself murdered?"

"Don't ask questions like that," Frank said. "It's none of our business."

"Isn't it?" she asked with a smile.

Before he could reply, the doorbell rang again. Frank chafed at the wait while their maid, Hattie, answered the door and dealt with the caller. In the old days, he would have opened his own door and known immediately who was there. On the other hand, Hattie could turn away people he didn't want to see. Being rich wasn't all bad.

Hattie came to the parlor door at last and said, "A Detective Sergeant O'Connor is here to see you."

Frank managed not to groan.

O'Connor was supposed to wait in the hallway until Hattie told him whether or not Mr. Malloy would see him, but he hadn't waited. He almost instantly appeared behind Hattie and slipped by her, stepping into the parlor with a brashness that annoyed Frank almost as much as it impressed him.

Frank and Gino rose to greet him. O'Connor was a big man and still young. He hadn't been a detective very long but long enough to have crossed Frank. He apparently hadn't yet recovered.

"Happy New Year, O'Connor," Frank said with far less enthusiasm than he'd greeted Gino.

"Same to you." O'Connor was busy looking around, taking in the furnishings and the paintings, things Frank and Sarah had bought in Europe on their wedding trip. Frank could see he was impressed and trying not to show it.

"What brings you here?" Frank asked.

"The Pritchard murder." His inspection of the room had noted the pile of newspapers, and he raised his eyebrows. "I went to see the family this morning, and they mentioned you'd seen Pritchard at the church that night. Ordinarily, I wouldn't have bothered tracking down a witness like that, but I couldn't pass up the chance to see how a millionaire lives."

But Frank and Sarah had deliberately chosen to live modestly, compared to most of the wealthy families in the city. "I hope you're not too disappointed."

"Not a bit. Nice house. Nice things. Nice wife. All bought and paid for."

Frank had actually taken a step toward O'Connor, ready to throw him bodily out of the house, but Sarah caught his hand and stopped him.

"Won't you sit down, Mr. O'Connor?" she said in a voice he seldom heard her use. It was the voice she'd learned at her mother's knee, her lady-of-the-manor voice.

O'Connor, bless his heart, responded instinctively. Something very like alarm flicked in his eyes and he sat. Frank and Gino did the same.

"Do you have a wife, Mr. O'Connor?" she asked.

"I . . . uh . . . Yes, I do," he said warily.

"And exactly how much did you pay for her?"

O'Connor's eyes grew round and he swallowed. "Uh, I beg your pardon, ma'am. Please excuse my manners. I'm, uh, not used to dealing with ladies."

"Obviously not, but if you think you can be civil, we'll be happy to answer your questions."

O'Connor cleared his throat and glanced at Frank. Satisfied that he wasn't going to do him bodily harm, at least not at the moment, he cleared his throat again and said, "So did you see Mr. Pritchard on the night he was killed?"

"Yes." Frank didn't let his anger show in his expression, because Sarah expected him to act like a gentleman, but he didn't even try to keep it from his voice. "We went down to Trinity Church to hear the bells, and we saw Pritchard in the crowd."

"How do you happen to know him?" O'Connor's confidence was returning. He pulled out his notebook and a pencil.

"His daughter married our neighbor, Nelson Ellsworth. We met the Pritchard family at the wedding, and we were invited to a dinner party last Friday that he attended."

"So you hadn't known him very long."

"No, we didn't."

"Did you speak to Pritchard when you saw him on New Year's Eve?"

"Yes, and we invited him to join us."

"We were in Mr. Malloy's motorcar," Gino offered with obvious satisfaction.

"Motorcar, eh?" O'Connor echoed with a frown.

"Yes," Gino said. "She's a real beauty. A tonneau with—"

"And you were there, too?" O'Connor said.

"Yes. Mr. Malloy lets me drive the motorcar and—"

"We thought Mr. Pritchard would like to sit down." Sarah shot Gino a warning look. No sense in antagonizing O'Connor more than necessary. "He didn't look well."

This got O'Connor's interest. "What do you mean?"

Sarah asked Frank a silent question and he nodded. No sense in hiding the facts from O'Connor either.

51

"He was approaching people and trying to talk to them, but . . . Did Mrs. Pritchard or her son tell you about Mr. Pritchard's interest in the turning of the century?"

Now O'Connor just looked confused. "The what?"

Frank quickly explained.

"But that was all settled," O'Connor said, still confused. "It's next year."

"Not according to Pritchard," Frank said.

"And we were worried about him approaching people to argue about it that night," Sarah said.

"We saw someone push him away, and he almost lost his balance, so that's when we called out to get his attention," Frank said.

"If you were so worried about him, why didn't you keep him with you?" O'Connor asked.

"We tried," Sarah said, "but he was only interested in informing people of his views. Malloy went after him but lost him in the crowd."

"You went after him?" O'Connor said with renewed interest.

"Don't get any ideas. I hardly knew the man, and I certainly didn't have any reason to kill him."

"Don't worry. I won't make the same mistake twice." O'Connor had falsely arrested Frank for murder a few short months ago, and he was probably still being razzed about it.

Sarah said, "We understand that Mr. Pritchard was strangled."

O'Connor looked at her in surprise. "That's right."

"We were just discussing how difficult it is to strangle someone, especially with so many people around."

"Is that what you talk to your wife about?" O'Connor asked Frank with amusement.

"That's what she talks to me about," he replied, even more amused.

"And I pointed out that strangling isn't what men do when they have a disagreement with a stranger. The usual reaction is a lot of pushing and shoving and at worst, a fistfight."

"She's right, too," Gino offered. "When you got here, we were trying to figure out why somebody would've strangled him and how somebody could've strangled him in that crowd without anybody noticing and stopping it."

O'Connor just blinked.

"What do the police think happened?" Frank asked after a long moment.

"That somebody strangled him," O'Connor said, obviously reluctant to admit his thinking hadn't gotten any further than that.

"Is it true he wasn't robbed?" Sarah asked.

"That's what the beat cop said."

"So he's the one who got Pritchard's watch," Frank said. It wasn't a question and O'Connor didn't bother answering. "You can tell him there's a reward for its return."

"The Pritchards didn't say anything about a reward," O'Connor said.

"His daughter is offering it." Frank pretended not to notice how Sarah raised her hand to cover a smile.

"Is she offering a reward for anything else?"

"I'll ask her."

They all knew O'Connor would work much harder at finding the killer if there was a reward. "You said you thought Pritchard didn't look right. Was he drunk?"

"What does Doc Haynes say?"

"He hasn't done an autopsy yet. Because of the holiday. I'm asking what you think."

"We thought he was ill," Sarah said. "I'm a nurse and a mother, and that's my considered opinion."

O'Connor didn't look like he wanted to argue about it, at least not with her.

"Have you found anybody else who saw him that night?" Gino asked.

"No. His family said he went out alone. They didn't mention this new-century stuff. Maybe he had some friends with him to help convince people."

Of course the Pritchards hadn't mentioned Clarence's hobbyhorse. "Maybe he did," Frank said, "but he was alone when we saw him."

"Did you say the daughter is your neighbor?" O'Connor asked.

Frank didn't want to subject the Ellsworths to O'Connor's questioning, but the police would naturally want to speak to everyone in the family, and O'Connor would want to investigate the possibility of a reward. "I'll take you over and introduce you." At least he could make sure O'Connor behaved himself.

And that Theda and Nelson understood they'd have to offer a reward to get her father's watch back.

Later that evening, Sarah was reading in her private parlor upstairs, enjoying the peaceful hour when everyone else had retired and she had the house to herself, when Hattie came up to tell her Mrs. Ellsworth and Mrs. Nelson Ellsworth had come to call.

"I would've told them you was already in bed," Hattie said, "but Mrs. Nelson is pretty upset, so I thought it might be important."

Sarah glanced at the bedroom door to make sure they hadn't disturbed Malloy, who must have already fallen asleep. "Thank you, Hattie. It probably is important."

Theda had been "pretty upset" ever since her father's untimely death, but if she felt compelled to seek Sarah out at this hour of the night, it must be something drastic. Could the police have discovered the killer?

Hattie had put the Ellsworths in the parlor.

"Oh, Mrs. Malloy," Mrs. Ellsworth said,

jumping to her feet. "I'm so sorry to bother you this late but—"

"It was my doing, I'm afraid," Theda cried. "They're ruining my father's reputation. Look at this!"

With a trembling hand she held out a newspaper. Her eyes were red and swollen, and her lips quivered as she fought back a fresh onslaught of tears.

Sarah took the newspaper and sat down in the nearest chair to read it. It was the evening edition of *The World*. This story was much longer than those from this morning and it was on the front page. The headline read, "Dairy Owner Murdered on Church Property," and beneath it in smaller letters, "New Century Heresy Brings Death." The story was accompanied by a picture of Mr. Pritchard. Newspapers couldn't print photographs, so they made engravings of the actual pictures, which meant the result wasn't particularly clear or detailed, but it was still Mr. Pritchard, all right.

"Where did they get a photograph of your father?"

"I don't know!" Theda wailed.

Sarah winced and concentrated on reading the article, which recounted Mr. Pritchard's accomplishments in business but ended with a mocking description of his obsession with the turn of the century. Supposedly, he had gone to Trinity Church to convince the revelers that they were actually celebrating the beginning of the twentieth century and ran into someone who disagreed strongly enough to murder him. The police, the story claimed, were looking for anyone who might have seen Pritchard that night or know who had killed him.

When she had finished reading, Sarah laid the paper in her lap and looked up to see both Mrs. Ellsworths watching her expectantly. "I'm so very sorry." She was, too. After all, she and Malloy were the ones who had told O'Connor about Pritchard's hobbyhorse. He must be the one who had told the newspapers, and he hadn't wasted any time in doing so.

"We have to do something," Theda said. "It's bad enough that my father was murdered. We can't let him become a laughingstock, too."

Sarah wanted to reassure her, but Theda was right. Once the newspapers got ahold of something like this, they'd never let go. They'd been known to invent scandals just to sell newspapers, and in this case, they had only to report the truth. "Did you have something in mind?"

Theda straightened and leaned forward in her chair. "We have to find the person who killed him."

"I'm sure the police are—"

"Oh, pish tosh, the police aren't going to do anything," Theda scoffed. "Did you see that detective Mr. Malloy brought to the house this morning?

He isn't a bit interested in finding the killer."

Sarah shifted uncomfortably in her chair. "Did Malloy explain to you that you need to offer a reward?"

Theda glanced at Mrs. Ellsworth. "Nelson already knew that, and we did tell the detective we'd give a reward for the return of my father's watch."

"An officer brought it to the house before supper," Mrs. Ellsworth reported sourly.

"I'm glad you got it back," Sarah said, "but to find the killer—"

"If I have to pay to find the killer, I'd rather pay someone I thought could really find him," Theda said. "That's why we'd like to hire Mr. Malloy."

"And Mr. Donatelli," Mrs. Ellsworth added.

"Don't you at least want to give the police a chance?" Sarah asked.

"After what they said about my father?" Theda gestured to the newspaper Sarah still held. "That detective was the one who told the newspapers about Father's interest in the new century. I know it was him. All he wanted to talk about was why my father was so interested in when the century really changes, and who else could have told the newspapers? My family certainly wouldn't have. The police and the newspapers are only interested in humiliating someone who can no longer defend himself. I'm not going to trust them to do anything to clear his name."

"I'm sure Malloy would be happy to help you, but you must understand, when the police find out Malloy is investigating, they'll probably stop."

"Good," Theda said. "Mother Ellsworth has told me Mr. Malloy is the best detective the New York City Police ever had. He's the one I want to find my father's killer."

Sarah turned to Mrs. Ellsworth. "The best detective they ever had?"

Mrs. Ellsworth smiled unrepentantly. "I'm sure it's true. I've never known him to fail."

Sarah had to agree that she and Malloy had enjoyed success on the cases they had solved together. She was certainly willing to do whatever she could for Mrs. Ellsworth, too, if that's what they really wanted, but she wasn't sure how much help they could be on this one. "You know we'd do whatever we can, Mrs. Ellsworth, but . . ."

"What is it?" Mrs. Ellsworth asked. "Do you think Mr. Malloy won't want to be involved?"

"I can't speak for Malloy, of course, but he'll probably tell you the same thing I just did, that the police should at least have a chance before you try elsewhere. And what about Nelson? Has he agreed to this?"

"We haven't told him yet," Theda said. "He'd already gone to bed, but Mother Ellsworth and I couldn't sleep, and when we saw your light was still on, I just couldn't wait. But I know Nelson will agree. He thinks even more highly of you and Mr. Malloy than Mother Ellsworth does."

Sarah knew why, too. She and Malloy had once saved Nelson's future, if not his very life. The Ellsworth family had reason to expect Malloy to save them again. Sarah only hoped they could.

# III

"I doubt anyone warned you about this when you got married, did they, Nelson?" Frank asked Nelson Ellsworth the next morning as they walked down Mulberry Street toward Police Headquarters. After learning of Theda Ellsworth's late-night request, Frank had convinced Nelson to try dealing with the police one more time.

"You mean that I'd be offering to bribe a police detective to investigate the murder of my father-in-law?" Nelson asked with a grim smile. "No, no one even hinted this would be one of my husbandly duties. I think it will be easier than explaining to Theda why I did it, though."

"Don't worry, I'll do that. Like I said before, I'll take all the blame and tell her I refused to take the case until the police at least investigated."

Nelson didn't look at all reassured. Frank knew a wife could make a man's life miserable if he displeased her—or at least he had observed it in others, having been lucky in his own choice of a wife—which was why he wasn't going to let Nelson suffer. But he also wasn't going to take on an investigation that rightfully belonged to the police. He'd already engendered too much ill will at the New York City Police Department, first by becoming rich and then by clearing himself of murder. No sense asking for more trouble.

Tom, the doorman at Police Headquarters, greeted Frank warmly. "I don't suppose you're coming back for good, are you, Mr. Malloy?"

"No, Tom, just visiting today."

"We surely miss you, Mr. Malloy."

Frank missed the department, too. Not everyone who worked there, of course, but he did miss the work and the camaraderie. "That's nice to hear, Tom. I'm wondering if Detective Sergeant O'Connor is here."

"I saw him come in earlier, but I didn't see him leave."

"Thanks, Tom."

Tom opened the door for them, and they stepped into the madhouse that was Police Headquarters. Someone was shouting and struggling with two patrolmen who were trying to subdue him. Several newly arrested prisoners sat on the benches beside the front door, looking dispirited and more than a bit afraid while uniformed officers swarmed around.

Frank took a minute to absorb the sights and smells, aware that Nelson wouldn't be quite as appreciative of their surroundings. Then he made his way to the desk, with Nelson at his heels.

The desk sergeant looked down his bulbous nose at them. "Malloy, is it? What in God's name are you doing here?"

"I've come to see Detective Sergeant O'Connor. Is he in?"

"That he is," the sergeant reported with a smirk. "He's probably upstairs licking his wounds."

"His wounds?" Frank didn't think they were actual wounds, but poor Nelson was looking a little pale.

"Yeah, the chief had to take him in hand this morning. Poor fellow won't be eating solid food for a while, I'm guessing."

"He's upstairs, you say?"

The sergeant nodded. "Be gentle with him, will you? He's just a boy."

Frank grinned and motioned for Nelson to accompany him.

"What did he mean? What happened to O'Connor?" Nelson whispered as they climbed the stairs to the second floor.

"Not what you're probably imagining," Frank said. "Chief Devery just called him on the carpet for something."

"Not to do with Mr. Pritchard's case, surely."

"I doubt it." Pritchard's death could hardly be important enough for Big Bill Devery to concern himself.

Devery had been the chief of police for a little over a year, after a notorious career that ended with him being convicted of bribery and extortion, of which he was more than guilty. When his sentence was overturned on appeal, he'd been reinstated on the force and promoted twice before being named chief of police in an effort by the politicians to undo all the reforms Theodore Roosevelt had made during his tenure as police commissioner. Devery was making a good job of it, too.

They found O'Connor at his desk in the detectives' room. Only two other detectives were at their desks and they studiously ignored the visitors. O'Connor had been staring glumly into space until he heard their approach. Then he scowled murderously.

"You started this."

"Started what?" Frank asked, pulling over a couple of chairs so he and Nelson could be comfortable.

"You're the one set the chief on me."

"Why would I do that? And the chief isn't likely to listen to me anyway."

O'Connor glanced at Nelson and frowned. "What are you doing here? You come to gloat?"

"Uh, no," Nelson said in surprise. "I came to . . . to offer a reward . . ."

"A reward for what?" O'Connor growled, angry now.

Nelson blinked rapidly. "For finding who killed Clarence Pritchard."

O'Connor gave a mirthless bark of laughter. "That's rich, especially when you know I can't even investigate that case."

"What are you talking about?" Frank asked.

"I'm talking about how you told Devery to take me off the case so you could take it on yourself."

Frank thumbed back the brim of his hat and scratched his head. "Why would I do that?"

"So you could get the reward yourself."

Frank exchanged a confused glance with Nelson again.

"That's not true," Nelson said with just a touch of outrage. "I tried to hire Mr. Malloy to investigate, but he said I had to give you a chance first, so that's why we're here, to tell you I'm offering a reward."

O'Connor frowned. "You are?"

"Yes, he is," Frank said. "Because I thought you should at least have a chance. This may surprise you, but I'm not interested in taking over all the crime investigations for the city of New York."

"Oh, that's right, you're rich, and you never need to work another day in your life," O'Connor said bitterly.

"No, I don't, so I brought Mr. Ellsworth down here to do the right thing, and here you are accusing us of . . . What exactly *are* you accusing us of, O'Connor?"

O'Connor shifted uncomfortably in his chair and glanced at Nelson warily. "You really came down here to offer a reward?"

Nelson was getting angry now, too. "Of course. Mr. Malloy assures me that is the expected thing."

O'Connor had the grace to wince. "Devery expects it, but this time he got the reward, not me."

"What does that mean?" Frank asked, rapidly losing patience.

"It means that somebody paid Devery not to look into Pritchard's death, so he told me to forget about it."

"Who would do that?" Nelson asked, obviously as confused as Frank.

"Devery don't confide in me, and I didn't think I should ask. Somebody with bigger moneybags than you, I'd guess, Mr. Ellsworth."

"So he took you off the case?" Frank asked.

"Me and everybody else. Nobody here cares who killed Pritchard."

Frank leaned back in his chair and considered this new development. "They'd care if somebody figures out who did it and the newspapers report it."

O'Connor brightened a bit at the thought. "That would be a bit embarrassing, wouldn't it?"

"It certainly would." Frank turned to Nelson. "I suppose this means I'm free to investigate Mr. Pritchard's death."

"I suppose it does," Nelson said a little uncertainly.

Frank turned back to O'Connor. "Maybe you'll tell me what you've learned so far."

"Not much more than what you told me, to tell

the truth. I didn't even get to talk to Doc Haynes about the autopsy yet."

"Do you have any idea why somebody wouldn't want you investigating?"

"No. As far as I know, Pritchard was just a businessman with really strange ideas about the centuries. The only person who doesn't seem to like him is his son." He apparently remembered that Nelson was family and shrugged apologetically. "I don't like my old man much either, come to that."

"You're right about the son," Frank said. "But sons don't usually kill their fathers, no matter how much they dislike them."

"That's true. Sorry I can't be more help, but like I said, I didn't have much time."

"If you think of anything, you know where to find me," Frank said, rising. "And I'll give you a nod when I know who the killer is so you can be ready when it hits the newspapers."

Plainly, O'Connor didn't like the idea of Frank doing favors for him, but he grunted his acceptance. Frank and Nelson left him to sink back into gloom.

"That was interesting," Nelson said when they reached the stairs. "Who would pay the chief of police to stop the investigation?"

"I'm guessing it's whoever killed Mr. Pritchard, so all we have to do is figure out who that is."

Nelson sighed. "One good thing, at least, now

I can tell Theda you're going to be doing the investigation."

Satisfied that Malloy and Nelson had the Pritchard situation in hand, Sarah took the opportunity to pay a visit to the maternity clinic she had opened on the Lower East Side a few months earlier. With any luck, someone there would be in labor, and she could help with the delivery. Although she thoroughly enjoyed her new life, she very much missed her old vocation of midwife.

She took the elevated train down. Gino would love to have driven her in the motorcar, but it caused too much of a sensation in that neighborhood. The children would run alongside, and she was terrified one of them would get run over.

She allowed herself a moment of pride as she caught sight of the formerly abandoned house that was now a bustling center of activity for the neighborhood. Pregnant women came for medical advice, and the resident midwives would go out for the deliveries of women fortunate enough to have a stable home, but their most important work was with those women who had no home and no one to care for them. Some had been deserted by faithless husbands while others had been thrown out by scandalized families because they had no husbands. No pregnant woman was turned away from this house, though, regardless of her situation.

The front porch had been recently swept and the

windows sparkled in the winter sunshine, making a stark contrast to most of the other dwellings on the street. Sarah rang the bell, silently lamenting the need to keep the front door locked. While the house held little worth stealing, the city's poor were often desperate enough to break in anyway. The clinic also had to worry about the occasional husband or lover who had had a change of heart and wanted to reclaim his paramour, whether she wished it or not.

The woman who answered the door was a stranger to Sarah. Although she was young, she seemed very self-possessed and her clothing had been made by a skilled seamstress, unlike the women who usually sought refuge here. Sarah introduced herself, but the woman gave no sign of recognition and made no offer to admit her.

"I founded the clinic," Sarah tried.

The woman blinked and said, "Oh, I'm so sorry," and stepped aside to allow Sarah to enter. The interior of the house was as spotless as the front porch.

Sarah pulled off her gloves as the young woman closed and locked the door behind her. Sarah took the opportunity to study her for a moment. She was fair, her hair the color of corn silk, with the alabaster complexion to match. Her hands showed no sign they had ever done any labor. Who was this girl and why was she here? "I don't believe we've met."

"No, we haven't. I'm sorry I didn't recognize you."

"There's no reason why you should, Mrs. . . . ?"

"Oh, it's *miss*." Color blossomed in her cheeks at the admission, although she refused to lower her eyes in shame. She wouldn't be in this house if she wasn't expecting, although she might just have been a little plump at this point. She hadn't even had to let out the seams of her dress yet.

"Miss . . . ?" Sarah prodded.

"Oh! You must think I'm a goose!" she cried, covering her scarlet cheeks with her hands. "Jocelyn Vane."

"Welcome, Miss Vane. I hope you've been made comfortable here."

"Oh yes. Everyone has been . . . very kind." But she didn't look grateful. If anything, she looked resentful.

"Is Miss Kirkwood or Miss Hanson available?" Sarah asked, thinking she'd ask one of the resident midwives about Miss Vane.

"They're both out, I believe."

"Who was that at the door?" another woman asked as she came down the hall from the kitchen, drying her hands on the apron stretched tightly over her expanded belly. "Oh, Mrs. Malloy. Good morning."

"Good morning to you, Stella," Sarah said. "How are you doing?"

Stella patted her belly. "We're both doing fine."

70

Jocelyn Vane frowned and eyed Stella warily, making Sarah wonder just how truly kind Jocelyn's reception had been.

"Perhaps you'd like some refreshment, Mrs. Malloy," Stella said.

"Something warm would be lovely," Sarah said.

Stella smirked. "Make Mrs. Malloy some tea, duchess. You know how to make tea, don't you?"

Jocelyn flushed again and sent Stella a murderous glare, but she said, "Of course I do." She turned to Sarah. "Please make yourself comfortable, Mrs. Malloy. I'll be right back."

Stella watched her go with apparent amusement. This wasn't good.

"Why did you call her duchess?" Sarah asked when Jocelyn disappeared into the kitchen.

Stella shrugged unrepentantly. "Because she acts like one. Showed up here in a big, fancy carriage with a trunk full of fancy clothes and thinks she's better than the rest of us, but she's here for the same reason we are, isn't she?"

"Thank you, Stella. I think I'll take my tea in the kitchen."

Leaving the girl staring after her, Sarah went down the hall and found Jocelyn arranging some tea things on a battered tin tray while a kettle of water heated on the stove. She'd done a good job of finding mismatched equivalents of the items that would normally appear on such a tray in the kind of house she'd obviously grown up in.

"I was going to bring the tray to the parlor," she said.

"I know, but you don't need to go to any trouble. I thought we'd be more comfortable here."

"All right," Jocelyn said uncertainly.

Sarah slipped off her coat and hung it on a peg by the back door while Jocelyn finished her preparations. She moved uncertainly, obviously not as comfortable in a kitchen as the other women here would be. She'd probably had servants and deportment lessons instead of learning to cook.

Sarah took a seat at the kitchen table, while Jocelyn finished gathering everything. By then the water was boiling, so she rinsed the chipped teapot and then put in the tea leaves and filled the pot with more hot water.

"How long have you been here?" Sarah asked when Jocelyn had set the pot on the table and taken a seat across from her.

"I . . . Two days."

"I don't want to pry into your business. I'm sure Miss Kirkwood and Miss Hanson told you that we don't need to know your circumstances unless you want to tell us."

"But you're curious about why a *duchess* needs to come to a place like this," she said bitterly.

"I'll speak to the other women about that. We do insist that everyone here be treated courteously."

Jocelyn waved away her concern. "It doesn't matter. Nothing matters anymore, really."

"Many things matter, Miss Vane. Your future welfare and your child's matter very much."

Jocelyn's hand went instinctively to the small mound beneath her skirt and her gaze darted away, as if from guilt. "My future welfare is assured. My parents are angry with me now, which is why they chose to humiliate me by sending me here instead of to Europe, which is where I am assured girls of my class who are in my condition are usually sent."

Sarah's heart clenched at a memory never far from her mind. They'd tried to send her sister, Maggie, to Europe, but she had defiantly run away to find her lover. If she had sailed that day, would she still be alive? The possibilities were too painful to contemplate. "I wonder how your parents knew of this place."

"Gossip, I assume. Some wealthy matron took it into her head to minister to the fallen women of the slums and . . . Oh," she said, suddenly realizing Sarah was that matron.

"Don't worry about my feelings," Sarah said. "What else do they say about me?"

"They're just jealous, I imagine," Jocelyn said, flushing once again.

"I doubt that, but I am curious what they think of the clinic."

"Oh, they're jealous, all right. They resent any-one not in society who might be richer than they are."

"What makes them think I'm not in society?" Sarah asked with amusement.

Plainly, Jocelyn didn't want to reply, but Sarah waited expectantly until she finally said, "Your name."

"Of course. I should have known. How had some Irish upstart gotten rich enough to do charitable works?"

"But you're not an Irish upstart," Jocelyn observed shrewdly. She had most likely noticed the same things about Sarah that Sarah had noticed about her.

Sarah merely smiled. "The tea is probably ready."

Jocelyn took the hint and filled two cups. Then she passed Sarah the sugar and the cream.

"This really is a charity," Sarah said when she'd prepared her tea. "If your parents could afford to send you to Europe—"

"Don't worry, they paid for me. My father and Miss Kirkwood had a brief conversation and *arrangements were made*. To her credit, she tried to talk him out of leaving me here."

Sarah truly hoped so. "This is very different from what you're used to, I'm sure."

Jocelyn smiled grimly. "I told you, it's my punishment. Fallen women don't deserve a grand tour."

"And what about afterward? Will they take you back?"

Jocelyn closed her eyes for a moment, as if considering the future was too difficult to bear. "Yes, or at least they assured me they would. I think they don't want to have to explain what became of me, so it's easier if I just return from visiting an aunt in Connecticut."

"And the child?"

Emotion flickered across her lovely face, but she had been trained since birth not to surrender to such nonsense. She raised her chin. "The child will be given to some deserving family."

Many young women would actually be thankful for the opportunity to resume their normal lives after a few months of inconvenience, unencumbered by the living reminder of their shame. Jocelyn Vane did not appear to be one of them.

"Would you like to keep your child?"

"Please don't ask me that when you know it's impossible."

Sarah sipped her tea, wishing she could tell Jocelyn it actually was possible. But if she hoped to return to the world into which she had been born, she could not bring her illegitimate child along. "There's no chance that the child's father . . . ?"

"No."

She offered nothing else, but the word itself was said with a finality that told Sarah all she needed to know. "You may find it difficult to make friends here." Sarah chose not to acknowledge

Jocelyn's bitter smile. "But I am always available if you need to talk to someone. Just ask one of the midwives to send for me."

Jocelyn blinked a few times as she absorbed that kindness. Then she said, "You really *aren't* an Irish upstart."

"My husband is. He was a policeman."

That shocked her, as Sarah had intended. Policemen were considered little better than street cleaners by the people who mattered in New York. "And your family accepted him?"

"They learned to, yes."

"But he's a fortune hunter!"

Sarah laughed at that. "Actually, the fortune is his. I was earning my living as a midwife when we married." Which was the truth.

Jocelyn frowned as she considered this. "So you founded this clinic because you were a midwife."

"Because I saw the need for a safe place where women in your situation could go."

"And what happens to them after? To the ones without wealthy families, I mean."

"We help the women find jobs and a place to live."

"What about the . . . the babies?"

"Sometimes the women keep them. Some charities provide child care for women who must earn their own livings."

"And the others?"

"We place them in orphanages where they'll be adopted."

"And are they? Adopted, I mean? Or do they spend their lives in some horrible place like the ones they write those awful novels about?"

"We don't send them to horrible places, Miss Vane, although I am sure there are many of those in the city. I don't suppose your parents would take the child."

"Never." That bitterness again.

"Or another family member, so you'd be able to see the child from time to time?"

She shook her head. "And don't suggest I find a job and make a life for myself. I'm not trained to do anything useful. I can barely make a pot of tea, as you saw."

Sarah sighed. "I was the same, until I trained to be a nurse."

"But you didn't have a child to provide for, did you?"

"No, I didn't."

"The only vocation for which I am fit is to be the wife of a wealthy man. If a breath of scandal touches me, even that prospect will be denied me, and I'll spend my days as the spinster aunt given a place to live out of pity."

And she would also know that her child, whom she would never see again, was out there somewhere. Sarah's heart wanted to break, but that wouldn't help Miss Vane in the slightest. "You'll have a lot of time to think about the possibilities while you're here. Perhaps a solution will present itself."

Jocelyn winced. "You mean a knight in shining armor will rescue me?"

"Or perhaps you'll figure out a way to rescue yourself."

Frank found Gino at the office, where he'd spent the morning writing up a report on the last case they'd handled. As a private investigator, Frank earned only enough to cover Gino's salary and some expenses, but that was just fine. His personal fortune more than provided for his own family and allowed him to accept only the cases that interested him. He couldn't imagine just sitting around being rich all day, and being a private investigator saved him from that fate. It also gave him some interesting mysteries to solve.

"Was O'Connor glad to see you this morning?" Gino asked after greeting him.

Frank hung his hat and coat on the coatrack. "Not at all. You won't believe this, but Devery ordered him off the case."

"Off the Pritchard case? Why would Devery care about that?" Gino asked in amazement.

"A very good question." Frank pulled up one of the chairs provided for waiting clients, turned it around, and straddled it, resting his arms on the back. "I'm starting to think Pritchard's murder was a lot more important that we imagined."

"If somebody paid Devery to stop the investigation, it must be," Gino marveled.

"So why would somebody with enough money and influence to bribe the chief of police be interested in a man who sells milk?"

Gino leaned back in his own chair to consider. "Maybe he sells more than milk."

"You met Pritchard. Did he strike you as somebody who would be mixed up in something illegal?"

Gino shrugged. "Can you really tell that just by looking at somebody?"

"Probably not, but I guess we'll have to find out, since Nelson has hired us to find Pritchard's killer."

Gino perked right up at that. "Really?"

"Yes, really."

"I guess his wife is happy. You said that's what she wanted in the first place."

"Nelson is even happier because he didn't have to tell her I refused. So we need to find out more about Pritchard."

"And more about his milk business. What could he be doing with that?"

"I have no idea, but if there's something fishy going on, I'll bet Harvey Pritchard knows all about it."

Gino nodded. "And Harvey and his father

79

weren't getting along very well the last time I saw them."

"So we should start with him. Why don't you go down to the dairy and see what you can find out? Talk to Harvey if he's there, and get a good look around."

"And if he's not there, I'll see what the gossip is. What will you do?"

"I think Sarah and I will pay a condolence call on Mrs. Pritchard and tell her Nelson has hired me to look into Pritchard's death since the police won't be doing it."

"That should be interesting."

Frank grinned. "I'm counting on it."

One of the midwives, Miss Kirkwood, had returned to the clinic just as Sarah and Jocelyn were finished with their tea and she gave Sarah a report on all the women currently in residence. Sarah was praising her efficiency when Jocelyn returned to the kitchen.

"Mrs. Malloy, there's a gentleman here to see you."

"A gentleman?" Who on earth could that be?

"You didn't let him in, did you?" Miss Kirkwood asked in alarm.

"Oh no. I left him standing on the porch." The rule against admitting men was not only for the safety of the women living here, but it also protected the clinic from gossip.

"It's not my husband, is it?" Sarah couldn't imagine who else would know to find her here.

"He didn't say."

Definitely curious now, Sarah followed Jocelyn through the house to the front door with Miss Kirkwood close behind to investigate this strange turn of events.

Sarah opened the door to find an old friend standing there.

Black Jack Robinson quickly removed his silk hat. "Mrs. Malloy, how are you?" He looked even more dapper than usual in a sealskin topcoat and leather boots so shiny, Sarah was sure she'd be able to use them to check the arrangement of her hair. His own hair was pomaded into an elaborate style, and his impressively appointed carriage stood waiting at the curb.

"Mr. Robinson, what a surprise."

"I heard that you were visiting the clinic and that you'd arrived on foot, and as I was passing, I thought I'd offer to drive you home. It's looking a bit like snow." He squinted and tipped his head a little as if he could check the sky from where he stood, although he would have had to go out to the middle of the street and look straight up to really do that.

"Are you having me followed, Mr. Robinson?" she asked in amusement.

He feigned shock. "Certainly not! But very little happens in my neighborhood that I don't hear about. Of course, if you haven't finished your business here yet, I can come back . . ."

Which meant he was very anxious to speak with her. He could have simply called at her house, although she supposed a man of his reputation would hesitate to call on a respectable lady unless invited. He had shown himself once before to be sensitive to the requirements of polite society, and he would care about imposing on her, even if she didn't.

"As a matter of fact, I was just finishing up here, and I would very much appreciate a lift home. If you'll just give me a few minutes to get my coat . . ."

"Of course."

"I'm sorry I can't invite you in to wait."

"That's all right. I understand completely. The charming young lady who answered the door explained your very sensible rules quite well." He smiled and turned his gaze to something behind Sarah. She glanced over her shoulder to see Jocelyn lurking just behind Miss Kirkwood and watching them with great interest.

"Thank you. I'll only be a moment." Sarah closed the door and turned to face Jocelyn and Miss Kirkwood.

"Is that Black Jack Robinson?" Miss Kirkwood asked with obvious disapproval.

"Yes, it is."

"How did he know you were here?"

"I imagine most of the children in this area earn their spending money by keeping him informed of who comes and goes in this neighborhood."

"Who is he?" Jocelyn asked, not disapproving at all. Jack was awfully attractive, Sarah had to admit.

"He's a criminal," Miss Kirkwood said.

"I don't think so," Sarah said kindly. "He's never actually been convicted of anything, but he does own a number of illegal businesses in the city. In fact, he used to own this very house before he sold it to me."

That shocked Miss Kirkwood into silence, allowing Sarah to take her leave. When she had fetched her coat from the kitchen and returned to the front door, Jocelyn was waiting to let her out.

"Is he very rich?" she asked in a whisper. "Mr. Robinson, I mean."

"I'm sure he is. Why do you ask?"

But Jocelyn only smiled and opened the door. Jack still stood on the porch, in spite of the wintery wind and the threatening snow.

"Thank you for waiting," Sarah said.

"My pleasure. And thank you for your help, miss," he added with a tip of his hat to Jocelyn, who simply nodded because it would have been improper to do anything more with a man to whom she had not been properly introduced.

Jack took Sarah's arm to help her down the porch steps and then assisted her into his carriage, which was even more luxurious inside than it was outside. He provided her a thick, fur lap robe before asking her the address. When they were on their way, he said, "Is that young lady one of your midwives?"

"What makes you think that?"

"Because she obviously isn't the type of woman who takes refuge in your clinic."

"You seem to know a lot about the clinic."

He smiled. "I have kept track of it, yes, and I must admit, I've heard only good reports. You're doing wonderful things there."

"That was my intention."

"Now that I know how much help it is, I realize I should have given you the house for nothing."

"If you're that grateful, you can make a donation. Most of the women there are unable to contribute to the cost of their support, so we rely on others to provide it."

"I will be happy to. I also wanted you to know that after . . . after what happened, I have closed all of my, uh, disorderly houses."

"I'm glad to hear that," she said, although she knew his gesture would make little difference in a city that had far more brothels than churches.

"Don't be too glad. I'm not becoming completely respectable. There are plenty of other sins that I can make a living on. I just couldn't bear the thought of making money from the misery of helpless females anymore. Your and Malloy's meddling has given me the beginnings of a conscience."

She found that amusing as well. "I hope you aren't finding it too much of a burden."

"Not likely. But enough about me and my conscience. You never answered my question about that young lady."

Sarah settled back against the leather seat and adjusted her lap robe as she studied Black Jack Robinson. Could he somehow be molded into a knight in shining armor?

# IV

"What do you think Robinson really wanted?" Frank asked when he'd returned and heard how Robinson had insisted on driving Sarah home.

"Oddly enough, I got the feeling he was simply lonely."

"How can a man like that be lonely?"

"Easily, I think. Remember, his fondest desire was to make a new life for himself and be accepted into polite society."

"By marrying a woman who would make him more acceptable." Frank well knew how much help the right woman could be to a man, so he couldn't fault Robinson for that.

"He may have lost the woman, but he apparently didn't lose his desire to become respectable. He told me he's closed all the brothels he owned."

"That's a step in the right direction, but I imagine the rest of his business is still pretty shady."

"I'm sure it is, but the same could be said for many men in the Social Register."

"So he's still looking for a proper wife." He gave her a suspicious frown. "I hope he didn't make you an offer."

That made her laugh, as he'd intended. "Not yet, but he did hint rather broadly that he'd appreciate any help I could give him in that direction."

"And I'm sure you know a lot of society women who would love to marry a gangster."

To his surprise, she smiled mysteriously. "I might know one or two. Now, tell me how your meeting with O'Connor went."

The Pritchards lived in the Lenox Hill neighborhood, which was home to many successful businessmen. Their town house was well kept and impressive, but not ostentatious, Sarah noted when she and Malloy arrived that afternoon. A mourning wreath hung on the door, and a maid admitted them.

She seemed a bit flustered. "I'll . . . I'll just see if Mrs. Pritchard is receiving."

"Please tell her we want to speak with her about the police investigation into her husband's death," Malloy said, which did nothing to reassure the poor girl.

She left them standing in the foyer when she scurried off.

"Did we break some etiquette rule by calling?" Malloy asked.

"No," Sarah said, still trying to figure out what was going on. "Maybe she's new and not sure about whether she should admit visitors when the family is in mourning."

"Wouldn't Mrs. Pritchard have explained all that to her?"

Before Sarah could reply, the maid came out

of the room into which she'd disappeared and hurried back to them. "Mrs. Pritchard asked would you make yourselves comfortable in the parlor and she'll be with you in a moment."

Without waiting for a reply, she opened the doors to the parlor in question, which was immediately to their right. Only belatedly did the girl realize she should first take their coats. When the coats were hung and they'd been escorted into the parlor, she disappeared again, closing the door behind her.

The room was formally furnished with a collection of matching plush sofas and chairs. Small tables bearing a large assortment of knickknacks were scattered around in convenient spots. Heavy velvet draperies hung at the windows, and darkly flowered wallpaper added to the overpowering dreariness of the decor. It was a room seldom used, but kept at the ready for formal visitors.

Mrs. Pritchard made them wait only a few minutes, and she also appeared a bit flustered when she finally came in. To make matters even more odd, a gentleman was with her. He looked vaguely familiar, but Sarah was sure they had never met.

"Mr. and Mrs. Malloy, what a surprise," Mrs. Pritchard said. She wore black, as Sarah had expected, but she looked no more grief stricken than she had on New Year's Day.

"We're sorry to intrude," Sarah said, "but Mr.

Malloy has some important news for you."

Mrs. Pritchard glanced at Malloy with what Sarah could only call alarm. "Annie said it was about the police investigation."

"Yes, I—"

"Why don't we all sit down," the man with Mrs. Pritchard said suddenly and with an air of authority. "And Ilsa, you can ring for some coffee. I'm sure your guests would appreciate something to warm them up."

"Oh yes, of course. What was I thinking?" Mrs. Pritchard said, casting him a grateful glance. "Please, sit down." She hurried over and pulled the bell cord.

"I'm Otto Bergman," he said, offering Malloy his hand.

"Oh, where are my manners?" Mrs. Pritchard said, hurrying back to make the introductions. "Otto is one of my oldest friends," she added when she'd finished.

"We grew up in the same tenement in Kleindeutschland," Bergman said, naming the predominantly German neighborhood in the heart of the city. He and Mrs. Pritchard exchanged a look of affection that told of years of pleasant memories. How nice that she had a good friend to comfort her.

Assuming, of course, that she needed comforting.

But how unusual that her good friend was a man.

Just as they had all finally sat down, the maid came in and was instructed to bring them coffee. When she left, Mr. Bergman turned to Malloy. "Did you say you had something to tell us?"

Sarah and Malloy were sitting on one of the sofas, and Mrs. Pritchard had taken a chair opposite them, while Bergman sat in a chair to Sarah's left. Although Bergman had asked the question—and had strangely used the word *us*—Malloy looked only at Mrs. Pritchard while he explained.

"Nelson wanted to hire me to investigate Mr. Pritchard's death," he began.

"It was actually Theda's idea," Sarah added.

Mrs. Pritchard looked alarmed again, but she nodded her understanding.

"I explained to Nelson that it was wise to allow the police to handle the matter and that he should use the money he would have paid me to offer a reward instead."

"Ah yes," Bergman said with a trace of irony. "The police do need encouragement, don't they?"

Malloy chose not to respond to that. "But when Nelson and I went to Police Headquarters today to speak with the detective in charge of the case, the detective informed us that he had been ordered not to investigate the case at all."

Both Mrs. Pritchard and Bergman exchanged a look of astonishment. "Not at all?" Mrs. Pritchard asked after a moment.

"Not at all," Malloy confirmed.

This time when she turned to Bergman, she actually smiled.

Before Sarah could figure out what that meant, Bergman said, "Why would that happen?" He was not smiling.

"We assume someone used their, uh, influence with the police chief."

"Who would do such a thing?" Bergman asked.

"We don't know, but we assume it was whoever killed Mr. Pritchard."

Bergman frowned, and he and Mrs. Pritchard exchanged another glance. Sarah thought they both looked very alarmed.

"But you don't have to worry," Sarah quickly assured them. "Because Nelson and Theda have hired Mr. Malloy to investigate after all, since the police won't."

Now Bergman and Mrs. Pritchard looked even more alarmed.

"Is that wise?" Mrs. Pritchard said. "I mean, is it *safe?* If someone doesn't want the police to . . . you might be in danger or . . . or something."

"I don't think so," Malloy said, "but I'm willing to take the chance."

"And we couldn't refuse to help Theda," Sarah added. "She's extremely anxious to find out who killed her father and see him punished."

"She and her father were very close," Bergman said flatly, as if he didn't approve.

"You mustn't . . . I mean . . ." Mrs. Pritchard

shrugged helplessly. "This is all so . . . so unpleasant, and I don't want to see her hurt."

"Do you have an idea why Mr. Pritchard was murdered, Mrs. Pritchard?" Malloy asked. "Something that might hurt Theda, for example?"

"Of course she doesn't," Bergman said too quickly. "But sometimes people have secrets they don't want their loved ones to know."

Mrs. Pritchard made a little sound of distress. She pulled a hankie from her sleeve and pressed it to her lips.

"If Mr. Pritchard had a secret, you should tell me now," Malloy said. "I promise to protect Theda if I can."

But Mrs. Pritchard only shook her head and began to weep softly into her handkerchief.

Gino was impressed. The Pure Milk Dairy took up a whole city block. The first floor housed the milk wagons and the horses that pulled them, while the upper floors contained the offices and the pasteurizing and bottling plant. The stables on the first floor were quiet this afternoon. The horses dozed in their stalls and the wagons were parked neatly in their rows. That seemed reasonable to Gino, since milk was delivered in the predawn hours, before the streets became impassable with traffic and pedestrians. A few men were working now, mucking out stalls and cleaning wagons, but none of them paid the slightest attention to Gino, so he decided to try his luck upstairs.

The bottling plant was bustling, and Gino blinked at the blinding whiteness of it all. The walls and floors were all tiled and scrubbed immaculately clean. The workers also wore all white and their reflections loomed large in the shiny metal vats that towered over them. This time one of the workers noticed him, a dark spot in all the gleaming brightness.

"You can't come in here without a uniform," the worker shouted over the din of the machinery.

"I'm looking for Harvey Pritchard," Gino shouted back.

The man made a face that might have indicated disapproval and pointed. "Upstairs."

Gino nodded his thanks and went back to the stairwell. Upstairs he found a suite of offices where a few clerks were busy doing whatever clerks did. A young man sitting at a desk guarded them against intrusion. Gino told him he was looking for Harvey.

"Do you have an appointment?"

"No, but I'm investigating Mr. Pritchard's death, and I need to ask him a few questions."

The young man's attitude changed instantly. "I'll tell him, uh, I'll just, uh, do you . . . ?"

Gino took pity on him and handed over his calling card. The young man frowned over it, probably expecting Gino to be a cop, but he carried it away to one of the private offices and returned shortly to escort Gino back.

Harvey sat behind a desk that obviously belonged to the owner of the dairy, and he looked somewhat lost behind it, as if even the desk knew he wasn't up to the job.

"Donatelli, I didn't expect to see you," he said, rising to his feet a little uncertainly.

Gino waited until the receptionist had left and then closed the door. "Nelson and Theda have hired our agency to investigate your father's death."

"Why would they do that?"

"Because when Nelson went down to tell the police he was offering a reward, they told him the chief of police had ordered them off the case."

This news obviously shocked Harvey, who plopped unceremoniously back down into his chair. Since Harvey was apparently too stunned to remember his manners, Gino pulled a chair over from where it stood against the wall and sat down facing Harvey across the desk. "Do you have any idea why the police would stop investigating?"

"What? Me? No, I have no idea at all," Harvey claimed, although Gino was pretty sure he was starting to sweat, even though the room was comfortably cool.

"I didn't either, so I've been trying to figure it out for a couple hours now. I used to be a cop myself, you see, and the only reason I can come up with is because your father was involved in something illegal, so if we find out who he was doing business with, we'll also find out who killed him. That person must have a lot of, uh, influence and they ordered the cops off the case."

"Oh no, that can't be it," Harvey said, shaking his head vigorously. "My father would never . . . He was the most honest man alive. Ask anybody."

"Are you sure? Because this looks very suspicious."

"I'm positive. He'd never do anything illegal. I'd swear to it."

But for someone who was so positive, he looked very nervous. "I guess we all want to think our fathers are the best men who ever lived, but you can see how I'd think something wasn't right. I mean, somebody bribed the chief of police to make sure nobody investigated your father's death."

"Bribed?" Harvey cried, obviously horrified. "You didn't say anything about a bribe."

"Didn't I? I guess that's because everybody knows that's the only reason the police do anything. Mr. Roosevelt tried to clean up the department when he was the police commissioner, you'll remember, but then he went to Washington and now he's the governor, so everything he did is being undone by Chief Devery and his cohorts."

Harvey pulled out a handkerchief and wiped his face, because he really was sweating now. "That's very disturbing."

"Yes, it is, especially when it means murderers can get away, but you don't want your father's killer to get away, do you, Harvey?"

To Gino's disappointment, Harvey had to think about that. Then he looked around, as if checking to make sure nobody was lurking who might overhear, even though they were the only two people in the room. "I ordinarily wouldn't say anything about this, but . . ." He looked around again.

"But what?" Gino asked with genuine interest.

"Well, you know how fanatical Pop was about the milk."

"He did seem to take great pride in how pure his is."

"Yeah, well, not everybody does."

"Not everybody does what?"

Harvey swallowed. "Not everybody keeps their milk pure."

Now, this was interesting. "Really? Isn't there a law now about how milk has to be pasteurized or something?"

"Oh yes. They have inspectors and everything, but that doesn't mean everybody follows the rules."

"And do you know somebody who doesn't follow them?"

Harvey leaned forward, as if confiding a deep, dark secret. "Pop found a dairy out in Brooklyn that still uses swill milk. That's when the cows are fed the mash that—"

"I know what swill milk is. What was he going to do about it?"

Harvey frowned. "I don't know. He didn't say, but he was plenty mad, and I think . . . I think he went to see the owner."

Now, this was *really* interesting. "What's the name of this dairy?"

"I don't know."

Gino managed not to sigh. "Can you find out?"

"I don't know. Maybe I could."

"What would happen to this dairy if your father reported them?"

"I don't know that either, but they'd be in trouble. Maybe they'd even have to shut down."

Gino could see that Harvey was just guessing, but it was a logical guess. At a minimum, exposure would surely result in lost business and maybe some fines. Did people kill over that?

People killed for all sorts of silly reasons, so why not that?

Gino gave Harvey his friendliest smile. "Could you find out the name of the dairy for me, Harvey?"

"I'll . . . Yes . . . Well, I mean, I'll try."

"Good. And Harvey, where were you on New Year's Eve?"

"New Year's Eve?" he asked suspiciously.

"Yes, the night your father was killed. You went out to celebrate, didn't you?"

"Of course I did."

"Were you alone?"

"What do you mean?"

"I mean, was somebody with you? Did you meet some friends? Where did you go?"

"Oh, I . . . Uh, yes, I met some friends."

"And where did you go with them?"

"I . . . To a saloon. I . . . More than one saloon, I think. We drank a lot that night. So I really don't remember."

"Maybe your friends will. Who are they?" Gino pulled a notebook and pencil from his pocket.

Harvey found that alarming. "I can't have you bothering my friends. What will they think?"

Gino flashed his smile again. "They'll think they are helping you prove you didn't kill your father."

Was Harvey looking a little pale? "That's ridiculous! I didn't kill my father. Why would I?"

"I don't know. I don't know why anyone would kill him, but if I can cross you off my list of suspects, that makes my job easier."

"I'll have to think about it. I don't know if my friends would appreciate being questioned."

Gino nodded his complete understanding. "Maybe you'd like to check with them first. That's fine. I'll come back tomorrow and you can give me their names and also the name of that dairy, while you're at it."

For some reason, Harvey didn't seem very excited by that prospect.

Frank waited to consult with Sarah until they were well away from the Pritchards' town house and he had managed to flag down a cab to take them home. Once securely inside the cab, they could speak freely, and he was glad to see Sarah still looked as baffled as he had felt in dealing with Mrs. Pritchard and her friend.

"So what do you think?" he asked.

"I don't know what to think." She shook her head as if to clear it. "She isn't too happy that you're investigating the murder, though."

"I noticed. Bergman isn't happy either."

"And who is he? And what gives him the right to be happy or not?"

"A childhood friend, she said."

Sarah frowned at such nonsense. "I had many childhood friends, but I didn't summon any of them to comfort me when my husband was murdered, especially not the men."

"So you don't think he's a childhood friend?" he asked with interest.

"Maybe he is or at least he once was, but he's more than that now. Did you see the way they looked at each other?"

"Yes, but . . ."

"But what?" she prodded.

"They didn't act like lovers, if that's what you mean."

She smiled smugly and leaned back against the seat.

"What did I miss?"

"They didn't act like lovers in the first flush of desire, it's true."

Frank winced. "Is that the way we act?"

"I'm sure we did on our honeymoon, but fortunately, we were in Europe so no one we knew saw us."

"And how do we act now?"

"Like a married couple who are very comfortable with each other."

Frank considered this for a long moment, remembering how Mrs. Pritchard had turned to Bergman time and again during their conversation. "You're right. But they're old friends. Wouldn't that account for it?"

She sighed in dismay and shook her head at his naïveté. "Imagine for a moment that I and—oh, whom shall I choose? Oh yes!—that I and Black Jack Robinson were closeted together after your death but before you were even in the ground, and that we were on such intimate terms that he felt comfortable questioning the authorities on my behalf about the details of your death."

Frank understood immediately. "I can't imagine it at all."

"Of course you can't, because women simply don't have that type of *friendship* with men, particularly married women with men to whom they are not married or otherwise related."

"So you think they're *lovers?*"

"I certainly think they are very close, and they have been very close for a long time."

"But wouldn't Pritchard have known? If it was going on for a long time, I mean?"

She gave him a pitying look. "Not all men are police detectives, Malloy. And I'm sure she and Bergman are very discreet."

He took a few minutes to consider this startling theory. "That could explain why the maid was so flustered."

"Servants always know everything, and this might have been the first time they had met alone at her house."

"Because it was the first chance they'd had, and now that she's a widow . . ."

"There's nothing to keep them apart, except the fear of gossip," Sarah mused.

"And maybe she no longer even cares about that," Frank said. "Her daughter is safely married off, and Harvey will be rich enough that a little scandal won't scare away too many eligible young ladies."

"And they must have been waiting for years already. I don't suppose Mr. Pritchard would give her a divorce."

"No, he didn't strike me as the type who would be understanding about his wife's desire to leave him for another man."

"Are there any men who *are* that understanding?"

"Maybe a few, but probably not many."

Sarah nodded sagely. "Which means she and Bergman could only wait around for him to die."

"And maybe they got tired of waiting and decided to help him along."

"Just what I was thinking. That would certainly explain their lack of enthusiasm at learning you are going to investigate. Where did Mrs. Pritchard say she'd spent New Year's Eve?"

Frank had to think back. "Didn't Mrs. Ellsworth say she was home alone and went to bed early, so she didn't even know her husband hadn't come home until the next morning?"

"I believe so. And if her husband wasn't home—which he wasn't because he was murdered that night—then there's no one to confirm that."

"Except the servants," Frank remembered. "They know everything."

"What do you want?"

Gino nearly jumped at the unexpected question. He'd been wandering through the dairy's stable on his way out of the building to see if he could spot anything out of the ordinary, and he hadn't realized anyone was near. He turned around to find an older man in dirty work clothes glaring at him. "I was just . . . I was upstairs meeting with Harvey Pritchard, and I thought I'd just . . . This is a really impressive operation you have here."

"Why were you meeting with Harvey Pritchard?"

Gino took a few seconds to size up his interrogator and decided he didn't look threatening, just concerned. "I'm a private investigator. I've been hired to find out who killed Mr. Pritchard."

The man winced and dropped his gaze for a moment. Was he mourning Mr. Pritchard?

"Have you worked here a long time?" Gino asked kindly.

The man looked up at that. He swiped a hand across his nose before he said, "Almost twenty-five years."

"You must've known Mr. Pritchard pretty well, then."

"I knew him from when he used to help load the milk wagons himself."

"He was very proud of the quality of his milk."

"Oh yeah, he never sold anything but the best."

"I don't suppose he had much patience for people who tried to cut corners, then."

The man frowned. "What do you mean by that?"

"I mean other dairies that aren't as careful."

"Oh. No, he didn't."

"Do you know any dairies in particular that he didn't approve of?"

The man shrugged. Plainly the subject didn't interest him. "Did you say *private* investigator? Why would Harvey need you? Aren't the police investigating?"

Gino smiled apologetically. "Uh, no. It seems they've decided not to." Gino glanced around to see if anyone else was around. "Would you have any idea why they did that?"

The man's eyes widened in alarm. "Me? No. I don't know nothing. I just do my job and don't ask questions."

"Is there something you'd like to ask questions about?"

He shook his head quite certainly. "No, and if you're smart, you won't either."

Harvey is definitely hiding something," Gino told Frank and Sarah. He'd joined them at their home after his conversation with young Pritchard at the Pure Milk Dairy.

"But what?" Frank asked as Sarah served Gino the coffee their maid, Hattie, had brought to them in the parlor.

"I thought he must have been involved in his father's death, but now I'm thinking he's just acting guilty because there's something going on at the dairy."

"Or it could be both," Sarah pointed out. "Nothing is ever simple, is it?"

No, it wasn't. "Mrs. Pritchard is hiding something, too, and we actually got to meet him," Frank said.

Gino perked right up at that. *"Him?"*

Frank nodded to indicate Sarah should tell the story of meeting Mr. Bergman.

When she'd finished, Gino sat back and considered it for a moment. "You think this Bergman and Mrs. Pritchard are lovers?"

"It seems obvious," Sarah said.

Gino winced. "But they're so old."

Both Frank and Sarah burst out laughing.

"What's so funny?" Gino asked, offended.

"They're not much more than forty," Sarah said.

"That's pretty old."

Frank caught Sarah's eye, and they enjoyed another good laugh. "I'll remind you of this someday," he promised Gino.

"I still don't see why it's so funny."

"At any rate," Sarah said, managing a straight face, "if they are lovers, one or both of them might have decided to get rid of Mr. Pritchard before they got any older."

"That's possible, I guess," Gino said. "And let's not forget about whoever owns this dairy that Pritchard was going to report to the authorities."

"If it really exists," Frank said. "Harvey might've been lying about that. We'll find out when you go back to see him tomorrow."

"In the meantime, we need to find out more about Mrs. Pritchard and this Bergman fellow,"

Sarah said. "I'm wondering if Mrs. Ellsworth knows anything about him."

Frank couldn't help smiling at that. "When has Mrs. Ellsworth not known everything there was to know about everyone she meets?"

Sarah waited until the next morning, when Nelson would be at work, to call on Mrs. Ellsworth. Nelson might not approve of them gossiping about his wife's family, so she didn't want to take any chances.

"Oh, Mrs. Malloy, I'm so glad to see you," Theda said when the maid escorted her into the family parlor where Theda and Mrs. Ellsworth were sewing. "Has Mr. Malloy found out anything yet?"

"He only started yesterday," Sarah said. "These things take time."

"I'm sorry, but I'm just so very anxious."

"Theda, go fix a tea tray and slice up some of that cake we made yesterday," Mrs. Ellsworth said. "Then we can have a nice chat."

Theda obediently hurried off, and Mrs. Ellsworth closed the parlor door behind her. "That will keep her busy for a few minutes, if there's something you'd like to talk to me about."

"How did you know?" Sarah asked in amazement.

Mrs. Ellsworth smiled mysteriously. "Let's just say I was hoping. Now, what is it?"

"Have you met Mr. Otto Bergman?"

Mrs. Ellsworth's eyes lit up. "*Uncle* Otto? Of course I have. He was at the wedding. Mrs. Pritchard's dear friend from childhood. May I assume you've met him, too?"

So that was why he'd looked familiar. Sarah had seen him at the wedding. "Malloy and I both met him. We called on her yesterday to let her know Nelson had hired Malloy, and he was there."

"*There?* At her house, you mean? Dear me, that's brazen of her."

"She's a widow now," Sarah said. "She doesn't have to worry about her husband finding out."

Mrs. Ellsworth glanced at the door as if to make sure it was still closed. "What is it you suspect?"

"Probably the same thing you suspect. Malloy and I think Mrs. Pritchard and Bergman are much more than friends."

"You mustn't mention that to Theda. She . . . Well, people often see only what they want to see, and of course we never want to think ill of our parents."

"How did you find out?"

Mrs. Ellsworth sighed. "Theda often mentions him because he is usually included in family gatherings. He is very fond of her and spoiled her a bit, I think. At first it just seemed strange to me that a man who is no relation to the family would be so involved with them, but then I saw the two of them together and . . ." She shrugged.

"Do you think Mr. Pritchard knew?"

"Heavens no! He never would have allowed the man near his family if he had. Not that he cared that much about his family, but you know how men are. Pride is everything. He wouldn't want it known his wife preferred another man."

Yes, too many men put pride before all else. "Do you think Harvey knew?"

Mrs. Ellsworth frowned at this. "I can't imagine. Children don't tend to think of their parents in that way, do they? Can you imagine your own mother having an affair?"

"Absolutely not."

"You see? And yet she's still a very attractive woman, and if she were unhappy with your father . . ."

Sarah gave a little shudder, although she had to admit Mrs. Ellsworth was correct. "I see what you mean, and love often drives people to do things they'd never otherwise do."

"Yes, and . . . Good heavens! Do you think Mrs. Pritchard and Bergman could have been driven to murder her husband?"

Mrs. Ellsworth certainly hadn't needed much encouragement to reach that conclusion. "I hope not, but we do have to consider every possibility."

"I know you do, but . . . Poor Theda!" Mrs. Ellsworth looked truly stricken.

"We don't have any reason to think it's true," Sarah added hastily.

"That's comforting, I suppose." Mrs. Ellsworth didn't look comforted, though.

Theda chose that moment to return. "Sally will bring the tray when the tea is ready. Did I miss anything important?" she asked, taking the seat she'd vacated earlier.

"Mrs. Malloy was just telling me she called on your mother yesterday. They wanted to tell her you'd hired Mr. Malloy," Mrs. Ellsworth said.

"How do you think she's doing?" Theda asked.

"Very well, I think. She's fortunate to have good friends to support her. A Mr. Bergman was there when we arrived."

"Oh yes, I should have known Uncle Otto would visit her. They're very old friends. Did she tell you?"

"She mentioned that they'd grown up together," Sarah said.

Theda smiled fondly. "In the old German neighborhood. Father didn't like being reminded that she was very poor, so she didn't talk about it when he was around, but Harvey and I loved hearing their stories about what their life was like back then."

"So your father's family was well-off?"

"Oh no, not at all! If anything, he was even poorer, but as I said, he didn't like being reminded."

Pride again. "I see. You seem very fond of Mr. Bergman yourself. Are you friendly with his family as well?" Sarah asked, hoping to nudge more information out of Theda without questioning her outright.

"He doesn't have any family, sadly. His wife died very young, and he never remarried."

"Which is probably why he doted on you and Harvey," Mrs. Ellsworth said.

The maid brought their refreshments then, interrupting what had become a promising exchange of information. When she'd gone and Mrs. Ellsworth was serving them, Sarah cast about frantically for an innocent-sounding question that would keep the conversation going in the right direction.

Before she could, Theda said, "It's funny to think of it now, but mother and Uncle Otto almost married once."

# V

Frank hadn't wanted to start his morning at the morgue, but he realized he needed to know some details about how Clarence Pritchard had died, and he'd already put it off long enough. He found Doc Haynes in his office at Bellevue, which was much better than finding him in the middle of an autopsy.

"Clarence Pritchard?" Doc muttered, sorting through the files scattered haphazardly across his desk. He pulled one from the mess and flipped it opened. "Oh yes, one of our New Year's Eve casualties." Doc peered at Frank over the folder. "What is your interest in him, if I might ask?"

"I've been hired to investigate his death because Devery has forbidden the detective squad from doing it."

Doc considered this. "How interesting. Do we know why?"

"You mean *why* besides some money changed hands? No, we do not."

Doc nodded and returned to perusing the file. "Strangled from behind with his own scarf, a good-quality piece of wool, I noted. It was still around his neck."

"Any other injuries?"

"Broken fingernails and scratches on his neck,

where he tried to pull the scarf loose. No bruised knuckles or any other marks on him to indicate a fight. It looks like somebody came up behind him, got ahold of his scarf, and choked him. And he was missing a shoe."

"A shoe?"

Haynes nodded. "They said his body was lying in some bushes, so probably whoever killed him did it nearby and then dragged the body to the bushes where it wouldn't be easily discovered. I figure his shoe came off during his death struggles or maybe when the body was moved."

What were the odds the shoe would still be there? Probably pretty slim after several days. "Any idea when he died?"

Doc shook his head. "He was pretty stiff when they found him the next morning, but rigor mortis wasn't complete. It was a cold night, though, so that would've slowed things down, which makes it hard to judge how long he'd been dead."

"I saw him the night he died between eleven thirty and midnight, so it was after that, if anyone asks you."

"You knew him?" Doc asked in surprise.

"I'd met him. His daughter is married to our neighbor. That's why they asked me to help when the police lost interest."

"I see. Well, I'm sorry I don't have more to tell you."

"How long would it have taken him to die?"

"A few minutes, but he wouldn't have been able to make a sound as soon as the scarf tightened around his throat. In the dark and with the noise from the crowd . . . I expect this could've happened with a hundred people within arm's length and they might not have noticed."

"That's what I was afraid of. And if anybody saw him lying on the ground after, they would've just thought he was drunk."

"There's a lot of that on New Year's Eve, although I've never understood what all the excitement's about."

"Just another excuse to drink, I'd guess."

"You're probably right."

"When are you going to release the body?"

"I already did. Sent word to the family and somebody picked it up first thing this morning."

"I need to find out when the funeral is, then. Thanks, Doc."

"Just let me know if this turns out to be interesting."

Frank grinned. "I certainly will."


"They almost married?" Sarah echoed, unable to believe she'd heard Theda correctly. A glance at Mrs. Ellsworth told her that her neighbor hadn't known this delicious piece of gossip either. How on earth had she missed it?

Theda smiled a little sheepishly. "Mother doesn't know that I know, and I never would have mentioned it when Father was alive, of course. Not that Mother ever gave him reason to be jealous, but . . . It could have made things awkward, couldn't it?"

"Absolutely," Mrs. Ellsworth said. "Men are such fragile creatures."

"Fragile?" Theda marveled. "Surely you're joking."

"Not at all. They can't stand the slightest challenge to their manly pride. You must have noticed."

Theda considered this for a moment. "Oh, I see it now. That explains poor Amelio."

"Amelio?" Sarah asked.

"Amelio Bruno. He works at the dairy. He . . . Oh, it's embarrassing now, and it sounds like I'm boasting, but he was quite infatuated with me at one time." She blushed prettily.

"How could we blame him?" Mrs. Ellsworth said.

Theda sighed at her memories. "I was so sorry for him. I didn't feel that way about him at all, and of course Father let him know he would never approve of him courting me, so that was the end of it, but I could tell Amelio was very hurt."

"I'm sure he was, dear," Mrs. Ellsworth said. "I can imagine how Nelson would have grieved if he had lost you."

"I suppose Uncle Otto was hurt, too, although

he must have recovered if he and Mother became such good friends," Theda said.

"How did you find out they'd almost married if your mother didn't tell you?" Sarah asked to return them to the subject she really wanted to discuss.

"My grandmother said something about it one time. She died years ago, when I was still a little girl, but I'll never forget what she said that day. Uncle Otto had just been to visit us. He'd brought me a doll, and she was so beautiful, which is why I remember. Grandmother told my mother she was sorry she hadn't let Mother marry him because he really had become successful after all."

"I wonder what she meant by that?" Mrs. Ellsworth said.

Theda sighed. "Grandmother was very ambitious for her children. She wanted Mother to marry well so she wouldn't have to struggle the way Grandmother did, and Father already had the dairy when they met. He was a bit older, you see."

"What does Mr. Bergman do for a living?" Sarah asked.

"He was a tailor, or at least that's how he started out. He was just an apprentice when Mother married Father, but now he owns several tailor shops around the city."

"So he's done very well for himself," Sarah said. "But your grandmother didn't know what would happen, so she encouraged your mother to marry Mr. Pritchard, who already owned a dairy."

"I think she did more than encourage it," Theda said. "Mother was young and so was Uncle Otto then—only seventeen or eighteen, I think—and they couldn't dream of disobeying their parents."

"But Mr. Bergman married someone else, too," Mrs. Ellsworth said.

"Eventually, yes. I suppose it was expected of a young man who was earning a good living. He and his wife were friends of my parents, or at least they saw each other socially. By then Uncle Otto had his own tailor shop, so even Grandmother couldn't object. But as I said, Uncle Otto's wife died young. No one spoke of such things, but I've always suspected she died in childbirth."

So many women did, and their babies along with them. "And you said Mr. Bergman never remarried," Sarah said.

"No, although he and Mother remained friends."

"And what about your father?" Mrs. Ellsworth asked. "Was he friends with Mr. Bergman, too?"

"I suppose, although Father was always so busy with the dairy, he didn't have much time for socializing. Uncle Otto would take us on outings when Father couldn't, though. I know Mother appreciated it very much."

"And your father didn't mind?"

Theda smiled a little sadly. "I think he was just

glad Mother wasn't nagging him to go places with us."

The doorbell interrupted them, and they waited in silence to see who might be calling at this unfashionable hour.

They heard the maid answer the door, and in a few moments, she brought in a telegram addressed to Theda. Theda tore it open and read it quickly. "It's from Mother. Father's funeral will be in two days."

"Saturday," Mrs. Ellsworth calculated.

The police would have released the body since they weren't investigating anymore.

"Oh dear, that suddenly makes it seem very real," Theda said, and burst into tears. Sarah and Mrs. Ellsworth spent the rest of the visit comforting her.

Frank caught the Third Avenue elevated train at the 28th Street station and got off at Fulton Street to walk the rest of the way over to Trinity Church. No one was working outside on this crisp January day, but the building wasn't locked. He easily found the church office and was soon directed to Mr. Quincy, who the church secretary assured Frank was the one who had found that poor man's body on New Year's Day.

Mr. Quincy was an older man in work clothes who at that moment was dusting the pews in the breathtakingly beautiful sanctuary. He looked up

119

in surprise when Frank approached and introduced himself.

"You're not with the police?" he asked, eyeing
Frank's card suspiciously.

"No. The police have decided not to investigate
Mr. Pritchard's death, so the family hired me to
see if I could find out who killed him."

"Poor fellow. That's no way to do a person.
They just threw him in the bushes like he was
trash they didn't want anymore."

"I was hoping you'd answer a few questions for
me."

Quincy shrugged. "Don't know much, but I'll
be happy to help."

"Could you show me where you found him?"

Quincy sighed. Plainly, he didn't relish the idea
of leaving the relative warmth of the sanctuary.
"Let me get my coat."

When Quincy had bundled himself against the
wintry winds, he led Frank through some hall-
ways and out a door that was probably seldom
used by worshippers.

"This here's the back of the church," Quincy
said as Frank took his bearings. "That street there
is Trinity Place."

Without waiting for a reply, he led Frank to
a clump of bushes and pointed. "That's where
I found him. We was cleaning up the grounds
that morning. Them people who come on New
Year's Eve to hear the bells, they don't care a wit

that this is God's house. They throw their trash everywhere. Liquor bottles mostly. And beer. And heaven knows what else. Filthy. We can't just leave it. What would people think? So we had everybody out that morning, picking up. I was working back here and saw his legs sticking out."

"Do you usually find a lot of drunks sleeping it off?"

Quincy shook his gray head. "Not in this weather. If somebody passed out, they'd freeze to death by morning. In fact, that's what I figured had happened, except for him being in the bushes, stuffed in like. Nobody would do that to themselves. I tried to pull him out, to see if he was still alive, but he was too stiff. I knew then there was no hope so I went to get help."

"Did you notice his shoe was missing?"

"Shoe?" He scratched his head. "I guess I did. Didn't think much about it, though."

"Has anyone found it?"

"I don't know. I can ask the other men."

"Would you?"

They started back to the door so Quincy could question the other men who cleaned the church. "I'm told he hadn't been robbed," Frank said as they walked.

"Oh no. Still had his watch and everything. I made sure nobody bothered him until the police took him away, too."

121

"I'm sure his family appreciates it."

Back inside, Quincy instructed Frank to have a seat in the back pew while he questioned the other men. Frank took the time to appreciate the soaring beauty of the sanctuary with its enormous stained glass windows. Even without the music and the candles and the fancy robes and the hundreds of congregants that must gather here on Sunday, the place was impressive.

A few minutes later, Quincy returned with a younger man who looked more than a little frightened.

"Allan here found the shoe," Quincy reported.

"I didn't know it was important or that it had anything to do with the dead man," Allan said, glancing nervously between Frank and Quincy.

"Of course you didn't," Frank said. "What did you do with it?"

"I gave it to the church secretary. I figured somebody had lost it during the bell ringing and they'd be back to look for it when they sobered up."

"Do you remember where you found it?"

Allan glanced at Quincy again, who nodded his encouragement. "By one of the benches."

Frank had noticed the benches on his first trip outside. "Can you show me which one?"

He did. The church had placed some benches around the grounds, where people could sit and rest or do whatever people did outside a church.

"It was just laying there. It was a nice shoe. If there was two of them, I might've kept them myself." He glanced guiltily at Quincy, who had accompanied them, but Quincy didn't chasten him. "I didn't know the dead man was missing a shoe."

"That's all right. Thanks for your help, both of you."

"Do you know who he was?" Quincy asked.

"Oh yes. Mr. Clarence Pritchard. He owned the Pure Milk Dairy."

"Really?" Allan said. "I see them wagons out all night long. Who killed him?"

"That's what I'm trying to find out," Frank said.

As he had promised the day before, Gino returned to the Pure Milk Dairy late that morning. The place was bustling with activity as the deliverymen were still unloading their wagons from the morning run. The milk was delivered in glass bottles, and customers would leave their empty milk bottles out on the stoop. The drivers would leave full bottles and collect the empty ones to be returned to the dairy, washed and refilled. The clink and clatter of hundreds of empty glass milk bottles rattling in their wire carriers and wooden crates was deafening, although the weary horses in their stalls nearby didn't seem to mind. Since none of the deliverymen looked interested in chatting, Gino made his way upstairs to the offices.

Once again the fellow at the desk stopped him, but after a reminder of who Gino was, he gave him permission to pass. Gino found Harvey Pritchard sitting at his father's desk again and looking even more bewildered than before.

"What are you doing here?" Harvey demanded.

"I came back to get the names of your friends, remember? You were going to make sure they were willing to vouch for you." Which wasn't exactly what Gino had asked for yesterday but what they both knew the friends would be doing. If they were good friends, they'd give Harvey an alibi for the time of his father's murder. Gino's job would be to find out if they were telling the truth.

Harvey's expression was momentarily panicked, but then he remembered something. "And you wanted the name of that dairy in Brooklyn, the one selling swill milk."

"That's right. Do you have it?"

Harvey began shuffling through the papers scattered across the desk and finally found the one he was looking for. "Here it is. Green Hills Dairy." He handed the paper to Gino. Someone had written the name and address of the dairy on it and nothing more.

Gino folded the paper carefully and put it into his pocket. "And the names of your friends?"

"You don't need to speak to all of them," Harvey

said with a confidence he obviously did not possess. "One should be enough. Amelio Bruno. He'll tell you we were together that whole night."

"All right. Where can I find Mr. Bruno?"

"That's easy. He's right outside. *Bruno!*" he added, shouting.

After a few moments, during which Harvey fidgeted nervously, a young man a few years older than Harvey came to the office door. Even without knowing his name, Gino would have recognized a fellow Italian. He wore a clerk's green eyeshade, and like the other clerks, he had removed his suit coat and had paper cuff protectors on his wrists. Oddly, his expression said he deeply resented the summons. "Yeah?" Which was hardly an acceptable response when speaking to your employer.

"Mr. Donatelli, this is Amelio Bruno. Tell Mr. Donatelli what we did on New Year's Eve, Amie."

He smiled grimly. He had apparently been prepared for this encounter. "Oh yeah. Me and Harvey went out to celebrate together."

Gino made a show of taking out his notebook and pencil and opening the notebook to a clean page. "And where did you go to celebrate?"

Bruno blinked in surprise. He obviously had not been prepared to be challenged. "What?"

"You said you went out to celebrate. Did you go to a party? To a saloon? Someplace else?"

Bruno glanced at Harvey but got no help there.

"I . . . To a saloon. To more than one saloon, in fact."

"Which ones?" Gino asked pleasantly, pencil poised to write down the names.

"I . . . I'm not sure."

"If you can't remember the name of the saloon, maybe you could just tell me where you were and then we can figure out which ones."

"We started out near Harvey's house, didn't we, Harvey?"

Plainly, Harvey was unprepared as well. "I . . . I think so."

Bruno shrugged and smiled a little sheepishly. "It's hard to remember. We were drinking a lot."

Gino nodded wisely. "I understand. Maybe we could go out together and retrace your steps."

"Why do you need to know where we were?" Harvey asked petulantly. "Amie told you we were together. That's all you need to know."

But Gino shook his head. "You might think so, but Mr. Bruno works for you, doesn't he?"

Harvey seemed surprised at that idea. "Well, I guess he does now."

Bruno seemed surprised as well, and not exactly pleased. "Yeah, I guess I do."

"So he'd want to stay on your good side, and if you asked him to say you were together, he would probably do it, even if it wasn't true and he knew he might be charged with perjury or even as an accessory to murder for doing it."

*"What?"* Bruno cried.

"He's not an accessory to anything because I didn't kill my father!" Harvey tried.

"Is that what this is about?" Bruno asked. "Because you didn't say anything about murder!"

"So are you saying that you really weren't with Harvey on New Year's Eve?"

Bruno gave Harvey an oddly superior grin. "We were together, but not until later. A few of us were at this saloon, but Harvey didn't join us until after one o'clock."

Gino showed no reaction to this at all. He merely turned back to Harvey, who was glaring at Bruno in return. "Maybe you can tell me where you were before you joined up with Mr. Bruno and his friends."

"Yeah, where were you?" Bruno asked, his tone still much too disrespectful for an employee.

Harvey needed another long minute to come up with an answer. "I was here."

Gino frowned. "Here? At the dairy?"

"Sure. People need milk every day, and we deliver every day except Sunday."

"Do you deliver the milk yourself?" Gino asked, happy to hear his voice sounded completely innocent.

"Of course not!" Because he was the owner's son, his tone said.

"Then why did you have to be here at that time of night? And even if you did deliver it yourself, I thought you delivered milk early in the morning, not at midnight."

Harvey opened his mouth to reply but nothing came out. He cast Bruno a frantic glance, but Bruno just shrugged. Finally, Harvey said, "They have to get the wagons loaded."

Gino gave them both a puzzled frown. "When do they start doing that?"

Harvey winced, but Bruno said, "Around four o'clock."

"In the morning?" Gino asked.

"That's right," Bruno confirmed, again a little smugly, proving Harvey a liar.

"If you don't do deliveries yourself," Gino said to Harvey, "and they don't even start until four o'clock in the morning, why were you here before midnight that night?"

Harvey looked hopefully at Bruno, who only shook his head. "All right, I was . . ." Harvey sighed in disgust. "I lied . . . I was out looking for my father."

Now, wasn't that interesting? "Why would you do that?"

"Can't you guess? You heard how he goes on about the turn of the century. I knew he'd be out there trying to convince everybody they were wrong and making a fool of himself, so when I found out he was going down to the bell ringing, I thought I'd go find him and bring him home before he got himself into trouble."

"That was very, uh, *noble* of you," Gino said, although *noble* wasn't the word he was thinking. "And did you find him?"

"No, I did not. I couldn't believe how many people were there, and I couldn't very well ask people if they'd seen an old man trying to convince everyone this was the beginning of the twentieth century."

"Were you alone?"

"Except for the thousands of other people there, you mean?" he asked bitterly. "Yes, I was alone."

"But nobody can confirm that you never found your father."

Harvey turned his murderous glare on Gino. "No, but I can promise you that if I *had* found him, I would've dragged him home and he'd still be alive."

Or maybe he did find Pritchard and that's why he's no longer alive, although why would Harvey have killed his father? Sons and fathers often didn't get along, but few of those sons resorted to murder. True, Harvey would apparently inherit the dairy, but was that enough motive? They'd need to learn more about Harvey before they could know for sure.

"Thanks for your help," Gino told the two men, closing his notebook and stuffing it back into his pocket. "I'll go check on this Green Hills Dairy."

"Green Hills? What for?" Bruno asked with a frown.

"Pop discovered they're selling swill milk," Harvey told him.

"And you think somebody there might've killed the old man over *that?*" Bruno scoffed.

"Don't you?"

Bruno merely shrugged.

Gino glanced at Harvey, who was glaring at Bruno again. "Harvey seems to think his father was going to report this Green Hills Dairy to the authorities."

"He was," Harvey confirmed defiantly. "And maybe they had somebody kill Pop before he could."

Bruno seemed to have a sudden change of heart. "Oh, I see. Yeah, that's probably it. If Mr. Pritchard reported them, they could get shut down."

But he didn't sound really convinced. Gino would have to come back and talk to Bruno alone. He might very well have something more interesting to say without Harvey around. Gino thanked the two men again and took his leave.

When he reached the first floor, he found that the activity had slowed significantly. The wagons had all been emptied and the drivers had gone home. A few boys were still grooming the horses and mucking out the stalls. Gino wandered around, looking for the man who had been willing to talk to him before or really anyone who might be willing to chat, but oddly, no one would even meet his gaze. They all just continued their work as if he weren't even there.

The warning he'd received yesterday echoed in his mind and the strange reactions of the stable boys confirmed his suspicions. Something was going on here that he needed to know more about.

Frank made it home in time for lunch with Sarah and Maeve. His mother was at Brian's school, but Maeve's duties ended when she dropped Catherine off at Miss Spence's School and did not begin again until she picked her up in the afternoon. They were going to have to find something to fill Maeve's time now that Catherine didn't need a nursemaid all day, because heaven knew what Maeve might get up to if they didn't.

They ate in the breakfast room, which was much more practical for three people than the dining room, and their cook, Velvet, served them a delicious Welsh rarebit.

Sarah described her visit with Mrs. Ellsworth and Theda that morning.

"How romantic," Maeve said when Sarah had told them about Mrs. Pritchard and Otto Bergman's thwarted plans.

"You think it's romantic that they weren't allowed to get married?" Frank asked, confused.

"No, that they've been in love all these years, in spite of everything."

"And murdered Mr. Pritchard so they could finally be together?" Sarah asked archly.

Maeve waved that theory away with both hands. "If they were willing to do that, why didn't they do it years ago?"

"Maybe because he never suspected them until recently," Sarah said. "If he just found out about the affair, he might have told Mrs. Pritchard she could no longer see Bergman."

Maeve shook her head this time. "You mean he told her that she couldn't see Bergman or else? Or else what? He'd divorce her? That's exactly what she wanted!"

"True, but he may have threatened her with something else."

"Like what?"

"Who knows? But Mr. Pritchard would have known what she cared about."

"Maybe, but I still think it's romantic."

Frank cleared his throat to remind them he was still there. "Well, I don't think it's romantic at all. I think it's sad. All of those people were miserable for over twenty years."

"He's right," Sarah told Maeve. "Mrs. Pritchard and Bergman might have enjoyed their stolen moments, but they would have lived in constant fear of being found out."

"I guess so, but you have to admit they must really love each other, and at least they can be together now."

"Unless one or both of them killed Pritchard," Frank reminded them. "And let's remember, we aren't even certain they were having an affair."

Maeve sighed in defeat. "Do we at least know where Bergman was that night?"

Frank exchanged a chagrined glance with Sarah. "No. We didn't even ask him."

"But only because we didn't know he might have a reason to want Mr. Pritchard dead," Sarah reminded him. "And Mrs. Pritchard claims she was at home in bed."

Maeve smiled wickedly. "Maybe Bergman was with her. Then they'd both have an alibi."

"An alibi we couldn't believe," Sarah pointed out.

"So we need to question Bergman a little more thoroughly," Frank said.

"And find out if Mrs. Pritchard really was home," Sarah said.

"Who can tell you that?" Maeve asked. "If she was alone . . ."

"The servants," Frank and Sarah said in unison.

"The servants always know everything," Sarah added.

"Sounds like a job for Gino," Frank said. "Maids love him. He'll need to go when Mrs. Pritchard isn't home, though."

"How about during the funeral service?" Sarah said.

"Do you know when it is?"

"Saturday. Theda got a telegram while I was there. Theda said her mother has decided to have it at their church."

"Perfect."

"So did you find out anything from the autopsy?" Sarah asked.

She'd waited until they had finished their Welsh rarebit to ask, Frank noticed. "Doc Haynes said somebody strangled Pritchard with his own scarf. From behind."

"That sounds familiar," Maeve said. They'd recently solved a murder that had hit very close to them in which the victim died the same way.

"But how could you strangle someone in a crowd like that without someone noticing?" Sarah asked.

"Doc said Pritchard wouldn't have been able to make a sound as soon as the scarf tightened around his neck, and it was dark and nobody was paying any particular attention. Remember how noisy it was, too, with all those tin horns blowing. I also figured out where he died."

"You mean besides near the church?" Maeve asked.

"Yes. He must have been sitting on a bench."

"How do you know that?" Sarah asked.

"Doc said he was missing a shoe, so I went to the church to see if I could find where he'd lost it. Turns out one of the maintenance men had found it under one of the benches. He didn't realize it belonged to Pritchard."

"So Mr. Pritchard was sitting on a bench and someone came up behind him and strangled him with his own scarf and he kicked off his shoe while it was happening," Maeve said.

"That's what it looks like," Frank confirmed. "Then the killer dragged the body over to a clump of bushes and stuffed Mr. Pritchard into them, mostly out of sight."

"Wait," Sarah said. "Did you say someone dragged his body away from the bench and hid it in some bushes?"

"Yes, that's—"

"That doesn't make sense," Maeve said.

"No, it doesn't," Sarah said. "Maybe nobody noticed when he was being strangled, but someone would have noticed a person dragging a body and hiding it, even in the dark."

"And it wasn't totally dark," Maeve said. "The streetlamps were lit and they're everywhere in that part of the city."

"Oh yes, I hadn't thought about the dragging part looking suspicious," Frank said.

Sarah frowned. "So if he was strangled while sitting on the bench . . ."

"Mr. Pritchard wasn't sitting on any benches when you saw him, though," Maeve said.

"What do you mean?" Frank asked.

"I mean he was going from person to person

explaining how this was the real beginning of the century and making everyone angry."

"That's right," Sarah said. "He was moving so quickly that you lost him in the crowd, too."

"So why would he have sat down with all those hundreds of people right there who might still be convinced?" Maeve asked.

"You're right," Frank said. "That doesn't make sense. And yet he did sit down, because that's where he was when he got killed."

"So if he wouldn't have sat down while there were people there still to be convinced, when *did* he sit down?" Maeve asked.

"After they had all left," Sarah said.

The others looked at her for a long moment.

"Remember, we waited while everyone was leaving to see if we could find him in the crowd," Sarah said.

"But we never saw him leaving," Maeve said.

"That's right," Frank said. "And that's because he never left. He would have been on the other side of the churchyard, over by Trinity Place, and we know he never left at all because he died there."

"So when all the other revelers were gone," Maeve said, "he might have been tired—"

"Or discouraged because nobody wanted to listen to his theories," Sarah said.

"Or sick, because remember you thought he looked strange," Maeve said.

"So he sat down on the nearest bench," Frank concluded.

"And someone saw him there and decided this was the perfect opportunity to kill him," Maeve said.

Frank and Sarah frowned.

"Don't look at me like that. It's what happened!"

"Yes, but why at that place and at that time?" Frank asked. "How could someone who just happened to want to murder Pritchard just happen to see him sitting there and decide this was his perfect opportunity?"

"That's easy," Maeve said. "The killer must have followed Pritchard there and waited for his chance."

"And I think that's exactly what happened," Gino said from the doorway.

# VI

Sarah got Gino seated at the table and Velvet immediately set about fixing him something to eat. While they waited for it to arrive, Gino told them about his visit to the dairy.

"So Harvey lied about where he was that night," Malloy mused.

"Yes, and he lied more than once, so now I can't even guess where he really was."

"So who is this Amelio Bruno to Harvey?" Maeve asked. "I mean besides one of the clerks at the dairy?"

"I gathered that he and Harvey are friends. They were going to celebrate New Year's Eve together, so Bruno must be more than just an employee."

"He was also once in love with Theda," Sarah said, shocking them all.

"Don't tell me it's another thwarted love affair," Maeve said. "This family seems to run to them."

"This one was very one-sided. Theda did not return his affections, and her father didn't approve of one of his clerks courting his daughter, either, but maybe his feelings for Theda make Mr. Bruno more willing to protect Harvey."

"Not necessarily. He might have lied for Harvey just to keep his job," Maeve said.

"But he wasn't too worried about losing his

job because as soon as I mentioned he might get arrested for perjury, he changed his tune pretty quick," Gino said.

"I was just telling the ladies about my visit to the morgue and to the church this morning," Malloy said.

"The church? You went back there?"

"Yes." He briefly explained how Doc had told him about the missing shoe and where it had been found.

Gino was nodding enthusiastically by the time Malloy had finished. "If Harvey had followed his father that night, he might have been keeping an eye on him the whole time, waiting for his chance."

"Or maybe he hadn't planned to kill his father but suddenly realized that would solve all his problems and took advantage of the opportunity," Maeve said.

"All what problems?" Sarah asked.

Maeve started to reply but stopped when she obviously couldn't think of anything.

"He'd inherit the dairy," Gino offered.

"Did he want the dairy?" Malloy asked.

"I don't know, but he doesn't seem too happy to have it," Gino admitted.

"He didn't get along with his father," Maeve offered.

"Is that enough reason to kill him, though?" Malloy asked.

Nobody had an answer.

"I think the more important question is why Harvey lied in the first place about where he was that night," Sarah said.

"He also lied in the second and third place. So far he's claimed to be out with his friends, at the dairy, and at the church where his father was killed," Gino said.

"That's a lot of lies for an innocent man, especially when nobody can confirm any of them," Maeve said.

"So it's possible he wasn't at any of those places, although it seems odd he'd finally claim he'd gone looking for his father when that makes him a better suspect in his murder," Malloy said.

"Maybe he didn't realize that," Sarah said.

"That's very possible. He doesn't seem very bright," Gino said.

"When he claimed he was at the dairy, what did he say he was doing there?" Maeve asked.

"That's the strange thing. Nobody should have been at the dairy at all so late at night except maybe a night watchman to keep an eye on things. The drivers come in very early in the morning to load up the milk wagons, and they go out around four o'clock. They deliver the milk, then come back and unload the empty milk bottles. They've got stable boys to take care of the horses, and by early afternoon, the drivers have gone home. I guess the men who pasteurize the milk and bottle it work until five or six o'clock, but after they go home, there's nothing happening until the drivers come back in the middle of the night. He tried to say he was there loading the milk wagons, but even I knew he was lying about that."

"So that was a really stupid lie," Malloy said.

"Yes, it was, except . . ." Gino paused when Velvet returned with his lunch. She'd made him a nice sandwich, since the rarebit was gone.

"Except what?" Maeve prodded while Gino took an enormous bite of the sandwich.

They had to wait while he chewed and swallowed. "Except it was his second story, and he seemed very pleased with himself, the way people are when you catch them in a lie and they finally tell you the truth and know it will get them out of trouble."

"But it didn't get him out of trouble," Maeve said.

"And then he changed his story again," Malloy mused. "Why did he change it that time?"

"Because I started asking him exactly what he was doing at the dairy at that time of night. I'd already gotten an idea of how things worked from my first visit, so it didn't make sense to me. Bruno was no help to him on this story, so he finally gave up and said he'd followed his father to the church for the celebration."

"Of course all three stories could be lies," Maeve pointed out.

142

"Or half-truths," Gino said. "Maybe Harvey did go to the church and kill his father and then went to a saloon to join his friends, but that story about being at the dairy seemed too strange to be made up."

"Especially when you know nothing happens at the dairy at that time of night," Malloy said.

"Nothing to do with the regular operation, no, but . . . I didn't mention this before because it was just a feeling, but I got that same feeling again today, so I should probably tell you. I think something is going on at the dairy that nobody wants me to know about."

"What makes you think that?" Sarah asked.

"Yesterday, one of the employees saw me looking around and he told me not to ask any questions."

"That's a strange thing to say to someone," Maeve said.

"I thought so. And today, nobody down in the stables would talk to me at all."

"Were you asking questions?" Maeve teased.

"No, as a matter of fact. I was just saying 'hello' and 'nice day,' but nobody acted like they even heard me. It was like they thought if they ignored me, I'd go away."

"Wishful thinking," Maeve said with a grin.

"Well, it's easy enough to find out if something is going on at the dairy," Malloy said. "We just go down there tonight and see."

## • • •

"Can you see anything?" Frank asked from beneath the heap of carriage robes he'd piled over him to keep out the wintry chill. Gino had convinced him to bring the motorcar to their late-night surveillance. Frank had to admit it was a good ruse. They'd parked down the street from the dairy, and Gino had hopped out and opened the hood, as if he were trying to fix something. Motors were always breaking down, so this was a common sight and no one would question their presence.

If only it wasn't so darned cold.

"Somebody just turned on some lights in the stable area," Gino reported from his position at the front of the motorcar. He stood on the sidewalk side so he had a clear view of the dairy without being too visible himself.

"Can you see what's going on?"

"Not yet, but . . . Wait, one of the doors just opened."

Frank could see the light spilling out into the street now. "Are they starting deliveries already?"

"It's way too early for milk deliveries," Gino said. It wasn't yet midnight.

They watched, however, as a milk wagon trundled out the open door and turned onto the street, coming toward them. They waited, with Gino continuing his pretended repairs to the motor. Frank raised a hand in acknowledgment to the

144

driver as the wagon trundled past them, but the driver ignored him, spitting over the side as if giving his silent opinion of the motorcar.

By then another wagon had come out and turned in the opposite direction. "Let's follow that one," Frank said when the first wagon was far enough away that the driver couldn't overhear.

Gino quickly levered the hood closed and gave the crank a practiced turn, bringing the engine to life.

"Notice anything funny about the wagon?" Frank asked as Gino eased the motor into motion.

"No. What?"

"It was empty."

Gino looked over in surprise. "How do you know?"

"The way it was riding, high and loose on its springs. Also, what's the first thing you notice about milk wagons?"

Gino considered for a moment. "Oh, the noise they make. All those bottles rattling."

"Yes, and that wagon didn't make a sound."

"So why would somebody be taking an empty milk wagon out at this time of night?"

"I don't know, which is why I suggested we follow one."

Gino was keeping a nice distance from the second milk wagon. Luckily, traffic was light at this time of night, so it wasn't hard to keep it in sight. "But you have a theory," Gino guessed.

"Let's just say that an empty milk wagon driving around late at night suggests a lot of things, none of them exactly legal."

"And where did it go?" Sarah asked while Malloy ate breakfast the next morning. He had not awakened her when he arrived home the night before, and she'd let him sleep in since he'd been out so late.

"We didn't want to get too close, and we certainly didn't want to see what they were really doing—"

"Because they wouldn't want any witnesses to what they were really doing," Sarah guessed.

"That did occur to us, and when we saw them heading down a dark street near the river where a lot of warehouses full of merchandise unloaded from the ships are located, we figured we'd seen enough."

"Do you think the wagons were stealing from the warehouses?"

"Not the wagons," Malloy said with a grin.

She waved away his correction with a flick of her hand. "The drivers, then."

"I don't want to accuse anyone of anything quite yet, but it looks like the Pure Dairy wagons are being used for something that might very well be illegal."

"The question is, did Mr. Pritchard know?"

Malloy frowned. "I can't imagine he did. Do

you think he would have been involved in something illegal?"

"Absolutely not! Do you?"

"No, I don't, and everyone else who knew him says the same thing. And yet just days after his death, this is happening."

"Could it have just started? Because he died, I mean."

Malloy sat back and sipped his coffee, giving the matter a few moments' thought. "That's definitely a possibility."

"So maybe they killed him so he wouldn't interfere."

"Or maybe he just found out it was going on, and they killed him so he wouldn't expose them."

Sarah sighed. This was all so ugly. "Either situation is a very good motive for murder."

"Yes, and it really doesn't matter which one it was. So we need to find out who is behind all this."

"Do you have any ideas?"

"It would have to be a person in authority at the dairy because someone is bound to notice the wagons are being used when the dairy is closed."

"If they bring the wagons back before the drivers arrive to load them with milk, how would anyone know?" Sarah asked.

"The wagons would either be dirty or freshly washed, if the person in charge of this is persnickety, which would be noticed, and the stable boys would know the horses had been used. They'd be tired and also dirty and in no condition to go back out for deliveries."

"What if they only used a few of the wagons and horses, though? The dairy probably has extras, because you never know when a horse will pull up lame or a wagon will lose a wheel or something."

"I'm sure you're right, but even still, somebody would notice that things were not in the same condition they'd been in at the end of the workday."

"And someone in authority would have to instruct the stable boys and the other drivers not to be concerned," Sarah said.

"But they would still know. This would also explain the feeling Gino got that something was going on."

"Yes, it would. But if the workers were already aware of it, surely it's been going on for a while, since Mr. Pritchard has only been dead for a few days."

"That means we have to find out how they kept it a secret from him, but most of all, we need to know exactly what they're doing and who is behind it."

"How are you going to do that?"

"I'm not sure yet. Meanwhile, Gino and I are going to Brooklyn today to visit the swill milk dairy that Harvey told us his father was upset about."

"Do you really think that has anything to do with Mr. Pritchard's death?"

"You saw how upset he got about the turn-of-the-century argument. He was probably even more obnoxious about somebody selling bad milk."

"You're probably right." Sarah sighed. "I just hope we don't find out the family is involved in any of this, for Theda's sake."

"Theda's the one who hired me, remember."

"Of course I remember, but I'm sure she had no idea her mother and Mr. Bergman were more than friends or that something odd was happening at the dairy."

"Do you think I should tell Nelson we can't find anything and just drop the investigation?"

Sarah considered his question for a long moment. "I'm afraid if we do, Theda will just hire another detective agency. At least we don't have to tell her everything we find out, especially if it has nothing to do with her father's death."

"That's true. A stranger wouldn't be interested in protecting her. We can at least do that."

"So go and visit your swill milk dairy."

Malloy smiled. "And what are you going to do?"

"I'm going to play matchmaker."

Frank and Gino took the motorcar to Brooklyn. Crossing the Brooklyn Bridge in a motorcar was a harrowing experience, with the wind howling as they raced across the enormous bridge at nearly ten miles per hour. Frank was sure human beings were never intended to travel so fast in an open vehicle. Trains and trolleys ran along their own tracks, and pedestrians walked in their special section above everything and down the very middle of the bridge, while wagons and motorcars were relegated to lanes on the outside edges, where they had a clear view of the East River far—too far—below. Gino thoroughly enjoyed the wind whipping around them, but Frank was grateful for the goggles they wore for protection because he could close his eyes rather than see how far above the water they were. One wrong move could send them catapulting over the edge into oblivion, and while Gino wasn't likely to make any such move, Frank was still grateful when they reached the opposite shore.

Brooklyn had flourished in recent years as the city grew and Manhattan island filled up. Factories and business had found more space across the river in what had recently been farmland. The Green Hills Dairy occupied a ramshackle warehouse in an industrial area with no visible hills, green or otherwise.

"How do they stand the stench?" Gino asked when he had parked the motorcar and they had sat for a few moments, sizing up the dairy.

"You get used to it, I guess."

"Pritchard's dairy doesn't smell much at all."

"He also doesn't keep cows."

"He keeps horses."

"They go out every day and his men keep the stalls clean and the horses groomed."

"That's right. But they don't have cows, because he gets his milk from farmers out in the country."

"And it comes in by train every day."

"Why would you keep cows, then?"

"I don't know," Frank said. "Let's ask . . . What's his name?"

"George Wolinski."

"Mr. Wolinski, if he's in, although if I owned this place, I'd stay as far away from it as I could."

As they had previously agreed, Frank went in search of Wolinski or whoever was in charge, and Gino headed for the dairy itself to get an idea of what was going on.

The offices, Frank discovered, were in a separate building, upwind from the dairy and protected by a large hedge. The smell wasn't nearly as bad here.

Two clerks were working diligently in the large, untidy main room when Frank entered the one-story, clapboard building. One of the clerks looked up from under his green eyeshade and scowled. "You a cop?"

"No, I am not. I'm here to see Mr. Wolinski."

151

The clerk didn't look like he believed Frank. "He expecting you?"

"Probably not."

"What's it about?"

Frank debated what he could say that would be most likely to interest Mr. Wolinski. "I wanted to talk to him about Clarence Pritchard's murder."

The clerk's eyes widened in alarm and he jumped up and scurried into one of the offices that opened off the main room. The other clerk was staring at him now, equally alarmed, although he uttered not one word.

A few moments later, the first clerk returned and said Mr. Wolinski would see Frank.

George Wolinski was just as untidy as his front room. A short, round man with bushy, dark hair and aggressive side whiskers clinging to his pockmarked face, he glared at Frank over his battered desk. He didn't stand up or invite Frank to sit down.

"Pete said you're not a cop, but you look like one."

Frank smiled. When he'd been a cop that used to annoy him. Now it just amused him. "Private investigator." He gave Wolinski one of his engraved cards instead of the cheap, printed ones, wanting to make a good impression.

Wolinski eyed it suspiciously. "Pete said you wanted to talk about Pritchard's murder, but all I know is what I read in the newspapers."

"Did you know Pritchard?"

"Sure. Everybody in the milk business knows everybody else."

"What did you think of him?"

"Not much. A holier-than-thou, straitlaced prig, but I didn't care enough about him to kill him, if that's what you're thinking."

"Even if he was planning to put you out of business?"

Wolinski found this hilarious, and he laughed until tears leaked out of his squinty little eyes. "Out of business?" he repeated when he'd gotten his breath back, and that set him off again.

Frank waited patiently.

"Sorry," Wolinski wheezed at last. "But . . . Pritchard couldn't put me out of business even if he tried."

"And did he try?"

"I don't know if he did or not."

"I was told he was going to report you for selling swill milk."

"He's perfectly welcome to do so. Or he was, at least."

"Isn't it illegal to sell swill milk?"

"Sure it is, but that's not what I sell. You can ask the inspectors." His grin told Frank the inspectors would say whatever Wolinski told them to.

"I see. So you weren't angry that Pritchard was going to report you?"

"It's annoying, but like anything else, you pay

off the right person and go on about your business. People like cheap milk. If I followed all the rules, I'd have to raise my prices, and my customers would be upset."

They'd be healthier, too, but Frank didn't think Wolinski would care. "Can you think of anybody who really was angry with Pritchard?"

"Angry enough to kill him, you mean?" Wolinski shook his head.

Frank had obviously wasted his time coming to Brooklyn. What else could he ask that Wolinski might know? Ah yes. "Any idea why somebody would be driving around the city at night in milk wagons that weren't delivering milk?"

Now he had Wolinski's serious attention. "Was Pritchard up to something?"

Maybe Wolinski was simply interested in another potential business opportunity. "Do you think that's a possibility?"

"With Pritchard? Not likely, but . . ."

"But what?" Frank asked with interest.

"Are Pritchard's wagons really driving around at night and not delivering milk?"

"Some of them are."

Wolinski gave this some thought. "I don't know. That son of his . . ."

"What about him?"

"If something is going on, I'd bet Pritchard didn't know a thing about it, but the son, he's a different sort altogether."

"In what way?"

"In every way. Now, I don't live in the city, so I just get my news secondhand, you understand. Even still, there's stories about the boy. What's his name?"

"Harvey."

"That's right, Harvey. He's a little wild, I hear."

"He must be very wild if you've heard about it all the way in Brooklyn."

Wolinski grinned. "We're not all rubes out here." His grin suddenly vanished.

"What is it?"

"Nothing," Wolinski said, and began to shuffle the papers on his desk.

"You remembered something. What is it?"

Wolinski looked up, his jaw set stubbornly. "I didn't remember anything."

"But you thought of somebody who might have been angry enough to kill Pritchard."

"Not angry, no. Those people are too smart to get angry. But . . . Well, if you want to know what's going on, you should probably ask Harvey himself. He's in charge now, isn't he? He's the one who would know."

As soon as Maeve got back from taking Catherine to Miss Spence's School, she and Sarah walked over to the elevated train station and headed down to the clinic. On the way, Sarah told Maeve her idea.

"I thought arranged marriages had gone out of style," Maeve said when she'd heard it. By then they were seated on the train that whisked them along two stories above the street.

"Not if the bride and groom arrange it themselves."

"This sounds like you're the one doing the arranging."

Which was what Sarah was trying to avoid. "I'm merely going to make the suggestion and see if both parties are interested."

"And what makes you think they will be?"

"If Miss Vane does not marry, she faces a bleak future. She will also be separated from her child, and she has indicated to me that would cause her great pain."

"I'll grant you Miss Vane has every reason to consider your suggestion, but why should Mr. Robinson be interested?"

"Mr. Robinson wants to rise in society, which is difficult for someone with his background."

"But not impossible," Maeve pointed out. "Most of the society families in the city got their start with somebody like Black Jack Robinson making a fortune by methods that wouldn't look too respectable today."

"Very true. Which makes them even more critical of others seeking to do the same thing. He is well aware of this, which is why he would like to marry a young lady from a good family."

"Which would give him a leg up," Maeve said. "I understand that perfectly."

"But of course the good families don't want their daughters to marry men like Black Jack Robinson," Sarah continued.

"Do you think Miss Vane's family will allow it, considering her circumstances?"

"I have no idea, but I think Miss Vane might be willing to disregard their objections if they are unwilling to give consent."

"I'm sure she would be, but you still haven't convinced me Black Jack would be willing."

"Did you forget? He was planning to marry a young woman in similar circumstances when we met him."

"And that ended very badly for the young lady, if I recall," Maeve said. "He wasn't too pleased either."

"Yet he sought me out the other day."

"Maybe he wants to marry you," Maeve said with a wicked grin.

Sarah did not find that amusing. "I'm sure Malloy would have a thing or two to say about that, but no, he isn't interested in me at all except as his only connection to the world he would like to be part of. I think he really wanted my advice."

"About what?"

"About how to accomplish his goals."

"Did you tell him about your plan?"

"Certainly not! I hadn't actually formulated

it yet, and I wanted to speak to Miss Vane first. But I think he would be interested. And after I've spoken to both of them, it will be up to them to decide."

Maeve shook her head. "I certainly hope you never decide I should get married."

"I wouldn't dream of interfering with your matrimonial status."

The look Maeve gave Sarah said that she didn't believe her for a moment.

On the walk from the El to the clinic, Sarah made sure to stop and speak to every group of children they passed, earning strange looks from Maeve, who knew perfectly well that was a good way to get your pocket picked or worse.

"What are you doing?" Maeve whispered after they'd engaged with the third group of ragtag street urchins.

"Ensuring that Mr. Robinson knows I'm at the clinic."

"Are you going to get them together today?" Maeve asked in amazement.

"No, I'm just going to approach her . . . or rather, you're going to since I can't be seen to show favoritism by singling out any one of the women with special attention."

"What?"

"All you need to do is chat her up and see if you can find out if the baby's father is a factor at all and then see how open she is to considering Jack."

"To considering an arranged marriage, you mean," Maeve said.

"Don't pretend you aren't thrilled that I've asked you to do this. Gino wouldn't have the first idea how to handle it," she added to remove any possible objection.

Maeve, knowing exactly how Sarah was manipulating her, groaned, but she said, "Does she have to decide today?"

"She doesn't have to decide at least until she's met Jack."

"Will she meet him today?"

"Of course not. Men aren't allowed in the clinic, and she certainly isn't going to traipse out to his carriage to show herself. If all parties are agreeable, I'll arrange something."

"I hope you learned something useful," Frank said when Gino finally rejoined him at the motorcar. As Gino climbed up into the driver's seat, Frank wrinkled his nose at the accompanying aroma. "I'm starting to be glad we're not in a closed carriage."

"I'm hoping the smell will blow off on the drive home, but I'll have to clean my shoes to get rid of it altogether. You will not believe what goes on in there."

"I know about the swill and—"

"You don't know anything." Gino shuddered. "Those cows . . . I wondered why they keep

159

them, and now I know. They don't have to pay to transport the milk and they don't have to worry about it going bad since it only takes a day or so to get it from the cow to the customer. That means they don't bother to pasteurize it either, which saves them even more."

"So Wolinski has plenty of profits to bribe the inspectors with."

"Do you really think inspectors ever come here?" Gino asked in wonder.

"Probably just to pick up their bribes."

"That makes sense, because the cows . . ." He shuddered again.

"What about them?" Frank asked, thinking he probably didn't really want to know.

"They never leave their stalls for their entire lives, and the stalls are . . . Well, just as filthy as you'd expect, and some of the cows are sick. Really sick. And if they get too sick to stand up, they put them in a sling and just keep milking them until . . ." He swallowed. "Until they die."

Frank glanced over at the dairy, seeing the run-down building in a whole new light. "Let's get out of here."

Sarah was disappointed to learn no one was in labor today, but at least she got to see two of the babies who had been born that week. Babies and mothers were all doing well, and the expectant mothers in residence seemed to be thriving.

Sooner or later a difficult birth or a mother too worn down by circumstances would result in their first disappointment, but so far the clinic was accomplishing its goal of helping mothers and their babies survive.

Sarah had greeted Jocelyn Vane and inquired about her health but had spent no more time with her than she had with any of the other women. Maeve, on the other hand, had managed a private visit with her, although Sarah noticed she managed to speak privately with at least two other women as well, so her conversation with Miss Vane would not appear extraordinary.

As Sarah had hoped, Black Jack Robinson knocked on the door a couple of hours into her visit, and they'd kept him waiting another hour before allowing him to take her and Maeve home. Sarah noticed Jocelyn Vane was on hand to escort them out. She and Maeve exchanged a conspiratorial look as she opened the door for them, and she waited there to watch Mr. Robinson emerge from the carriage and help Sarah and Maeve inside. She also noticed him noticing Jocelyn with appreciation.

Sarah introduced Maeve as her nanny. "Although she often helps Malloy and me in our investigations."

"Are you investigating anything interesting at the moment?" Mr. Robinson asked, already interested.

"I'm not sure how interesting it is, but a friend's father was murdered on New Year's Eve, and she asked Malloy to help find the killer."

"The man who owned the dairy? What was his name?"

"Clarence Pritchard."

"That's right. I saw it in the newspaper. What a dreadful thing when people aren't safe on a church lawn."

"We don't believe it was a random act," Sarah said, realizing Black Jack Robinson might have some insights into at least part of the mystery of Mr. Pritchard's death.

"Really? He wasn't the victim of an overzealous thief?"

"No, he wasn't even robbed. In fact, we've found several people who might have had a reason to get him out of the way. And, uh . . . May I ask you a question without giving offense?"

This amused him. "I'm not sure. I suppose that depends on the question."

"Then I'll ask and you may choose to be offended and not answer."

"By all means. You have me intrigued now, Mrs. Malloy."

"Can you think of a reason why someone would need the use of a milk wagon in the city late at night?"

# VII

Mr. Robinson was even more amused now. "May I assume this wagon is not delivering milk?"

"Yes, you may assume that. And you may also assume more than one wagon is being used. They leave the dairy with nothing in them at a time when the dairy is usually closed."

Mr. Robinson leaned back against the fine leather upholstery of his luxurious carriage and gave the matter some thought. "Do we know where the wagons go?"

"Toward the river."

"Milk wagons," he mused. "How clever."

"Then you have an idea."

"A theory, although I'm willing to bet I'm correct. You see, stealing merchandise is only the beginning of the process. A thief who hopes to profit from stealing it must transport the merchandise from its original location to a place where it can be safely stored and then disposed of—all without being caught."

"By *disposed of,* I assume you mean sold to someone else."

"Exactly. It may be sold many times after that, but moving it the first time is the most dangerous part of the process. Someone is always going to notice merchandise moving through the city at odd times."

"Unless it's in a milk wagon," Sarah guessed.

"My thought exactly," Mr. Robinson said.

"Because no one notices milk wagons," Maeve added.

"Except to curse them for blocking traffic," Mr. Robinson said. "They can also hold a lot of merchandise."

"And no one can see what's inside them," Maeve said.

"Another advantage. I could be wrong, of course. Do you think this Pritchard was operating his dairy to cover up his real business?"

"Oh no," Sarah said. "Mr. Pritchard was far too honest and upright to be involved in anything illegal."

"But someone may have been taking advantage of him," Maeve said.

"I see," Mr. Robinson said. "And he wouldn't have allowed it if he knew, so . . ."

"Yes," Sarah said. "If he found out, someone may have killed him."

"So you *are* investigating something interesting. Why did you think I might be offended?"

Sarah shrugged. "My question implied that you would have knowledge about illegal activities."

"But I do have such knowledge, even though I can assure you moving stolen merchandise is not one of my business interests. And I'm happy to help, after the, uh, kindness you and your husband once performed for me." Jack had once loved a young woman named Estelle whose privileged upbringing had masked a horrible secret. Sarah wasn't sure she considered solving Estelle's murder a kindness, but she was glad Jack did.

"I think Mrs. Malloy would like to perform another kindness for you," Maeve said slyly.

Sarah glared at her, but she grinned back, unrepentant, and once again Mr. Robinson was amused.

"Would she?" he asked. "And what kindness do you think I need?"

Sarah managed not to sigh. At least she didn't have to worry any longer about how to broach the subject. "From what you said the last time I saw you, I gathered that you are still interested in . . . shall we say, becoming more respectable?"

His amusement vanished. "Of course I am, but you know how difficult that would be without . . ."

"Yes, without a wife to lend you some respectability," she said, thinking of how he had lost the young woman he had once planned to marry, the woman who might have given him entrée into that world. "Mr. Robinson, I know you are a practical man."

"I believe I am."

"And your original plan was very practical."

"I thought so."

"What if I suggested it might still work?"

Robinson frowned. "But . . ."

"With a different young lady," Sarah hastily added. "I don't for a moment suggest that another young woman could take her place in your *heart,* but perhaps she could help you achieve your goals."

Mr. Robinson considered her through narrowed eyes. "Did you have a particular young lady in mind?"

He glanced speculatively at Maeve, who shook her head decisively. "I'm really just a nanny. I wouldn't be any help at all."

"I do know another young lady who would be, however," Sarah said.

"And what makes you think she would be interested in a man like me?"

Sarah turned to Maeve. "Perhaps you should tell Mr. Robinson what you learned today."

Maeve straightened importantly. "Mrs. Malloy asked me to speak with Miss Vane to see if she might be willing to consider an arrangement that could be mutually beneficial."

"Miss Vane?" he asked Sarah.

"You asked me about her the last time you met me at the clinic."

"The young lady who answered the door?" he remembered with obvious pleasure. He would also remember he had recognized her good breeding.

"Yes, the one you thought must be one of the midwives, but she is not."

"Then what . . . ?"

They gave him a moment to figure it out.

"She's confined there, then," he said thoughtfully.

"Yes. She comes from a socially prominent family, and her condition would be an embarrassment to them."

"And it would ruin her reputation forever if it became known," Maeve added. "So her father sent her to the clinic to hide her away."

"Which would seem to solve her problem," Mr. Robinson said. "No one is likely to recognize her here and her secret will remain undiscovered."

"Perhaps," Sarah said, "although there is no guarantee. People talk, and gossip like that might find its way out. In any case, Miss Vane would have to give up her child, and she cannot bear the thought of it."

"Then she must be attached to the child's father, which makes me wonder why he has not taken responsibility."

"I can assure you she is not attached to the child's father," Maeve said. "In fact, she loathes him."

"He forced her, then," Robinson guessed.

"No, he *tricked* her," Maeve said, her own loathing obvious. "It's an old story: an innocent girl flattered by the attentions of a man from a family with far greater wealth and social position. After he'd taken advantage of her, she learned he had become engaged to someone else."

"But surely . . . Doesn't he know about the child?" Robinson asked, as outraged as Sarah could have hoped.

"He denies everything and says he refuses to be coerced into marrying a harlot and giving his name to some other man's by-blow."

Sarah winced at Maeve's frankness, but Maeve only shrugged by way of apology.

"If she chooses to keep her child," Sarah said, "her family will disown her. She might find some kind of work, but trying to support herself and take care of a baby is extremely difficult for a woman alone. Besides, as she pointed out, the only job she is trained for is to be the wife of a wealthy man."

"I certainly qualify as wealthy," Mr. Robinson said with a frown, "but . . . her family is hardly likely to approve a match with a man whose fortune comes from saloons and gambling dens."

"Her family is hardly in a position to be particular," Sarah said.

"And she is perfectly willing to overlook any objections they might have," Maeve said with a grin.

"You've already approached her about this?" Mr. Robinson seemed shocked by the very idea.

"There was no point in discussing it with you if

she wasn't willing to consider it," Sarah said.

"Oh yes, I suppose I can see that," he admitted reluctantly.

"And if you do marry, there will be a scandal, of course," Sarah continued, as if such a thing were commonplace. "You'll have to elope so the exact date of the marriage will forever be in question, but when the baby is born, everyone will assume you seduced poor Miss Vane to force her into a marriage that gave you every advantage and her none at all."

But Mr. Robinson smiled at that. "Which will only enhance my reputation as a man to be reckoned with, Mrs. Malloy."

"I'm glad you find that an appealing prospect. And of course Miss Vane herself will enhance your reputation in other ways. She will be the perfect hostess, and many of her old friends will want to meet her notorious husband, giving you entrée into that world."

"But," Maeve said, "she must be allowed to keep her child. That is the only reason she would consider this at all."

"That speaks well of her, don't you think?" he said. "Most women would be happy to walk away from a child in these circumstances. My own mother did," he added with more than a trace of bitterness.

"Don't judge her too harshly, Mr. Robinson," Sarah said. "Life can be cruel to a woman alone."

"Yes, I suppose it can," he said. "So now that you've spoken to both of us, what are you planning to do next?"

Sarah blinked in surprise. Had he just agreed to consider taking Jocelyn Vane as his wife? "I thought I would host a small dinner party where you and Miss Vane could meet."

"How very respectable," he said, amused again.

"I thought so. Are you by chance free on Sunday?"

"Maeve and I can pick her up in the motorcar," Gino said when Sarah had explained to him and Frank what she and Maeve had accomplished that morning. They had found her at home when they returned from Brooklyn.

"I think that's an excellent idea," Sarah said.

"Don't you think you'd better ask Maeve first?" Frank asked, thinking she was brave indeed to speak for the girl, who was not present because she'd gone to fetch Catherine from school.

"She'll see the wisdom of it. She'll tell them at the clinic that Miss Vane's family wants her to come home for a visit, and she was sent to escort her."

"Why not just say she's coming to your house?" Gino asked.

"Because that would look like favoritism," Sarah explained. "And poor Jocelyn is already finding it difficult to fit in with the other women because of her privileged background. We don't want to make things worse by having the other women think I show her special attention."

"But you *are* showing her special attention by trying to find her a husband," Frank pointed out.

"Believe me, I would do the same for every unmarried woman at the clinic if I could, but I fear there is a limited supply of suitable men. And don't forget that we already do whatever we can to help every unmarried woman find work and a safe place to live and whatever help she needs when she leaves the clinic. This is actually just another form of making provisions for one of our patients."

"I guess it is," Frank said. "I just find it difficult to believe Black Jack Robinson would agree to something like this."

"You told me yourself that he once said he wouldn't mind marrying another young woman under similar circumstances. He actually told me he admires Miss Vane's determination to keep her child, since his mother apparently gave him up."

"Yes, but claiming another man's child as your own . . ." Frank said, shaking his head at the very thought.

"Catherine is another man's child," she reminded him with a smug smile. "She's another woman's child, too, and yet we both love her as our own."

"And Brian isn't Mrs. Frank's son, but she loves him, too," Gino reminded them both.

Frank found he had no arguments left. "When you put it that way . . ."

"Exactly," Sarah said. "And Mr. Robinson would be getting a wife with many accomplishments who can repay his kindness by introducing him to society, which is his fondest wish."

"Although I can't imagine why he'd want that," Frank said with a shudder.

"Neither can I," Sarah said, "and he may change his mind later, but at least it will be his decision. Now, did the two of you learn anything interesting in Brooklyn?"

Frank told her about his conversation with Wolinski and the man's suspicions about Harvey.

"Which reminds me," she said. "I asked Mr. Robinson if he had any idea why the milk wagons would be out at the wrong time of night."

"And did he?" Frank prodded when she hesitated.

"As you already guessed, he thought they might be being used to transport stolen merchandise."

"Yes, but who at the dairy would have been involved? We're pretty sure it wasn't Pritchard himself, but it had to be someone with enough authority to convince the other employees to ignore what was going on."

"And now we think that's Harvey," Gino said.

"But how would he get involved in something like that?" Sarah asked.

"And even if he did, does it have anything to do

with why Pritchard was killed?" Frank added. "I don't think Harvey would tell me if he's involved with a ring of thieves, and if his mother or sister know anything, would they tell us if it implicates Harvey?"

"I know who *would* tell us, if she knows," Gino said with a sly grin.

"Mrs. Ellsworth," Sarah guessed. "I should probably call on her, but that's going to have to wait now. The funeral is tomorrow."

"That's right," Frank said. "Everyone will be at the church for the service, won't they?"

"I'm sure they will, except the servants who'll be setting up the repast for afterward," Sarah said.

"Which will give Gino a perfect opportunity to pay the servants a visit to find out if Mrs. Pritchard really was at home on New Year's Eve."

"You don't really imagine she followed her husband down to Trinity Church and strangled him, do you?" Sarah asked, obviously skeptical.

Frank was skeptical himself. "Stranger things have happened, but what I really want to know is if she was with Bergman that night."

"Oh, I see. That would give her an alibi," Sarah said. "Him, too, I suppose."

"Or maybe she and Bergman went down to Trinity Church together," Gino said.

Sarah was spared replying because Mrs. Malloy arrived home just then with Brian, who wanted to tell them all about his day at school. While Mrs. Malloy was interpreting the new signs he'd learned that day, Maeve also arrived home with Catherine, who had stories of her own to tell. All discussion of murder had to wait.

Gino didn't bother going to the front door at the Pritchard house. He wasn't a visitor or a mourner come to pay respects. He knocked on the kitchen door and was admitted by a young maid who smiled flirtatiously. "And what would you be wanting?"

"I'm a private investigator. I've been hired to investigate Mr. Pritchard's murder."

He handed her one of his cards and was gratified to see she was impressed.

"The family isn't here. The funeral is today, you see, and they've all gone to the church."

"I know. That's why I came. I wanted to ask the staff a few questions when the family wasn't around."

"But we're busy getting ready for the funeral dinner," she protested.

Gino glanced past her into the kitchen, where an older woman, another maid, and a middle-aged man sat around the table, obviously not working very hard at getting anything ready. "I only need to ask a few questions."

"What's he want?" the older woman called. Gino figured she was probably the cook.

"Says he's an investigator," the maid called back. "He's got a card and everything."

"What're you investigating, young fellow?" the older woman demanded.

"Mr. Pritchard's death. I hate to bother you at this sad time, but my boss told me I had to come see you when the mistress isn't here," he added quickly before she could dismiss him out of hand.

"And why would you need to see the likes of us?" she asked with a frown.

Should he be honest or lie? She didn't look like the kind of woman who enjoyed being lied to. "Because my boss says the servants always know everything that's going on in the house."

That made the old woman laugh, and the others joined her. "Bring him on in, Daisy. We've got everything ready, and we were getting bored just sitting around waiting."

Daisy took his coat and Gino thanked them as he took a seat at the table.

"Daisy, bring the boy some coffee. He looks froze clean through," the old woman said.

Daisy brought him coffee and some fruitcake while they introduced themselves. Mrs. Young was indeed the cook, and she'd been with the Pritchard family long before the current Mrs. Pritchard had come along. Mr. Zachary had served Mr. Pritchard and Harvey as a valet and sometime butler. The other maid was Penny.

"I don't know if Mr. Harvey will keep me on

175

now," Zachary said with a sigh. "He thinks I'm too old-fashioned."

"I guess Harvey doesn't like anything that's old-fashioned," Gino tried.

"Oh no, not Mr. Harvey."

"He and his father disagreed a lot, I hear," Gino said, dropping the pebble in the water to see where the ripples would go.

"Where'd you hear that?" Mrs. Young asked.

"Here and there, but I actually saw them going at it last week. I was at a dinner party at Nelson Ellsworth's house—"

"You went to a party at Miss Theda's house?" Daisy asked, wide-eyed.

"She's Mrs. Nelson now," Mrs. Young said. "And why would *you* be invited there, young man?"

"My boss is a good friend of Mrs. Ellsworth's. They're neighbors. Anyway, Mr. Pritchard got mad at something Harvey said and stormed out of the house."

The servants exchanged uneasy glances, but said nothing.

"Look, I'm not here to gossip," Gino said, trying out his abashed smile on the ladies. He figured Zachary would be immune. "But I need to ask you a few things."

"What things?" Mrs. Young snapped. "And don't go asking us if somebody in this house killed Mr. Pritchard because we won't believe it."

Gino chose his next words carefully. "I just need

to verify where everyone was that evening Mr. Pritchard died." He reached into his coat pocket and pulled out the small notebook he carried and a pencil stub. He licked his thumb and carefully turned the pages until he came to the last one where he had jotted down the lies he had decided he would tell to get them to talk. "According to what Mrs. Pritchard told us, Mr. Pritchard left the house around nine o'clock that evening."

The women all turned to Zachary, who nodded reluctantly. "That's about right, I guess. He said he wanted a chance to speak to as many people as possible at the church, so he needed to get there early. I believe . . ." He cleared his throat and looked embarrassed. "I believe he intended to approach each person as they arrived to tell them his theory about . . . uh . . . about the turn of the century."

Gino pretended not to notice his chagrin and simply made a notation: *Pritchard, nine o'clock.* "And Harvey left shortly afterward. Is that correct?"

It was only a guess. Surely, if Harvey had followed his father to the church, he would have left after Mr. Pritchard, but not long after.

But Zachary was shaking his head. "Oh no, Mr. Harvey had already gone. Said he was meeting some friends. He didn't want any supper or anything."

That was interesting. "About what time did he

177

leave, then?" Gino asked, pencil ready to jot it down.

"I'd say around eight o'clock. I didn't check the clock or anything, but I'd just finished helping him dress when Mr. Pritchard called for me. It usually takes an hour to get Mr. Pritchard into his formal dress, and if he was ready at nine . . ."

Gino nodded, making another note. How strange. If Harvey really had left an hour before his father, how could he have followed him to the church? Then again, if he knew that's where his father was going, he wouldn't have needed to follow him at all.

"And how long after Mr. Pritchard went out did Mrs. Pritchard leave?" Gino gave them his best innocent, questioning smile because this was the biggest test of all. Mrs. Pritchard had claimed to be home and to have gone to bed early that night.

The servants wouldn't know that, however, and they all looked at Daisy, who scratched her chin nervously, as if she'd been asked to give the answer to a very difficult arithmetic problem. "Not too long after Mr. Pritchard left, it was. She told me to tell her when he was gone, and then I helped her with her dress. She was all ready except for her gown."

Gino nodded as if this confirmed what he already knew, even though his heart was hammering away with excitement. Mrs. Pritchard had lied. "Did someone call for her?"

Daisy shook her head. "She just walked down to the corner like she usually does."

"Like she usually does?" Gino asked, trying not to sound too shocked.

"Mrs. Pritchard is very independent," Mrs. Young said, giving Daisy a sharp warning glance. Maybe the girl really didn't know that ladies did not *usually* leave their houses alone and walk off unaccompanied into the night. "And before you ask, she arrived home shortly after midnight."

"Alone?" Gino asked, still smiling.

"Of course alone," Mrs. Young said before anyone else could reply.

"Does anybody remember what time Harvey got home that night?" Gino asked.

"I waited up for him and Mr. Pritchard," Zachary said, his expression bleak. "Mr. Harvey came in just after four, but Mr. Pritchard . . ." His voice broke, and a twinge of guilt twisted in Gino's stomach for causing him pain.

"You must've been worried."

"Of course I was. Mr. Pritchard had never stayed out all night before without telling anybody."

"And his family must have been worried, too."

"Mrs. Pritchard was when she found out," Mrs. Young said a little defensively. "But what could she do? He's a grown man, and if he wanted to stay out all night, that was his business."

"Did she consider notifying the police?" Gino asked.

179

"Because a grown man stayed out all night on New Year's Eve? Not likely."

"And how did Harvey react?"

"When he woke up, you mean?" Daisy asked, and they all laughed.

"I suppose he slept pretty late," Gino said.

"And he didn't feel too well when he did wake up, either," Daisy said. "I doubt he was thinking about his father at all."

So Harvey didn't express concern over his missing father. Was that because he knew where his father was or because he just didn't care?

"I've been hearing some stories about Harvey," Gino tried.

Mrs. Young frowned her disapproval. "Have you, now? And what kind of stories have you heard?"

"Oh, mostly just people shaking their heads and saying Harvey is kind of wild or that he made his father worry."

"His poor mother, too," Mrs. Young said.

"I don't think we should be gossiping about Mr. Harvey's behavior with this young man," Zachary said with a frown.

"You're absolutely right," Gino said, "unless he was involved in something that led to Mr. Pritchard's death."

They all gaped at him, suitably shocked.

"What do you mean by that?" Mrs. Young asked.

Gino tried to look abashed and thought he probably succeeded. "Maybe you folks don't know, but something was going on at the dairy, something illegal."

"What could have been going on at the dairy?" Zachary asked, outraged now.

"That's what I'm trying to find out. I don't expect that Mr. Pritchard would have put up with somebody using his milk wagons for something illegal, would he?"

"Certainly not!" Zachary said, looking to Mrs. Young for confirmation.

"What makes you think something like that?" she asked.

"Because I saw the wagons going out just before midnight, which is much too early for milk delivery, and besides, the wagons were empty."

"We don't know anything about what goes on at the dairy," Mrs. Young said, angry now.

"I didn't think you did, but you do know things about the family."

Zachary shook his head. "If you're trying to get Mr. Harvey in trouble—"

"I'm trying to figure out who killed Mr. Pritchard, and if something Harvey did got his father killed, then I need to know it."

"Maybe you do and maybe you don't," Mrs. Young said, "but you won't find it out from us."

Mr. Pritchard had been a man of impeccable character and unwavering rectitude, if what Sarah had heard about him at his funeral was any indication. Of course, hardly anyone mentioned a person's faults at his funeral. It simply wasn't done. Sarah wondered idly if that was all part of the superstition that forbade speaking ill of the dead or if it was simply good manners practiced to spare the family additional grief.

And, speaking of the family, Theda surely was grief stricken. She wept through the entire service. Poor Nelson comforted her as best he could, and Sarah was glad at least one person truly mourned Mr. Pritchard. His wife, as they say, was holding up well. Others would probably comment on her dignity and refusal to publicly show her grief, but Sarah knew she probably wasn't showing much private grief either. Harvey, too, was trying to maintain his dignity, but he looked ill. Malloy would probably say he had a hangover, and maybe he did, but he might also finally be realizing his father was truly gone.

When all the tributes had been given—Mr. Pritchard apparently had many friends who thought quite highly of him—and the hymns sung and the prayers said, Sarah and Malloy and Mother Malloy waited while the family followed the coffin out. Mrs. Ellsworth had sat with them near the front, not thinking it proper to sit with the family.

"Poor Theda," Mrs. Ellsworth murmured as she and Sarah walked down the aisle together.

"I surely hope you can figure out who killed her father and put her mind at ease. I don't think she can even begin to recover from this until the killer has been punished."

Sarah couldn't help thinking Theda might not be as comforted as she expected by seeing the killer identified if it proved to be a member of her family. She decided to see what Mrs. Ellsworth's opinion might be about that. "Harvey seems to be taking it hard as well."

Mrs. Ellsworth looked at her in surprise. "You're right, he is. I would have expected him to be relieved. They really didn't get along, as you undoubtedly noticed, but Theda says he's actually been getting more upset as the days go by."

"Perhaps he's just beginning to realize what his father's death means for him. He'll have to run the dairy now, won't he?"

"Or sell it, although it wouldn't bring all that much and I can't think what he'd do for a living if he did sell."

Still, Harvey was young for so much responsibility, and Malloy had already observed that he didn't seem pleased to have it.

A line of rented carriages carried the mourners out to the cemetery for a brief graveside service and then back to the Pritchard house, where a buffet had been set. Otto Bergman, who had been discreetly invisible at the church, now made his presence known, making sure the widow was comfortable and got something to eat and that Nelson was adequately looking after Theda. His attentions, while marked, were also perfectly proper. Casual acquaintances would probably think him a beloved uncle or close family friend, which of course he was.

Sarah could clearly see what would happen now. Mr. Bergman would continue to be of service to his dear friend Mrs. Pritchard. Their long friendship would gradually blossom, and they would quietly marry when the proper period of mourning had passed. No hint of scandal would touch them unless they had conspired together to murder Clarence Pritchard and happened to be found out.

"What are you thinking?" Malloy asked, coming up behind where Sarah stood, absently eyeing the dessert table.

"Just how awful it would be for Theda if her mother was involved in her father's death."

"Excuse me."

They both looked up to find Nelson Ellsworth looking apologetic at having interrupted them.

"Nelson, how are you holding up?" Sarah asked.

"I'm fine, but . . . Do you know who that is talking to Theda?"

They glanced over to see a young man leaning over a seated Theda, speaking somewhat urgently to her. She looked distressed and a little panicky.

"That's Amelio Bruno," Malloy said.

"Who?"

"He works at the dairy," Malloy said.

"And he once fancied himself in love with Theda," Sarah added, remembering the story.

"So he's the one," Nelson muttered, moving quickly to rescue his wife.

"Theda, are you all right?" Nelson asked a little louder than necessary.

Bruno's head jerked up, and he scowled at Nelson's interference.

For her part, Theda gave Nelson a grateful and loving smile. "Oh yes. Mr. Bruno was just expressing his condolences," she said with an uneasy glance at him.

"Your mother was asking for you," Nelson said. "If you'll excuse us, Mr. Bruno."

Plainly, Mr. Bruno did not want to excuse them for anything, but he stepped back so Theda could rise from her chair. Nelson took her arm tenderly and led her away. He didn't see the fearful glare Bruno gave him as they walked off.

"Oh my, I don't think Mr. Bruno is quite over his infatuation with Theda," Sarah said.

"Maybe he thinks now that the old man is dead, he stands a chance with her," Malloy said.

"But she's married."

"Maybe he doesn't care about that."

Before Sarah could reply, they were distracted by an argument taking place at the other end of the room. In deference to the solemnity of the occasion, conversations were hushed at events like this, and Harvey was trying to keep his voice down but with limited success.

"What are you doing here?" he demanded.

The gentleman to whom he spoke was middle-aged and well dressed, but something about him seemed out of place. Sarah couldn't put her finger on it, but she was sure her mother could have told her instantly what it was that set him apart from the other mourners. All Sarah could manage was a deep sense that he was not one of them.

"I just came to pay my respects, Pritchard," he said with what appeared to be the proper amount of reverence, but something in his voice was off as well. He didn't really consider Harvey worthy of concern and he didn't really feel any sense of loss over the deceased. Sarah could not have said how she knew this, but she did, instinctively.

"You can't just walk in my house and pretend we're friends," Harvey said.

"He's drunk," Malloy whispered to her. "Should I stop this before he makes a complete fool of himself?"

Sarah glanced around. The other people who had been in the room, including Amelio Bruno, had discreetly wandered out, but anyone might walk in at any moment. If Harvey raised his voice any higher, a lot of people would. "Yes, please."

Sarah had missed what the man said in reply to Harvey's last challenge, but it hadn't placated him at all. Fortunately, Malloy reached the two men before Harvey could respond.

"Harvey," Malloy said sharply, to get his attention. "Oh, excuse me," he said to the well-dressed man. "I didn't mean to interrupt, but Harvey, your mother was asking for you."

If it had worked for Nelson . . .

For a few terrible seconds, Sarah thought Harvey would ignore Malloy and go back to his argument with the strange man. But with one last, furious glance at the man, Harvey downed the dregs of the drink he held and marched out of the room in search of his mother.

Malloy, God bless him, turned to the man and grinned in a way that usually intimidated even the most hardened criminals. "It would be a shame to cause a disturbance at a funeral. Think how upsetting it would be for the widow."

"That would indeed be a pity," the man said. "I would never want to cause her any concern." With a curt nod, he turned and left, passing a small group of mourners coming into the room in search of something to eat.

"My hero," Sarah said when Malloy had made his way back to her.

He grinned for real at that. "And I wouldn't worry about Theda. I'm afraid her brother is the one we have to worry about."

# VIII

Gino came by on Sunday morning and picked up Maeve and the motorcar for the trip down to the clinic. Maeve had insisted on an early start because she assumed Jocelyn Vane would want to spend a little time getting ready once she understood the real purpose of this outing.

Everyone at the clinic understood that Maeve had come to fetch her for a visit with her parents. That, Maeve thought, would explain Miss Vane's anxiety and desire to look her best. Miss Vane, however, was told the truth, so her anxiety and desire to look her best were much greater than anyone suspected.

Only when they were in the motorcar, bundled in their dusters and goggles and lap robes and heading north to Bank Street, was she free to really question Maeve. "So this Mr. Robinson knows all about me and . . . and my situation?"

"Yes. Mrs. Malloy and I told him everything. He thinks you're very honorable for wanting to keep your child."

"He does?" she asked in patent disbelief.

"Yes. He was . . . Well, his mother wasn't married either, and she abandoned him."

"Oh."

"But you'd never guess he came from a background like that. He takes great pride in behaving like a gentleman."

"Did you tell her about the girl he lost?" Gino called.

"Yes, I did."

"So I know he's still mourning her," Miss Vane said with resignation. "I don't expect to fall in love, in any case."

"He's very charming, though," Maeve said.

Miss Vane didn't look like she believed that for a moment, so Maeve would just let her be surprised.

"He's still . . . I mean, he owns gambling dens and saloons," Miss Vane said.

"And he's very rich and has a lovely home."

Miss Vane simply looked determined. And a little terrified.

Sarah had started to wonder if she should offer Jocelyn Vane a small dose of laudanum to calm her down. She'd been pacing their parlor for nearly an hour, occasionally stopping to glance out the front window and then moving toward the mirror to check her appearance yet again, all the while asking myriad questions about Black Jack Robinson without really listening to the answers. Finally, the doorbell rang, right on the dot of noon, when they had asked him to arrive.

Malloy went to greet him while Sarah and Maeve arranged themselves on either side of

Jocelyn on the sofa. Gino took his place by the fireplace. Malloy's mother had chosen to have dinner with the children in her rooms. She had no desire to witness the awkwardness that surely would occur when two strangers met to consider an arranged marriage, and the children would have been too much of a distraction.

Sarah heard Jocelyn's breath catch when Mr. Robinson and Malloy came into the parlor but she somehow managed to appear completely composed.

Mr. Robinson, for his part, had also taken great care with his appearance. He wore a tailor-made suit in a tastefully muted pattern and a modestly sized diamond stickpin in his tie. His shirt and collar were blindingly white. He came straight to Sarah and gave her a small bow.

"Mrs. Malloy, thank you so much for the invitation. I hope you're well." She noticed he had barely glanced at Jocelyn, which she thought very gentlemanly of him.

She gave him her hand. "I'm very well, thank you, and I'm glad you were able to come. You remember Miss Smith and Mr. Donatelli, I'm sure."

"Of course. So nice to see you both again."

Maeve smiled and Gino smirked from where he stood on the other side of the room, but neither of them said a word.

"And this is Miss Vane."

Finally, Mr. Robinson turned his full attention to her, and to give her credit, she met his gaze without flinching, although her color was a bit high. She also offered her hand, which he took in both of his. "So nice to meet you, Mr. Robinson."

"I'm very pleased to meet you, too, Miss Vane."

For a long instant, no one moved or even breathed, and then Robinson released her hand and stepped back. Sarah exhaled the breath she had been holding and thought everyone else did the same.

Malloy once again came to the rescue, offering Mr. Robinson a drink, which he declined—"A little early for me"—and getting him seated. So far he was doing well, and Sarah couldn't help thinking how nervous he must be, too.

"Mrs. Malloy," he said when an uncomfortable moment of silence had passed, "I am hearing good things about the clinic. I believe it is raising the entire tone of the neighborhood."

"Really?" Sarah replied, surprised he would mention such a potentially embarrassing subject in front of Jocelyn. "In what way?"

"Your midwives, for one. They have caused quite a revolution in the way children are being cared for."

"Already?"

"Oh yes. They're holding classes, I hear."

"Indeed they are. Does anything happen in that part of the city that you don't know about?"

"Very little of importance," Mr. Robinson said with remarkable humility.

"Maybe we should be asking Mr. Robinson's advice on some other things," Maeve said to Malloy.

"I was thinking the same thing," Malloy said. "But that can wait. How are these classes changing things?"

"Let's just say we have never seen so much soap sold in that part of the city."

"Then the classes are having the desired effect," Sarah said.

"You seem to take an unusual interest in the children of that neighborhood, Mr. Robinson," Jocelyn said.

Sarah saw her own surprise reflected on Malloy's face. She had assumed Jocelyn would be too nervous to engage in conversation.

To his credit, Mr. Robinson didn't seem surprised at all that she had addressed him. "I do, as a matter of fact. I spent a good part of my youth on those very streets."

"That must have been difficult."

"I survived, although many others didn't."

"And you've done well for yourself, it appears."

He smiled at that, although it was just a small twist of his lips. "Yes, I have."

"And yet, as you say, some did not even survive. To what do you credit your success, then?"

He leaned back and considered her question

for a long moment, during which she continued to hold his gaze with a confidence Sarah could only admire. Although Sarah knew Jocelyn was anxious, she betrayed none of that. If she'd thought Jocelyn Vane would be a good match for Black Jack Robinson, she was sure of it now.

Mr. Robinson said, "I think I must have been too stubborn to die."

"But you did more than just not die."

"And I was willing to work hard and do whatever came to hand. It wasn't always legal, I'm afraid."

"Don't be afraid," she said with a small smile of her own. "I'm not sure everything my father does is legal either."

"It probably isn't, although I'm surprised you realize it."

"Why? Because I'm a female?"

"Not at all. I've learned never to underestimate females. I just meant a loving daughter often doesn't see her parents' faults."

"I think a loving daughter simply chooses to overlook them."

"If I'm ever fortunate enough to have a daughter, I hope she will do the same for me."

They never knew how Jocelyn might have replied to that, because their maid, Hattie, chose that moment to announce dinner was served. Sarah bit back her disappointment and ushered her guests into the dining room.

She seated Mr. Robinson beside Jocelyn on

one side of the table. Gino and Maeve sat on the other side with Malloy at the head and herself at the foot. The dinner conversation was lighter, as Maeve and Gino spoke of the weather and Malloy's motorcar—which Mr. Robinson expressed a strong desire to see—and the latest scandals being reported in the newspapers.

Sarah noticed that neither Jocelyn nor Mr. Robinson had much of an appetite but that they frequently looked at each other. Jocelyn asked him the occasional question, and he responded as if somehow honored to be the object of her attentions. Perhaps he was.

Sarah had given considerable thought to how they might profitably spend the time after dinner. A game seemed like a good way to get people to relax and talk, and Sarah thought she knew the perfect one.

"What's this?" Malloy asked when he brought Gino and Mr. Robinson into the parlor when they'd finished their after-dinner drinks.

"The Checkered Game of Life," Sarah said.

"It's such fun," Jocelyn said.

"And I'm very good at it," Maeve informed Gino in a clear challenge.

"Are you familiar with it, Mr. Robinson?" Sarah asked.

"Parlor games aren't too popular with people who don't have parlors, and I didn't have one until recently," he said apologetically.

"Don't worry," Jocelyn said. "I'll teach you how to play."

That was all the encouragement he needed.

All six of them sat down around the game table, and true to her word, Jocelyn explained the basics of the board game to Mr. Robinson.

When she demonstrated the teetotum to him, he frowned as he spun the cardboard hexagon bearing the numbers one through six that was mounted on a wooden stick and used to determine how many spaces a player could move.

"Why don't they just use dice for this?" he asked.

"Because they're associated with gambling and many people will not have dice in their house," Jocelyn told him with mock solemnity.

"I see," he replied, equally solemn.

He had no trouble picking up the rules of the game, convoluted as they were, though. The object was to move from "Infancy" to "Happy Old Age," but one could not achieve happy old age without also accumulating at least fifty points along the way. Spaces such as "Success," and "Honor" and "College" could earn points. Spaces like "Crime" sent you to "Prison," and "Gambling" led to "Ruin."

Gino and Maeve were enjoying the competition and teased each other unmercifully over their decisions. Maeve moved two spaces, landing on the one occupied by Gino's disk. "You go to jail."

Gino sighed dramatically. "I still have more points than you."

"I think you're cheating. Every time I look away, you move your dial up a notch."

"I do not. Mr. Robinson is keeping too close an eye on me."

"Indeed I am, Miss Smith, because he's keeping a close eye on me, too," Robinson said.

At one point, Mr. Robinson spun a one.

"That allows you to move one space up or down," Jocelyn said, consulting her "record dial" card.

Without hesitation, Mr. Robinson moved to the "Matrimony" space.

Jocelyn frowned. "I'm not sure that was the best strategy, Mr. Robinson. While it does get you closer to 'Happy Old Age,' it also doesn't earn you any points. You could have moved to 'Happiness' and gotten five."

"Yes, but I should hate to reach old age without matrimony, Miss Vane," he told her with a smile. "And I expect happiness will come along with it."

Sarah always claimed that was the moment he won her.

Frank usually didn't enjoy board games, but he had found this one extremely entertaining. In spite of his inexperience and Maeve's and Gino's intricate strategies, Robinson managed to win. A gambler's luck, he had claimed, to everyone's amusement. While Frank had been skeptical of Sarah's plan to bring him and Jocelyn Vane together, he couldn't deny it seemed to be working.

After the game, they had all enjoyed some coffee, and then Sarah announced it was time to take Miss Vane back "home." The men took that opportunity to show Robinson the motorcar, since Gino had to fetch it from the mews behind the house, where it was stored.

Gino led the way, and as they walked down the alley, Robinson fell into step beside Frank. "Mrs. Malloy told me you're investigating the death of that man who owned the dairy."

"That's right. Clarence Pritchard. His daughter married one of our neighbors, and she asked me to help when the police dropped the case."

"Do you know why they dropped it?"

"Because somebody bribed Chief Devery, but I haven't figured out who yet."

"I might have."

Frank gaped at him. "Why would you have done that?"

"Because Mrs. Malloy asked if I had any idea why somebody would be using milk wagons late at night."

"And you just happened to know?"

Robinson smiled. "I'm not that good, but I did ask around about the dead man's son. His name was in the obituary, and in my experience, the sons of wealthy men often get themselves in trouble."

"And is Harvey Pritchard in trouble?"

"He's in debt, which can lead to all sorts of trouble. The boy likes to gamble, you see."

"Is he in debt to you?"

"No, more's the pity. I'm a reasonable man. He's in debt to Lou Lawson."

Frank groaned.

"Yes, it's unfortunate," Robinson agreed. "Harvey should have just confessed all to his father and begged him to pay the debt."

"Yes, he should. Oh, I just remembered something that suddenly makes sense. I witnessed an argument between Harvey and his father. Harvey had said something offhandedly about how he'd bet his father would do something or other, and his father became furious. Pritchard said Harvey would bet on anything, or words to that effect. So he must have known about the gambling."

"And if it made him that angry, he must have known about the debts, too. When was this?"

"Just a few days before Pritchard was killed." Frank now had to rethink everything he knew about Harvey.

"Mrs. Malloy said Pritchard was a painfully honest man," Robinson said as they reached the former stable where the motorcar sat. Gino had already opened the door and stood waiting for them.

"Yes, he wouldn't have been happy to learn his son was in debt to a man like Lawson."

"And I've been thinking," Gino said, obviously eavesdropping. "If he'd been afraid to tell his father about the debt, at least at first, he might've come up with some scheme to raise the money himself."

"Like using the milk wagons to move stolen goods, you mean?" Frank turned to Robinson. "My wife said you also thought that's what was happening."

"It does seem logical. The question is, did Harvey think of that himself or did Lawson force him to do it?" Robinson said.

"I guess I'll have to ask Harvey," Frank said.

"And if he won't confess?"

Frank hadn't even considered such a thing. "I guess I'll have to ask Lawson, then."

"I'd like to see that," Robinson said.

"You don't think I'd do it?" Frank asked, more than a little offended.

"I suppose you could try, but not many people get to meet Mr. Lawson. He's notoriously shy."

"Shy?"

"I'm being diplomatic. He can't be bothered. He lets his henchmen handle the dirty parts of the business."

"Is this a dirty part?"

"Probably. Look, do me a favor. If you do need to talk to him, let me arrange it and go with you."

"That's very generous of you," Frank said, although he was more than a little insulted.

But Robinson just shrugged. "Mrs. Malloy has been very kind to me. I would hate to see her widowed."

When the men had gone, Jocelyn sank down onto the sofa and placed a hand over her heart, as if trying to hold it in her chest.

"Are you all right?" Sarah asked, sitting down beside her.

"I don't know. What do you think? Did he like me?"

"I think he liked you very much. The question is, did you like him?"

"I hardly know. You were right, he's very charming."

"And intelligent," Maeve added. "And rich. He's not bad-looking either."

"I think he's kind, too, in his own way," Sarah said. "Or at least kind to those he cares about."

"I would be forever in his debt, and my child, too. Some men would never let a woman forget that."

"But he wants something from you in return, something you are well equipped to give him, too," Sarah reminded her.

"Respectability?" Jocelyn scoffed.

"Or what passes for it in high society," Sarah said with a smirk. "You understand that world, and you know how to navigate it."

"So will you take him?" Maeve asked.

Jocelyn smiled sadly. "He hasn't asked me to take him yet, but if he does, I don't have much choice, do I? I'm not likely to get another offer."

"You do have choices," Sarah reminded her, "although the others aren't what you want either. Your parents will let you come home and resume your life, as long as you give up your baby. Some would consider that an easy choice."

"But I *know* that they will never let me forget what they did for me. So I'll have to live with their smug sanctity and without my child, always wondering what became of him. Or her. And if I ever get an offer of marriage, assuming we are able to keep my downfall a secret, I will have to decide whether to tell him and risk being scorned or not tell him and risk having him learn the truth later. You're right, none of those is what I want."

"And somehow I don't see you working in a factory while you leave your baby at a Salvation Army creche," Maeve said.

Jocelyn shook her head. "Even if they'd hire me at a factory, my parents would probably force me to come home and take the child anyway. They'd never let me disgrace them like that."

"Don't judge Mr. Robinson too harshly," Maeve said. "I think he might be as grateful to have you accept him as you would be to have his protection."

*"His protection,"* Jocelyn echoed sadly. "That sounds like a melodrama."

"He really would offer protection," Sarah said. "He would protect your reputation and never allow your parents to force you to do anything."

"Not only that, but I'm pretty sure he wouldn't allow anyone else to hurt you either," Maeve said.

"Wouldn't that be lovely?" Jocelyn sighed.

"This is a fine machine, Malloy," Robinson declared when Gino had driven them around to the front door. "I might need to get one myself."

"I'd be happy to help you choose one," Gino said. "I've studied up on the various kinds, and I think we got the best one there is."

"I'll certainly take you up on that, Donatelli."

Gino stayed with the motorcar while Frank and Robinson went back inside. Jocelyn and Maeve were already bundled into their coats and dusters. Frank noticed that Jocelyn wasn't smiling. The spirit she had shown all afternoon seemed to have evaporated.

Robinson went directly to her. "I'm very happy to have met you, Miss Vane. Perhaps, if you're willing, we could speak again very soon."

The color blossomed in her cheeks, and she almost smiled. "I . . . Yes, I . . . If we can arrange it, that would be fine." She turned to Sarah. "Thank you for having me, Mrs. Malloy."

"It was my pleasure," Sarah assured her.

After another round of good-byes, Maeve

escorted Jocelyn out. Gino saw them tucked into the rear seat of the motorcar, and then they were on their way.

"And I must thank you, too, Mrs. Malloy," Robinson said. "I believe you have done me a great service."

"I hope so, Mr. Robinson."

For a moment, he looked a little unsure of himself, an expression Frank suspected not many people ever saw on him. "Did she . . . ?"

Sarah took pity on him. "She found you charming, Mr. Robinson. I believe she would welcome an offer from you."

His sigh of relief was almost comic, although neither Frank nor Sarah showed any amusement. "What do you advise me to do, then?"

"I don't think we need to stand on ceremony. I can arrange for Miss Vane to visit here again, and the two of you can speak privately."

"I should like a few days to prepare," he said. "Perhaps we could set Wednesday for our next meeting."

"I'll make the arrangements."

When he had gone, Frank turned to Sarah. "What do you think he needs to prepare?"

"I don't know, but I'm looking forward to finding out."

The next morning, Sarah went to visit Mrs. Ellsworth and Theda. Theda looked a little better than she had at the funeral, but she still wasn't her usual self. They'd been baking and gladly took a break to visit with her. They insisted that Sarah have some cake and coffee with them.

"I'm so glad you came, Mrs. Frank," Theda said when they were seated at the kitchen table. "We've been desperate to know if you've made any progress."

"We've learned a lot, but we don't know if any of it is important yet," Sarah said. "I know it's difficult to wait, but these things take time."

"At least the newspapers have seemed to lose interest," Mrs. Ellsworth said. "I would so hate for this to become a scandal."

Sarah would hate that, too, although she had to bite her tongue to keep from teasing Mrs. Ellsworth, who usually loved a good scandal when it didn't involve her own family. "Harvey told Malloy about a dairy in Brooklyn that still sells swill milk. Apparently, your father was going to report it to the authorities."

"That sounds just like Father," Theda said, tearing up. "He was so proud of the quality of his milk."

"He had every right to be," Sarah said.

"Do you think the owner of that dairy might be responsible for Mr. Pritchard's death?" Mrs. Ellsworth asked.

"Malloy doesn't think so, but this man did say . . . Well, this is awkward, but he hinted that

Harvey might have been involved in something
. . . embarrassing."

"Embarrassing?" Theda echoed in surprise.
"What do you suppose he meant by that?"

"Perhaps Mrs. Frank is just being discreet," Mrs.
Ellsworth said. "Do you mean something that
might have caused embarrassment to his family?"

"Embarrassment or distress," Sarah clarified. "I
hate to remind you of it, but the night we were
here for supper, Harvey and your father had a . . .
a disagreement."

"I'm so sorry you had to see that," Theda said,
tearing up again. "They never used to argue like
that. I don't know what got into them."

"So the . . . the tension between them was a
recent thing?" Sarah asked.

"Yes, just in the past few months. I confess,
I was so distracted by the wedding plans that I
didn't take much notice at first. Harvey had
always been such a quiet boy, so when he was
sent home from school, it was a surprise."

"From school?"

"Yes, he'd started college in the fall, but . . . I
don't know. There was some to-do and Harvey
had to leave the school. He said it was all a
mistake. He said some other boy had done something but they blamed him for it. Father was very
angry, but he put Harvey to work at the dairy and
everything settled down again, or at least I thought
it did. After Nelson and I married, I wasn't at

home anymore, you see, so I didn't know . . ."

"You didn't know what?" Sarah asked gently.

"I didn't know that they were still at odds. Mother wouldn't tell me a thing like that, of course. She wouldn't want me to be unhappy."

"But they were at odds," Sarah guessed.

"Apparently."

"Do you know why?"

"No one would tell me exactly. It turns out Harvey really did do whatever they'd accused him of at school, and then he did something here that made Father even more angry."

Sarah silently debated "guessing" it might be gambling, but she didn't want to alert Mrs. Ellsworth to that possibility if it turned out to be untrue. "I see."

"But that couldn't have anything to do with Father's death, could it? Harvey certainly didn't kill him."

Sarah only wished she could be sure of that.

Frank and Gino went to the Pure Milk Dairy to see if Harvey would verify the story Jack Robinson had heard. The weather was a bit milder, so Frank didn't suffer quite so much on the drive over, although he still wasn't completely convinced the motorcar was a better mode of travel than a horse-drawn vehicle. The milk wagons were still out on their morning deliveries, so Frank went upstairs to the offices while Gino strolled around, looking for anyone who might want to chat.

As Frank had hoped, Harvey was in his office. This morning he looked a little more at home. He was actually reading some papers when Frank came in, and the desk had been cleared a bit.

"Mr. Malloy, what brings you here?" He didn't sound very happy to see Frank.

Frank took a seat, even though Harvey hadn't offered it. "I wanted to have a quick word with you about the investigation into your father's death."

"I don't . . . I mean, I already told you everything I know."

Frank doubted this very much. "Are you aware that some of your milk wagons are being taken out late at night?"

Harvey's hands clenched where they rested on the desktop, but he said, "Of course they are. That's when we deliver the milk."

"No, I don't mean in the early-morning hours. Someone is taking a few of them out around midnight."

"I . . . You must be mistaken. We have very strict rules. I would know if that was happening."

"Is that why you went to the dairy on New Year's Eve? To make sure the wagons went out?"

"I don't know what you're talking about."

"You told my associate, Mr. Donatelli, that you were at the dairy that evening."

"I most certainly did not."

Had Harvey forgotten? Or was he simply lying?

"Where were you, then?"

"As I told Donatelli, I was with my friends. We met for a late supper and celebrated together."

Except Harvey had joined them only later. "You left the house at eight o'clock, but you didn't meet your friends until after midnight."

"Who told you that?"

"A number of people."

"They're lying. I was with my friends."

"Then your friends will confirm that."

"They'd better."

Frank blinked in surprise but managed not to laugh out loud. His friend Amelio Bruno had already failed to confirm it, Harvey had refused to name any other friends he'd been with, and then Harvey had changed his story a third time to say he'd followed his father to Trinity Church. "Are you much of a card player, Harvey?"

"What?"

"You know, cards. Gambling."

"I . . . I don't play cards. My mother doesn't approve."

"Really?" Could Black Jack Robinson's information be wrong? "A young man-about-town like you? I thought all the young bucks like a game of chance on occasion."

"Oh well, I do buck the tiger now and then," he admitted a little reluctantly.

"Ah, faro," Frank said. "But . . . isn't that a card game, too?"

"It's not *playing cards*. Not like poker or . . . It's just played *with* cards."

Frank thought that a hairsplitting difference, but he didn't argue. "It's exciting, though, isn't it?"

"I . . . I suppose."

"Where do you play?"

"Lots of places."

"I hope you don't go slumming down on Bowery. You're likely to get skinned down there."

"Oh no. There's plenty of nice places around."

"They cater to the rich, I suppose."

Harvey found this distasteful. "They're in respectable neighborhoods, if that's what you mean."

"But they can still cheat you."

Harvey also found this distasteful. "They use a dealing box so the dealer can't palm the cards and cheat."

Did Harvey really not know all the possible ways a dealing box could be rigged? "So I suppose you win as often as you lose."

This was the most distasteful of all. "Why are you so interested in my hobbies, Mr. Malloy?"

"I'm investigating your father's murder. I have to figure out who might have profited from his death."

"You really don't have to figure out anything at all. In fact, I would be happy to pay you to drop your investigation altogether."

"Would you, now?" Frank said with genuine surprise. "Are you the one who paid the police to drop theirs?"

*"What?"*

"Did you bribe the police to stop investigating?"

"Of course not! Why would I do something like that?"

"I don't know. But somebody did, and it seems logical that whoever did is the same person who killed your father."

Harvey opened his mouth to protest, but nothing came out. He closed it almost instantly.

"You do know it's dangerous to get into debt to a gangster," Frank tried.

"He's not . . . What do you mean, a gangster?"

"A man who makes his living by illegal means, such as running a faro board."

"I'm not in debt."

"That's not what I heard."

Harvey blanched at that. "Where did you hear something like that?"

"From a reliable source."

"Well, he's not all that reliable. My debts are paid."

How interesting. "Did your father pay them?"

"That's none of your business."

"It's my business if it has anything to do with your father's murder."

"It doesn't."

Frank stared at Harvey for a long moment,

trying to decide what to ask that would get him the information he needed. "Did paying your debts have anything to do with the milk wagons going out at midnight?"

"I don't know who told you that, but it isn't true. It isn't happening. Nobody is using the wagons for . . . for anything anymore."

*"Anymore?"* Frank asked.

The office door flew open and Amelio Bruno said, "What's going on in here?"

"Harvey and I are just having a friendly discussion," Frank said.

Color flooded Harvey's face and he jumped to his feet. "You have no business here, Malloy. Get out. Get out now before I throw you out."

# IX

"I think I need to talk to Lou Lawson," Malloy said.

They'd all gathered at the house when Sarah had returned from her visit and Malloy and Gino got back from the dairy. Maeve had been kicking her heels all morning, waiting for them after returning from taking Catherine to school.

"Is that a good idea?" Gino asked. "Mr. Robinson said—" He stopped short when Malloy shot him a black look.

"What did Mr. Robinson say?" Sarah asked, giving Malloy a black look of her own.

"I told you, he said Harvey was in debt to Lawson," Malloy said.

Sarah glanced at Gino, but he just shook his head. He wasn't getting involved in this. *"Malloy,"* she said by way of warning.

"He just offered to go with me if I met with Lawson," Malloy said, as if that were the most natural thing in the world.

"And why would he do that?" Sarah challenged.

"Because he's such a kind and thoughtful man," Maeve supplied when Malloy couldn't come up with a plausible lie quickly enough.

Sarah continued to glare at Malloy. "Was he thinking he needed to protect you somehow?"

"I don't need protection. I was a New York City Police detective, for heaven's sake."

"And I'd go with him," Gino said.

"But still Black Jack Robinson offered to accompany you."

Malloy shrugged with unconvincing nonchalance. "I think he likes feeling important."

"All right," Sarah said. "Suppose we do decide you need to speak to this Lou Lawson. Do you really think he'll admit it if he's using the Pure Milk wagons to move stolen goods?"

"And that he bribed the chief of police to stop the investigation into Mr. Pritchard's murder because he had him killed?" Maeve added with a little too much glee.

Sarah sighed. "Yes, I can see where you might need protection. What man is going to answer questions like that?"

"I can understand your concern, but who else could have arranged to use the milk wagons, had Clarence Pritchard killed when he objected, and convinced Big Bill Devery not to investigate?" Malloy said.

"And what's to stop a man like that from killing *you* for asking too many questions?" Sarah replied in exasperation.

"She has a point," Gino said with a smirk.

"I'm certainly not going to accuse him of killing Pritchard right to his face," Malloy replied, equally as exasperated.

"Then, what would you accuse him of?" Sarah asked sweetly.

This time Malloy sighed. "All right, I can see your argument."

"Maybe we can find out more if we go back to the dairy tonight," Gino suggested. "We could barge in and see who's there and question *them,* at least."

"That does sound a little safer than bearding Lou Lawson in his den," Maeve said.

In the end, that's what they decided to do.

This time Gino parked the car around the corner, out of sight of the dairy, and they walked over. Lights blazed in the stable area and they could see men moving around inside. Since it was only a little after eleven, they knew it wasn't the regular drivers getting ready for the milk deliveries. They'd discussed several possible ways to approach this and had chosen to simply walk in, as if they had every right.

At first no one even noticed. A few stable boys were harnessing horses to about half a dozen wagons, and some older men were making sure the wagons were completely empty. Finally, one of the men stopped what he was doing and said, "What do you want?"

That made everyone else stop and turn. Frank just stood there with his hands stuffed into his overcoat pockets and smiled. "Is Harvey here?"

"What's going on?" someone called from the back.

No one answered, and hurried footsteps told them someone was rushing up to find out. When he came into view, Frank's smile broadened.

"Hello, Mr. Bruno."

Amelio Bruno stopped abruptly at the sight of Frank and Gino. He still wore the suit he'd been wearing earlier today, but now straw clung to it in unlikely places, as if he'd spent more time in the stable than a man wearing a suit usually did. "What are you doing here?"

"We'd like to have a little chat, if you don't mind."

"I do mind. You have a lot of nerve showing up here. Mr. Pritchard threw you out earlier today."

"Which is why I came back."

Bruno frowned. "That doesn't make any sense."

"When he threw me out, I knew he must be doing something he didn't want me to know about, so I came here tonight to find out what it was."

Although no one said anything, Frank felt a wave of tension go through the room.

"What's going on here?" another man demanded. He'd also come from the back, and he also wore a suit. His was much cleaner, however, and much more expensive. It might even have been the same one he'd worn to the funeral on Saturday.

"We meet again," Frank said. He was the man

Harvey Pritchard had accosted on Saturday. "But I don't think we were actually introduced. I'm Frank Malloy."

"Oh yeah, the detective," he said with distaste. "And what do you think you're detecting here?"

"Some unusual activity, and I wonder if Harvey Pritchard knows about it."

"You can wonder all you like—" Bruno began, but the other man stopped him with a raised hand.

He glanced around at the men and boys who were still watching them and listening to every word. "Let's go upstairs and talk about this in private."

Bruno led the way, with the other man following behind Frank and Gino. They went to the third floor, where Harvey Pritchard's office was, but Bruno didn't take them any farther than the reception area. He just stopped there and crossed his arms belligerently. The other man also stopped, but he didn't appear to be as upset as Bruno.

"There's nothing going on here that should concern you, Mr. Malloy."

"And why should what's going on here concern *you?*" Frank asked him.

That stopped him for a moment. "I . . . What do you mean?"

"I mean, who are you and what are you doing here after hours when the dairy is usually closed and what is going on with those wagons downstairs?"

"I think that is between Mr. Bruno and myself," he replied, his poise restored.

"But I don't think that at all. You see, the owner's daughter hired me to find out who murdered her father, so if something unusual is going on at his business, it's my duty to investigate. It's also my duty to find out if it has anything to do with Mr. Pritchard's murder."

"But it doesn't, so you can go," the man said.

Frank pulled his hand out of his pocket and rubbed his chin thoughtfully. "Maybe you'll tell me who you are and what you're doing here, and if that impresses me, then maybe I will go."

The man sighed. Everything about him told Frank he was confident in his power and his ability to handle any situation. Frank could also see he wasn't used to being challenged. "All right, Mr. Malloy. My name is White, and I'm, uh, advising Mr. Bruno."

"Advising Mr. Bruno about what?"

"About a way to increase the dairy's profits."

Frank considered this for a long moment. "And does Harvey Pritchard know about this?"

"Of course he does," Bruno said before White could reply.

"What about Clarence Pritchard? Did he know?" Frank asked.

"He certainly did," White replied before Bruno could. "He was quite pleased with our arrangement."

"What exactly is your arrangement?" Frank asked. "What are you using the wagons for?"

"Deliveries," White said without hesitation. "The wagons would just be sitting idle otherwise, and this time of night, the traffic is much lighter."

"Deliveries of what?"

Mr. White smiled. "Merchandise, Mr. Malloy. Now, that should answer all your questions, although Mr. Bruno is correct, this is really none of your business."

"So if I ask Harvey Pritchard about this, he will confirm what you've told me?"

"Of course he will," White said, although Bruno shifted uneasily, Frank noticed.

"That's funny, because he just told me this morning that your little arrangement had ended."

White frowned and glanced at Bruno, who flinched slightly. When he turned back to Frank, he said, "I'm sure you misunderstood him."

"And Harvey will confirm that his father knew about it, too?"

"I can't speak for what Harvey knows, but I assure you, Mr. Pritchard was well aware of our partnership."

"*Your* partnership?" Frank said with interest. "Does that mean you're the one in charge of this enterprise?"

Frank could see White struggling with his answer. He wouldn't want to admit to being second fiddle, but he also wouldn't want word to get back to his employer—if his employer really was who Frank thought he was—that he was claiming to be in charge. "I manage this enterprise, as you call it," he finally said.

Frank nodded as if he were satisfied with that answer. "Fair enough. But could I ask you a favor?"

"You can ask. I make no promises," White said, obviously relieved to be back on firmer ground.

"Would you tell Lou Lawson that I'd like to verify all of this with him?"

"And what did he say to that?" Sarah asked. She'd waited up for him, too worried to sleep until she knew he'd gotten home safely.

"Not much. He tried to laugh it off, like it was a joke, but he turned a little green when he realized I knew Lawson was behind all of it." She'd been sitting up in their private parlor but now they'd moved into the bedroom so he could start getting ready for bed. He shrugged out of his suit coat and started removing his shirt.

"You don't really think you'll hear from Lawson, do you?"

"Who knows? I can't imagine his little deal with Pritchard's dairy is all that important to a man who controls half the crime in New York City."

"Does he really?" Sarah asked in amazement.

"I don't know. That's probably an exaggeration,

but he controls a lot of it. How much stolen merchandise can he be moving in a few milk wagons?"

"I suppose that would depend on what he was moving."

Malloy paused in the process of unbuttoning his pants. "What do you mean?"

"I mean you could fit a lot of diamonds in a milk wagon. Or jewelry. Even bolts of silk and other fine fabrics. Small things that are very valuable. And who would think to look in a milk wagon?"

"Not many, and no one if they've been paid to look the other way."

"Exactly."

"Then maybe I *will* hear from Lou Lawson."

Sarah removed her warm robe and quickly slipped into bed. "So if this is your last night on earth, we should probably make the most of it," she said with a coy smile.

As she had expected, he needed no further invitation.

The next morning, Malloy went to his office to meet Gino. Since Sarah wouldn't hear of him going to see Lou Lawson and having nothing else in particular scheduled for the day, he thought perhaps he and Gino might go over everything they knew once more to see if they'd missed anything. Maeve had gone shopping, and Sarah was preparing to go to the clinic. She knew two of the residents were due to give birth any day, so she was hoping to be there for a delivery. She also needed to check with Jocelyn to make sure she had gotten the message Sarah had sent and was prepared to meet with Jack Robinson tomorrow. She was almost ready when Hattie came in to tell her Mrs. Pritchard had come to call.

Since it was much too early for "morning calls," which took place in the afternoon, Sarah was consumed with curiosity and hurried down to the parlor to greet her guest.

"Mrs. Pritchard, what a pleasant surprise. I hope nothing is wrong."

Mrs. Pritchard wore her severest widow's weeds, her cheeks rosy from the wintery winds, and she didn't smile. "I beg you to forgive me for calling at such an unfashionable hour, Mrs. Malloy, but Theda came to see me yesterday afternoon, and I felt I should speak with you privately."

"Of course. I've asked my maid to bring us some tea or would you prefer coffee?"

"Tea is fine, thank you."

Sarah seated her in front of the fireplace. Hattie had laid a fire, but it wasn't lit since Sarah was going out and the central heat kept the house comfortably warm without it. Sarah struck a match and touched it to the kindling. A blaze would be cheerful, at least. She took a chair opposite her guest and gave her an encouraging smile, which Mrs. Pritchard still did not return.

"Theda told me what you said when you called on her yesterday."

Sarah tried to remember what she might have said that could have alarmed Mrs. Pritchard. "Yes, I knew Theda would be anxious to find out what we'd learned about her father's death."

"She said you had more questions than answers, though."

"That's probably true, since we're still trying to piece everything together."

Mrs. Pritchard drew what sounded like a fortifying breath, and Sarah suddenly realized that her grim expression concealed anger, not concern. "Mrs. Malloy, I will thank you to leave my children out of your *investigation*." She said the word as if it left a bad taste in her mouth.

Sarah let a few moments go by before replying to that remarkable statement while she tried to decide what was really behind Mrs. Pritchard's ire. "I'm sorry if Theda was upset. She certainly didn't seem to be, and she didn't say—"

"If she wasn't upset, she should have been. Mrs. Malloy, I assure you, my children had nothing to do with my husband's unfortunate death. It's bad enough that he was murdered in such a . . . such an *unseemly* way that it must necessarily reflect badly on all of us who survive, but I will not have them suspected of having a hand in it. Is that understood?"

Sarah began to think she did understand. "Does that mean you know more about your husband's death than you've told us?"

Her eyes widened. *"What?"*

Sarah feigned her own surprise. "You just assured me that your children had nothing to do with your husband's death. Naturally, that made me think you know who did."

"Of course I don't know. I have no idea!"

"Forgive me, then, but if you don't know who is guilty, how can you be certain who is innocent?"

"I . . ." She gaped at Sarah for a moment and then burst into tears.

Sarah knew a moment of guilt herself for having distressed the poor woman, but she had no idea how she could have avoided it.

Just then Hattie came to the door with the tea tray. Sarah jumped up and took it from her, telling her to shut the door behind her to spare Mrs. Pritchard any more embarrassment. She set the tray down on a low table and proceeded to pour a cup for her guest while Mrs. Pritchard fished out her black-bordered handkerchief and blotted her tears.

When she finished, Sarah handed her the cup. "I put extra sugar in it. That helps with shock."

Mrs. Pritchard took it gratefully and sipped carefully while Sarah prepared her own tea.

"I know this is a very difficult time for you, Mrs. Pritchard," Sarah said, giving her guest time to compose herself. "And of course we don't suspect Theda of anything since she is the one who hired Malloy in the first place."

Mrs. Pritchard cleared her throat. "But you do suspect Harvey."

Oh dear, how to get around that one? "We suspect everyone connected with your husband, Mrs. Pritchard. And of course we have to consider that Mr. Pritchard might have been killed by a stranger, too."

"But you saw that argument between Harvey and his father, of course, and that has made you especially suspicious of him. That argument doesn't mean anything at all, though. Fathers and sons argue all the time."

"Yes, they do, and very few fathers get murdered as a result. We know all that, but when a man is killed, we do have to at least *consider* everyone. Tell me, Mrs. Pritchard, do you know why Harvey and his father were at odds?"

"At odds? What do you mean?"

"I mean that they hadn't been getting along for some time, according to what we've learned."

"Did Theda tell you that?" she asked with a frown.

"Theda said she hasn't lived at home since her marriage and for several months prior to her wedding, she was distracted with her own concerns, so she didn't notice anything unusual."

All of which was true, as far as it went, but

Mrs. Pritchard seemed oddly relieved. "I see."

"So *do* you know why Harvey and his father were arguing?"

Mrs. Pritchard didn't answer right away, telling Sarah she knew perfectly well and was trying to frame an answer that would satisfy Sarah but not incriminate her son. "Harvey is . . . Do you have brothers, Mrs. Malloy?"

"No, I don't."

"I didn't either, so raising a boy was a rather new experience for me. Boys aren't . . . Well, they aren't as governable as girls."

Sarah remembered her sister, Maggie. Her parents would have said Maggie had not been governable at all, but Sarah simply nodded encouragingly.

"Harvey has . . . He hasn't met his father's expectations."

"Theda said he was sent home from college last fall," Sarah said to test the waters.

Mrs. Pritchard winced at that. Plainly, she did not think it appropriate to tell a virtual stranger something so unflattering about one's family. "That was the disappointment. His father never had the opportunity for an education, and he wanted his son to have every advantage."

"I understand he was gambling," Sarah tried, although no one had actually said this was the reason he was sent home from school.

Color flooded Mrs. Pritchard's lovely face.

"How dare you?" she asked, nearly breathless with fury.

"Theda doesn't know," Sarah added quickly. "I practically begged her to tell me the reason Harvey was sent home, but she truly has no idea. I don't think she really wants to know, quite frankly."

"Then how did you find out?" she demanded.

Sarah debated for a moment and decided to test Mrs. Pritchard further. "I didn't. It was just a guess, because Mr. Malloy recently learned that Harvey had incurred gambling debts here in the city."

"Oh," she said in dismay, her eyes filling with tears again.

"I'm so sorry," Sarah said quite sincerely. "I can't imagine how difficult this must be for you."

"No, you can't. First Harvey returned home after being expelled, or whatever they call it, from college and then we learned he's been gambling at some notorious house here in the city and has lost thousands."

"So you knew about his debts?"

"Not at first. And not about the gambling either, or at least not that he was doing it here. He swore he would stop when he came home from school. He was like a little boy who has been caught stealing cookies from the kitchen. He begged us to forgive him. He even wept. I truly believed he was too ashamed to ever go back to it."

"I'm told it's quite thrilling. Some people find it impossible to resist."

"How could losing thousands of dollars be thrilling?" Mrs. Pritchard scoffed.

"I understand that they let people win for a time, at least at first, to draw them in, and then occasionally, to give them hope."

"You mean . . . ? I thought they were games of chance. Are you saying those places control who wins and loses?"

"The people who operate gambling dens control every aspect. No one ever comes out ahead except the owner."

"How horrible! Someone should do something," she cried.

"They did do something," Sarah said. "They made gambling illegal."

Mrs. Pritchard's color blossomed again as she realized the irony. "Oh."

"Yes, but of course there are still hundreds of places in the city where you can play any possible game of chance, as you call it, and thousands of people still frequent them. But we aren't worried about them. We're only worried about Harvey."

"Clarence was furious when he found out Harvey was still gambling, and that he'd lost so much money."

"Did your husband refuse to pay Harvey's debts?"

Mrs. Pritchard set down her now-empty cup.

"He threatened to, I know. He would have liked to teach Harvey a lesson, but he also realized the men he was dealing with were dangerous. They wouldn't stop at hurting Harvey."

"So he did pay the debts?"

She started to reply, but stopped herself.

"What is it?" Sarah asked.

"I just realized I'm not sure."

"What do you mean, you're not sure?"

Mrs. Pritchard shook her head. "I don't really know what happened. I mean, I know the debts were settled. Clarence told me that much, but . . . He seemed angry about it. I supposed he was angry about throwing money away on something like that. Maybe that's why he was even angrier at Harvey afterward."

"And when did all this start? His anger toward Harvey, I mean."

"Just a few weeks ago, right before Christmas. That was when . . . Well, I don't know exactly what happened, but suddenly Clarence was furious and berating Harvey for his gambling debts every time they were in the same room. That was the first time I knew anything about the debts, and I'm sure it was the first time Clarence did because he probably would have been angry earlier if he'd known."

"When they argued, what did they say?"

"Clarence would accuse Harvey of ruining everything Clarence had worked all of his life to build and destroying his reputation, although I can't see how a few gambling debts could do that."

"If they were high enough, it might," Sarah suggested.

"I suppose. But neither of them would discuss it with me. I just had to try to calm them both down so we could eat the occasional meal in peace."

"Mrs. Pritchard, where were you on New Year's Eve?"

She looked up in surprise at the sudden change of topic and grew instantly uneasy. "I . . . I told you. I was at home in bed."

"No, you weren't. We know you went out somewhere. Perhaps you went to a private party or to visit some friends. They could vouch for you."

"Vouch for me? Why do I need anyone to vouch for me?" she asked, angry again.

"As I explained earlier, we have to be suspicious of everyone."

"You can't think I followed Clarence downtown and murdered him!" she insisted. "I was at home, asleep."

But Sarah shook her head. "It's actually better if you tell us where you really were. Mrs. Pritchard, we know about Mr. Bergman."

"Of course you do. I introduced you to him."

"No, I mean we know you and Mr. Bergman have been . . . in love for a long time."

This time her face turned scarlet. "I don't know

where you got an idea like that! How dare you!"

"And we suspect that you and Mr. Bergman were together on New Year's Eve. We have no desire to embarrass you or judge you. If the two of you were together, you can vouch for each other."

"Why would Otto need anyone to vouch for him?" she asked, trying to be outraged.

"Because the two of you have been lovers for years, and if your husband had finally found out, he might have put a stop to your assignations, which would give Mr. Bergman a reason to kill him."

"I . . . I . . ." She snatched up her handkerchief and pressed it to her lips while she squeezed her eyes shut against a fresh onslaught of tears.

"I'm terribly sorry. I know this must be embarrassing for you, Mrs. Pritchard," Sarah said, "but no one else needs to know you were together that night. No one needs to know anything at all about your private affairs."

"*Affairs,*" she snapped. "You know nothing about it."

"I don't pretend to."

"We should have been married. Otto and I. We'd decided that when we were twelve years old, but my parents . . ." She had to apply the handkerchief again.

"I'm sure they thought they were doing what was best for you."

"Of course they did. Clarence had his own

231

business. He was already a success. Otto was still a boy."

"But he proved himself in the end."

"Yes." She dabbed at new tears. "But Clarence would never have given me a divorce. Not that I ever dared ask for one, but he was outspoken on the subject. I knew what he thought of women who divorced their husbands. He would have blackened my name and taken my children and made sure I never saw them again. Otto wouldn't ask me to make a sacrifice like that, even if I'd been willing."

And if she'd simply deserted her husband and lived in sin, the scandal would have ruined her children's chances of making a decent marriage. Women really had no options for ending an unhappy union. "So you were with Mr. Bergman that night?"

"Of course I was. I knew Clarence would be out for hours trying to convince people of his ridiculous theories, so he'd never miss me. I'd just have to return before he did. Sometimes I came in later, by accident, but he never knew. We'd had separate rooms for years, and he wouldn't pay any attention to whether I was home or not. He was so sure of me, he never even thought to suspect me."

"Where did you go that night?"

She winced again. "I'd like to tell you we went to some restaurant and enjoyed a lovely evening out, but we couldn't ever be seen in public. We didn't dare go to his house either. Servants gossip and neighbors do, too, you know."

How well Sarah knew that.

"Surely, you didn't go to a hotel," Sarah said, wondering what kind of place would allow such goings-on.

"Oh no, nothing so outrageous. Otto bought a small house out in Harlem. No one knows us there. He has a housekeeper who lives in and turns a blind eye. But that's only been since . . . He was married, too. Did you know?"

"Theda told me."

"When he became successful, he decided to make a home for himself. He wanted a family, and he was always faithful to her. We were both faithful for years. Then she died, and . . . We had never stopped loving each other for all that time. But we were always friends, so Clarence never suspected a thing. I don't suppose he could imagine anyone wanting me in that way. At any rate, Otto bought the house so we could have a place to be together. I don't know how I would have survived without that."

"How did Mr. Pritchard find out?"

Mrs. Pritchard had been lost in her memories and she looked up with a start. "What?"

"How did Mr. Pritchard find out you were lovers?"

"He didn't. He never knew."

"But—"

"He didn't, Mrs. Malloy. Some men might have suspected but decided not to raise a fuss and just tolerate it, but not Clarence. He was . . . Well, you know how he was. He was always right, about everything. He was right about how milk should be produced. He was right about when the new century began. He was right about how long a sermon should be in church. He was right about how people should conduct themselves, and he wasn't shy about telling them, either. If he had suspected for one moment that I had betrayed him . . ." She shivered.

"Then you must have been terrified he would find out," Sarah tried.

"At first I was. I made myself sick with worry, but time passed and he never even noticed. We were careful, of course, but still, he never even objected to Otto coming to the house or escorting me and the children to things. I think Clarence was actually grateful that he didn't have to bother with us."

What a sad commentary on her life. "I gather your children are fond of Mr. Bergman."

"Of course they are. He was good to them. Better than their own father in many ways."

"And what were your plans?"

"Plans?"

"For the future? Sooner or later Mr. Pritchard would have found out."

She smiled sadly. "And perhaps he would have been so outraged that he would have finally divorced me, but I doubt it. He would more likely have refused, knowing that he'd be denying me any hope of happiness."

"You don't have to worry about the children anymore," Sarah reminded her.

"No. I could have simply left him, I suppose. I would have hated the scandal, especially dragging Otto into it, but Theda is married now, and Harvey . . . Well, boys aren't tainted in the same way, are they?"

"No, they aren't." And Harvey had sins of his own to atone for. "So you didn't really have any plans?"

"I suppose I always thought . . . Clarence is older than I. Almost ten years. I suppose I thought someday he would die."

And now he has, but Sarah didn't distract her by pointing it out. "So you and Mr. Bergman were together on New Year's Eve at your house in Harlem."

"Yes, we were. We couldn't have killed Clarence."

"And I suppose the housekeeper was there and can verify that."

"Uh . . . She . . . Otto gave her the night off, because of the celebration. But Otto and I can vouch for each other."

Which really wasn't much of an alibi at all.

# X

Frank and Gino went to the house for lunch because they knew Velvet's cooking would beat anything they could find at a restaurant near their office. Indeed, she'd put the leftover roast from Sunday's dinner into a stew with carrots and potatoes and served it with a fresh loaf of bread. Maeve was home, too, so while they ate, they all got to hear Sarah's account of her amazing visit with Mrs. Pritchard.

"So she admits to the affair with Bergman," Frank said.

"I don't suppose there's a reason to deny it any longer," Maeve pointed out reasonably.

"I doubt she's going to announce it to the world," Sarah said, "but she did feel obligated to explain it to me. Besides, she needed an alibi for the night her husband was killed."

"It's not much of an alibi," Gino said.

"Do you really think they'd lie for each other?" Maeve asked in mock astonishment.

"If they wouldn't, it wasn't much of an affair, was it?" he retorted.

"How romantic," Maeve said with a wince.

"Which is exactly why we can't rule either of them out," Frank said.

"Do we really think Mrs. Pritchard followed her

husband down to the church and strangled him?" Sarah asked.

"Are you going to claim a woman couldn't do something like that?" Maeve asked with a grin.

"Of course not, but we have to decide if *Mrs. Pritchard* could have done it."

"Mrs. Frank is right," Gino said, probably just to disagree with Maeve. "Not many women would go downtown alone at that hour of the night to find their husband in a huge crowd and strangle him."

"But it wasn't just any night," Maeve pointed out. "Lots of respectable people were on the streets because of the celebrations. She could have taken a cab, which would be fairly safe and not particularly unusual. Apparently, she often went out alone to meet her lover. And who says she went down there intending to kill him? Didn't Harvey claim he went down to bring his father back before he got himself in trouble? Maybe she did the same thing, and when she saw him sitting on the bench, she just . . ." She shrugged.

"She just suddenly decided she'd be better off if he was dead?" Gino scoffed.

"Or maybe something happened that we don't know about," Frank said. "Maybe her husband did finally figure out she was having an affair, so she suddenly had a good reason to do something she wouldn't normally have done."

"Let's hope killing one's husband isn't something a woman would normally have done," Sarah teased.

"I *always* hope that," he replied.

"Mr. Malloy is right, though," Maeve said. "We only have her word that her husband didn't know about the affair, and she'd have every reason to lie about that if it's the reason she or Mr. Bergman killed him."

"Which reminds me," Frank said. "Mrs. Pritchard didn't have to go downtown alone at all that night. She could have taken Bergman with her, and they could have killed him together."

"Or Mr. Bergman might have done it alone," Sarah said.

"How would we ever find out, though?" Gino said. "They aren't going to admit it."

"He might say something incriminating, if you get to him before she can warn him," Maeve said.

"Do you think you could?" Sarah asked Frank.

"I could try, but I don't have any idea where to find him."

"He's probably listed in the City Directory," Maeve said. "I'll get it."

"Even if she manages to warn him," Gino said while they waited for Maeve to return, "it would be good to see his reaction when you ask if they were together that night."

"That's true. I'd also like to hear his justification for having an affair with another man's wife for all those years, too."

239

Maeve returned with the City Directory, and they found a home and business address for Otto Bergman. Frank and Gino decided to head out to find Bergman while Sarah finally was able to leave for her visit to the clinic. Maeve remained behind to do her nanny duties and pick Catherine up at school.

Sarah was once again disappointed that no one was in labor when she arrived at the clinic, but she did get to visit the little girl who had been born overnight. To her surprise, she found Jocelyn holding the child while the mother slept.

"I never knew much about babies," she said to Sarah when she'd returned the infant to her cradle. "They're really rather helpless, aren't they?"

"Completely. They're also demanding. Are you having second thoughts about your decision?"

"Second and third and fourth thoughts," Jocelyn confided as they slipped out of the room. Jocelyn led Sarah to her own room, where they could speak privately. "I change my mind a dozen times a day. But in the end, I always have to admit that the thought of never seeing my child again makes me want to scream, so I think I must do whatever I can to keep it."

When they were in her room with the door closed, Sarah said, "Did you get my message about Mr. Robinson wanting to see you again?"

"Oh yes, which is why I've been thinking

so much. You're sure he is going to propose marriage?"

"I don't think he would violate my trust by suggesting anything else, although I suppose anything is possible."

"I couldn't help him rise in society if I was only his mistress, which makes me think his intentions are honorable, at least."

"And you're willing to accept him if he does propose?"

Jocelyn sat down on her bed and closed her eyes for a long moment, as if trying to shut out whatever she was thinking. "Suppose I marry him, and when the child is born, he decides he doesn't want it after all? I'd be powerless to prevent him from simply giving it away."

Oh dear, she really had been thinking about this. Sarah considered the question for a few moments before replying. "I don't think he could expect you to fulfill your part of the bargain if he didn't fulfill his."

"I suppose you're right, but it's also possible he won't find being accepted into society as rewarding as he imagines."

"He may not, but that won't be your fault either."

She smiled sadly. "I've noticed that doesn't stop most men from casting the blame anyway."

"Jocelyn, this is a big decision, and I can't make it for you. I do, however, think you would do well to raise all these issues with Mr. Robinson. You may find he has considered them himself. For example, what is to stop you from leaving him once your child is born? You'll have the protection of his name for the baby and only a divorce to cause you any scandal. While that's considered a serious breach in some circles, a few women have managed to maintain their social standing after obtaining one and even to make a good second marriage."

"I hadn't thought of that. You're right, of course." She smiled a little less sadly. "I didn't realize he might also be worried."

"I've been married twice, and I believe I can safely say that men often worry just as much as women do. The best way to deal with it is to talk about it."

Frank and Gino easily found Bergman's home on a quiet street in the Lenox Hill neighborhood, not far from the Pritchards'. It was just what Frank would have imagined a successful businessman would own, a brownstone town house with a tiny but tidy front yard fenced in wrought iron. The maid told them he was not at home, and she felt sure they could find him at his office. She even confirmed that they had the correct address, which was a building a few blocks away on Sixth Avenue.

The office building had a directory in the lobby, telling them Mr. Bergman's office was on the third floor. The elevator operator took them up, and a discreet sign beside one of the doors in the hallway said BERGMAN ENTERPRISES.

They entered to find a girl secretary typing at a desk in the nondescript reception area. She was a strapping Irish girl with a mass of auburn hair only slightly tamed into a bun and green eyes that told them instantly she would brook no nonsense from them. A brass nameplate on the desk said she was Kathleen Denson.

"May I help you, gentlemen?" she asked without the slightest indication she wanted to help them at all or even that she really considered them gentlemen.

"We'd like to see Mr. Bergman, if he's in," Frank said, trying a little of his charm, although Sarah had warned him it wasn't nearly as good as Gino's.

"I don't suppose you have an appointment," Miss Denson said, "because if you did, I'd know about it."

"No, we don't, but we're here on some business for Mrs. Pritchard, so we thought he might see us anyway."

"Mrs. Pritchard, is it?" Kathleen obviously did not approve, although Frank had no idea what it was she did not approve. The affair? Mrs. Pritchard in general? The fact that Frank had mentioned her name? Or just Frank in general? "I'll see if he's available."

She rose and walked to one of the doors leading to what must be adjoining offices. She tapped lightly and entered without waiting for a reply. She also closed the door behind her, which Frank found excessively discreet. Was Bergman concerned about being overheard when he refused to see visitors?

Before Frank could really consider his own question, the door opened again and Miss Denson said, "Mr. Bergman will see you."

Frank exchanged a glance with Gino, who looked as intrigued by all this as Frank was, and then Gino followed him into Bergman's office. This space was also modestly furnished. Frank had carefully considered the decoration—or rather the lack thereof—for his own offices, not wanting to mislead potential clients with lavish furnishings. As a businessman, wouldn't Bergman want to give the opposite impression, that he was highly successful and had money to waste on carpets and draperies? But maybe Bergman wasn't as successful as they had been led to believe, although his suit was certainly well made. Of course a tailor would own nice suits, he supposed, no matter what his income.

"Mr. Malloy," Bergman said without much enthusiasm. At least he rose from his chair and put out his hand for Frank to shake. Frank introduced Gino, and when they were seated in the visitor's chairs in front of Bergman's desk,

Bergman took his own seat and stared at them in uncomfortable silence for a long moment. "My secretary said Mrs. Pritchard sent you," he said at last.

"I said we needed to see you on some business for Mrs. Pritchard," Frank clarified. "She doesn't know we're here."

"I see." Although plainly, he did not.

"We need to ask you where you were on New Year's Eve."

"Why?"

Not any of the possible answers Frank had been expecting. "Because we are checking on the whereabouts of everyone who might have had a reason to kill Clarence Pritchard."

Frank had to give him credit. He looked truly astonished. "And you think I am one of those people? What possible reason could I have for killing him?"

Frank leaned back in his chair and let some seconds tick by before he said, "Because you have been having a love affair with Mrs. Pritchard for a number of years."

"Who told you such a scandalous lie?" Bergman asked with credible outrage.

"Mrs. Pritchard." As expected, this silenced Bergman. He stared back at Frank in shock, and Frank let him absorb the information before adding, "So you see, we need to know where you were the night Pritchard died."

245

Bergman shifted uncomfortably in his chair. "I was . . . at home."

"You didn't go out to celebrate?"

"I've always felt it was silly to celebrate the New Year. It's really just another day."

"Were you alone?"

"What does that matter?"

Frank smiled benevolently. "Can anyone else verify that you were at home?"

"No," he said tightly.

"Not even your servants?"

"I gave them the night off."

"The servants at *both* of your houses?"

Frank watched in fascination as the color rose in Bergman's face. He was hating this, and even worse, he was furious, which meant Mrs. Pritchard had definitely not yet told him about her conversation with Sarah.

"What do you mean by that?"

"Mrs. Pritchard also told us about the house in Harlem," Frank said, keeping his voice free of all emotion.

"And did she tell you where she was on New Year's Eve?"

"She did, yes." Frank had no intention of revealing what she'd said.

"Then you know we were together."

He did, of course, but exactly *where* were they together? "Can anyone else confirm that?"

"I don't know why anyone else would need to

confirm it." Bergman was no longer bothering to hide his annoyance. "You have our word. We were together, so we can vouch for each other. Neither of us killed Pritchard."

"Did Pritchard know about your affair?"

"What kind of a question is that?"

"An important one, I think."

"Not that it's any of your business, but since it eliminates any reason I might have had for wishing him harm, no, he did not."

Of course, it didn't really eliminate *all* the reasons he might have had for wanting to kill Pritchard. "Are you sure?"

"Yes, I'm sure. Had he known, he never would have allowed me in his house again, and he probably would never have allowed Ilsa out of it."

"But what if he'd only just learned of it that day, so he hadn't had time to take any action?"

"He would have made the time. Believe me, Clarence Pritchard was not a man to postpone his vengeance, and if he knew he'd been cuckolded, he would have sought immediate vengeance on everyone involved."

"Do you know of any other reason someone might have killed Pritchard?"

Bergman sighed in exasperation. "I've been very patient with you, Mr. Malloy, because I care very much for Theda and I know she wants justice for her father, but I will not submit to any more of this. I will also thank you to leave Mrs. Pritchard alone. Neither she nor I had anything to do with Clarence's death, and I won't have her upset any more over this."

"Does Mrs. Pritchard know you have appointed yourself her protector?"

"Really, Malloy, you are trying my patience. You come in here and insult Mrs. Pritchard with your innuendos and practically accuse me of murder, and then you don't even notice when you've been warned off. Well, let me make it perfectly clear. I will not tolerate you meddling in the Pritchard family's affairs any longer. I want you to tell Theda you've been unable to solve her father's murder and you are withdrawing from the case." He actually took a breath, as if preparing to say more, but he seemed to catch himself.

Frank waited, but he appeared to be finished. "Or what?"

"What do you mean?"

"I mean that usually when somebody gives me an order like that, they follow it with a threat of what will happen if I don't obey."

Was Bergman actually grinding his teeth? Frank thought so. "I am a man who is used to being obeyed simply because I give the order, but if you want a threat, I'll give you one. Your two-bit detective agency will be finished. No one in this city will ever hire you again. Is that good enough for you?"

Frank managed not to sigh. "I guess it will have to be."

"And now you'll leave and never come back here."

He must have pushed some kind of alarm because Miss Kathleen Denson opened the office door and stepped in. "This way please, gentlemen."

Frank and Gino rose and followed her out. She opened the door to the hallway for them and closed it rather firmly behind them.

"That was interesting," Gino said as they waited for the elevator.

"It certainly was. Did he strike you as a tailor?"

"A tailor? Oh, that's right, he owns a bunch of tailor shops."

"That's what Theda or Mrs. Pritchard said. I forget which one. He started out as an apprentice and eventually opened his own shop and now he owns several in the city."

"Why isn't his office in a tailor shop then?"

"Maybe he likes his privacy."

But Gino shook his head. "He doesn't talk like a tailor either."

"How many tailors do you know?" Frank asked with interest.

Gino grinned. "Just the one who made my good suit, but I don't think tailors—even ones who own several shops—expect people to run and hide when they order them to."

249

"He didn't order us to run and hide."

"Practically. He ordered us off the case, which is pretty bold of him since he didn't put us on it in the first place."

"I thought so, too."

"And that threat . . ." Gino shook his head again and made a rude noise.

"You're right. It was pretty weak. From the look on his face, I was expecting a lot more."

"Yeah. He should have at least threatened to beat us up or something. But maybe being put out of business is a pretty scary threat to some people."

"I guess he doesn't know the detective agency doesn't support me."

"Even so, how does he think he can keep clients from hiring us?"

"I don't know, but I'd like to find out. I think we need to know a bit more about Mr. Otto Bergman."


"How will you find out more about him?" Sarah asked. Gino had joined them for supper that evening, and Malloy had told her and Maeve about their visit with Bergman. Mrs. Malloy chose to have supper with the children rather than listen to the details of their investigation.

"Not from his secretary," Gino said with a grin. "So don't even suggest I might try to charm her into talking about him."

"Nobody was going to," Maeve said, earning a scowl from him.

"She's a rather formidable Irish lass," Malloy said, "and apparently very loyal to Mr. Bergman."

"You'd probably have better luck at his shops, then," Maeve said. "Employees always like to complain about the boss, and since he isn't on the premises, they wouldn't be shy about talking."

"That's what we were thinking," Malloy said. "Except we'll need to find out from Theda where his shops are. We couldn't find any tailor shops in the City Directory with his name on them, and we even stopped at my own tailor's shop on the way home to see if he could help, but he never heard of Otto Bergman."

"That's strange, but maybe there are just too many tailors in the city for all of them to know each other," Sarah said.

"Bergman isn't just a tailor, though," Malloy reminded her. "He's supposedly very successful and owns several establishments."

"He didn't look all that successful to me," Gino said. "His office wasn't even as fancy as ours, and he lives in a town house in Lenox Hill. And tell them about his threats."

"He threatened you?" Sarah asked, aghast.

"Not really," Malloy said with an odd little grin. "He ordered us to leave Mrs. Pritchard alone and stop investigating or else he'd make sure my detective agency went out of business."

"How does he propose to do that?" Maeve asked. Malloy shrugged. "He didn't say."

"The funny part," Gino hastened to explain, "is that Mr. Malloy and I both expected him to really threaten us. He was furious and he ordered us off the case the way somebody who was used to ordering people around would do it, but then he stopped. Mr. Malloy had to remind him that he needed a threat to make us do what he wanted."

"And he couldn't come up with anything worse than putting you out of business?" Maeve asked, enjoying this thoroughly.

"If he could, he decided not to mention it," Malloy said. "So naturally, we have no intention of giving up the case. Tomorrow, we're going to track down Bergman's tailor shops and find out what we can about him."

"Gino can't go," Sarah reminded him. "He has to take Maeve down to the clinic in the motorcar to fetch Jocelyn tomorrow morning."

"Oh, that's right. It's the big proposal tomorrow," Malloy said with a smile.

"We hope so, at least," Sarah said. "Maybe you can start your morning with a visit to Mrs. Ellsworth and ask Theda if she knows where Mr. Bergman's shops are. You won't need Gino for that, at least."

"No, and with any luck at all, I'll have visited all of them by the time Gino has returned Jocelyn to the clinic," Malloy said.

· · ·

Jack Robinson arrived before Jocelyn the next morning. Hattie showed him into the parlor, where Sarah was waiting. He'd obviously taken great pains with his appearance again today. She thought his suit might actually be brand-new. She wondered idly who his tailor was.

"I'm early, I'm afraid."

"I hope that means you're anxious to see Miss Vane."

"More than anxious." He was carrying an attaché case, and he laid it down on the sofa beside him. "I hope she's anxious, too."

"I'm sure she is, although the prospect of marrying a total stranger must be terrifying to you both."

"How kind of you to consider my feelings as well, Mrs. Malloy," he said.

"I'm not kind at all, just realistic. I saw Jocelyn yesterday, and she has many concerns. She was afraid you might change your mind about allowing her to keep her child, and she was surprised when I suggested you might be concerned that she would take the child and leave."

He smiled slightly. "I've been disappointed once, and you're right, I'm not eager to be disappointed again. But I've given the matter considerable thought, and I think I have found a solution that will allay her fears and mine as well."

"I'm glad to hear it," Sarah said, glancing at the attaché case and wondering if that had anything to do with his solution.

"How is Mr. Malloy coming with his investigation?" he asked.

"Sadly, we haven't made much progress. Malloy told me you offered to accompany him to visit that Lou Lawson."

"Did he?" Mr. Robinson seemed to find that amusing.

"Actually, Gino told me. I don't think Malloy would have mentioned it otherwise."

"Ah, that makes sense. I couldn't imagine Mr. Malloy would have admitted it to you, but then, I don't know much about how married couples behave with each other, so I couldn't be sure."

"I don't think there is any one way that married couples behave with each other, Mr. Robinson. It depends on the individuals involved. I think you'll find that if you treat your wife with respect and consideration, you will be rewarded with the same in return."

"I have a feeling that is excellent advice."

"I certainly hope so."

They heard the motorcar pulling up outside, its rattle unmistakable. Mr. Robinson instantly jumped to his feet, betraying the anxiety he had managed to keep controlled until now.

"Please sit down and let me go to meet Miss Vane," Sarah said. "She'll want to freshen up before she sees you, I'm sure. Riding in the motorcar leaves one a bit windblown."

He looked as if he wanted to argue with her but at last he nodded, taking a seat again only when she left the room, closing the door behind her.

Jocelyn was definitely windblown but still lovely. The ride had brought color to her cheeks and a brightness to her eyes, which widened in sudden apprehension when Sarah said, "He's already arrived."

But Sarah and Maeve rushed her off to Mother Malloy's apartment so she could remove her duster and hat and make repairs to her hair.

"Has he said anything?" Jocelyn whispered to Sarah when she was finally ready.

"He's nervous, too. I told Hattie to bring in some tea when you arrived, so you'll have something to do. If you need anything, you can ring or just call. Maeve or I will hear you."

Jocelyn nodded and then lifted her chin and drew a fortifying breath. "I'm ready."

Sarah escorted her in and saw the tea service delivered. Then she left them to it. Gino took the motorcar to the garage and spent the time tinkering with it. Maeve went to her room and Sarah retired to her private parlor to write some letters. She'd left the door open, so she heard Mr. Robinson call for her nearly two hours later.

She had to force herself not to run, especially when she saw Mr. Robinson's expression as he gazed up at her from the bottom of the stairs. He was fairly beaming, and Sarah couldn't help but beam right back at him.

"Are congratulations in order, Mr. Robinson?"

"I believe they are, but I'll let Jocelyn tell you herself."

Jocelyn was also beaming, although her eyes were a bit red and she was clutching a handkerchief.

"She says I shouldn't worry because she's crying," he whispered to Sarah.

"I'm sure they're happy tears," Sarah said. "Ladies who are in a delicate condition are often more emotional than usual, too."

"I can't seem to help it," Jocelyn said, dabbing at her eyes.

"Of course you can't. Mr. Robinson tells me you have news."

She drew another fortifying breath. "We have decided to be married on Saturday at Mr. Robinson's home."

"I've asked a friend of mine who is a judge to officiate," he said.

Sarah was a bit astonished to learn Black Jack Robinson was friendly with a judge, but that would no doubt be advantageous to a gangster.

"It will be a private ceremony, of course," Jocelyn said. "An elopement, really, but we would very much like to have you and Mr. Malloy stand up with us."

"Normally, I wouldn't speak for Mr. Malloy, but in this case, I'm sure he will be as honored as I am to be asked. Of course we will stand up with you. We'll also be happy to collect Jocelyn at the clinic and bring her to your home, Mr. Robinson."

"There's no need for that. I can fetch her in my carriage," he said.

"But you can't see the bride before the ceremony," Sarah said. "That's bad luck. Let us bring her to you."

"We don't want to start with bad luck, so I'll accept your offer," he said. "And we'll have a wedding breakfast afterward. My cook is already baking the cake. I believe you know her, Mrs. Malloy."

"I do?"

"Yes. I hired Tom and Marie O'Day when they found themselves, uh, without employment."

The O'Days had worked for Estelle's family and been her only protectors when she was young. They had also been very helpful to Frank and Sarah during that case. "You did? How delightful."

"I've thought so. Marie is an excellent cook, and Tom is a font of information."

"I'm guessing she will enjoy having a young woman to look after again, too."

"She assures me that she will, so long as the young woman doesn't want to run her kitchen."

"I wouldn't dare," Jocelyn said.

Sarah took a seat and they spent a few minutes finalizing plans. Jocelyn had packed nearly all her belongings when she moved to the clinic, not knowing where she might end up after the baby was born, so she had a dress that would serve for the ceremony. They determined that on Saturday, they would bring her and her trunk in the motorcar first to the Malloy house so she could get dressed, and then on to Mr. Robinson's house.

When everything was settled, Sarah invited him to join them for lunch, but he begged off. "I'm afraid if I spend too much time with Miss Vane before the ceremony, she'll change her mind." That made Jocelyn laugh, as he had meant it to.

Mr. Robinson then took his leave, being so bold as to raise Jocelyn's hand to his lips, a gesture that obviously thrilled her. Sarah saw him out. At the door, he said, "I am indebted to you, Mrs. Malloy."

"Nonsense. No one is happier than I that the two of you have found each other."

"It's not nonsense, and I always pay my debts. My offer to assist Mr. Malloy still stands, and you may call upon me for anything that is within my power to do."

"That's very generous, Mr. Robinson, but totally unnecessary. You may repay me simply by making Jocelyn a good husband."

"I will do my best."

When he had gone, Sarah went back to the parlor, where she found Jocelyn perusing a sheaf of important-looking papers, and Sarah realized he had left the attaché case behind.

"What's that?"

"Oh, Mrs. Malloy, you won't believe what he's done. Now I know why he wanted a few days to prepare. He proposed to me, but not before he explained all this." She held up the papers. "He had an attorney draw them up. He has settled a sum of money on me. The money will be mine upon our marriage and remain mine no matter what, so that if I'm unhappy in the marriage, I can leave him and make my own way in the world, me and my child, and we'll always be taken care of."

That didn't sound right to Sarah. "So he's already decided that you're probably going to want to leave him someday?"

"Oh no! That's not it at all. Don't you see? He's done the kindest possible thing that he could think of for me. He's eliminated the one thing that terrified me, which is being left alone and helpless and unable to take care of my baby. I never have to worry that he'll leave me penniless. And he also pointed out that this will keep him on his good behavior because if he displeases me, I won't have to stay with him. How could I help but love a man like that? And how could I ever want to leave him?"

259

Sarah wasn't sure she saw the logic of that, but Maeve did, and the two of them marveled over Jack Robinson's generosity, which Sarah supposed was good. When Gino came in, he shared Sarah's confusion but was wise enough not to argue with the young ladies. Hattie had just told them luncheon was ready when Malloy returned.

They didn't want to discuss Pritchard's murder in front of Jocelyn and ruin her wonderful morning, but Malloy did manage to tell Sarah that Theda had no idea where Bergman's shops were located, and he'd had no luck in finding them himself yet either.

Malloy did accept the invitation to stand up with Mr. Robinson, and he was even more enthusiastic than Sarah could have wished. Most of the meal was devoted to hearing Jocelyn's opinion of Mr. Robinson's thoughtfulness and kindness. Sarah was glad to see Gino managed not to roll his eyes and Maeve at least pretended an equal enthusiasm. Sarah had no idea how she really felt, but no doubt Maeve would tell her later. They were just finishing their meal when someone started pounding on the front door.

"What on earth?" Sarah said, but Malloy was already out of his chair.

"I'll get it, Hattie," he called to the maid, who had hurried out of the kitchen in response.

Hattie stopped in the dining room, and they

all waited, frozen by the implied urgency of the pounding. It stopped abruptly, and they heard a woman's voice raised in anguish.

"That's Mrs. Ellsworth," Sarah said, and they all hurried out to see what was wrong.

Mrs. Ellsworth was weeping and trying to speak but not making much sense. Malloy had put his arm around her and was guiding her into the parlor. Sarah took her arm and together they got her seated on the sofa.

"What's happened?" Sarah said, sitting beside her and taking her hand.

"Oh, Mrs. Malloy, it's terrible. It's Harvey. He's been murdered, too."

# XI

Sarah had Mrs. Ellsworth drink a few sips of brandy while they waited impatiently for her to calm down enough to tell them what had happened.

"They found him at the dairy this morning," Mrs. Ellsworth said when she could speak coherently. "I don't know all the details, but I gathered he had been there for a long time, maybe overnight. It took a while before someone thought to inform Mrs. Pritchard, and of course she was completely distraught. She must have sent for Mr. Bergman, and he was the one who came just now to inform Theda. Her mother thought Theda should be informed in person, but she was much too upset to come herself."

"Do they have any idea who killed him?" Frank asked.

"I don't know. I don't even know if they sent for the police, although I suppose you have to when someone is murdered."

"And they're sure he was murdered?"

Mrs. Ellsworth winced. "That's what Mr. Bergman said. I don't think he would have put it like that if they weren't sure."

"I'm so very sorry," Sarah said. "Poor Theda."

"Losing her father was awful enough," Mrs. Ellsworth said, "but her brother . . . He was so young, with his whole life ahead of him."

Frank noticed Maeve trying to get Sarah's attention, so he gave her a little nudge. When Sarah looked up, Maeve indicated Jocelyn, who was watching the whole scene with dismay.

"Malloy," Sarah said, "would you look after Mrs. Ellsworth for a moment while I see to our guest?"

With an efficiency that made Frank marvel, Sarah swept Jocelyn out of the room and organzed Gino and Maeve to return her to the clinic, all in the time it took for Frank to pour Mrs. Ellsworth some more brandy. By the time they were out the door, the additional brandy was doing its work, and Mrs. Ellsworth was almost calm.

"Where is Theda now?" Sarah asked when she returned.

"Mr. Bergman took her back to Mrs. Pritchard's house, and we sent word to Nelson to join her there. Before she left, Theda asked me to tell you what happened, Mr. Malloy, but I don't know what you can do."

"Not much at the moment, I'm afraid," Frank said. "We have to at least give the police time to investigate."

"Do you think they will?" Mrs. Ellsworth asked.

"I suppose we'll have to wait and see." It would depend on whether someone paid off the police commissioner again, though. Had the same person killed both Pritchard and his son?

Frank couldn't quite convince himself that two members of the same family had been murdered by different people in the course of two weeks. And if the same person had killed both men, would he use the same method to ensure he wasn't caught this time, too?

"But shouldn't we be doing something?" Mrs. Ellsworth asked.

"You should be going to bed," Sarah said. "I'll take you home and make you some warm milk."

"You can't expect me to rest with all that's happened, and besides, it's the middle of the day," she protested.

"I know, but you need to conserve your strength. You'll have to deal with Theda when she returns, and that will be difficult."

"Yes, it will. Poor child, she takes everything so hard, and this will be unbearable."

"Come along, I'll take you home."

While Mrs. Ellsworth was buttoning her coat, Sarah pulled Frank aside. "What will you do?"

"I think I'll go over to see what's happening at the dairy. Somebody will be willing to gossip."

By the time Frank reached the Pure Milk Dairy, things were very quiet. No crowds stood gawking. All the milk wagons had returned from their deliveries and were tucked away. The horses had been groomed and fed and stood dozing in their stalls. No policemen lingered. No coroner's black ambulance waited for its cargo. Frank made his way unchallenged into the building and up the stairs.

The workers were laboring away at pasteurizing the milk and bottling it in their snow-white cavern, although Frank thought the workers were quieter than usual. That would be only natural, under the circumstances. On the floor above, the clerks really were quieter, and they didn't seem to be working quite as industriously as Frank had seen them work before.

The young man at the front desk looked up, bleary-eyed, and frowned. "Who are you?"

Frank decided to play dumb. "Frank Malloy. I'd like to see Harvey Pritchard, if he's in."

A spasm of pain flickered across the young man's face. "You've been here before. I remember now."

"Yes. I'm investigating Mr. Pritchard's death."

"Just . . . Just a minute," he said, rising rather uncertainly to his feet. "Don't go anywhere."

He moved in the opposite direction of Harvey's office—presumably the office where his body had been found—to one on the other side of the room. He stepped into it and had a whispered conversation with someone. In another moment, he returned, followed by Amelio Bruno, who was scowling ferociously.

"Mr. Malloy, what are you doing here?" Bruno asked.

"I had a few more questions for Harvey. Isn't he here?"

"No, he's . . ." For a moment, Frank thought he would blurt it right out, but then Bruno glanced around and saw that every clerk had stopped even pretending to work and was watching eagerly to see what he would say. "Maybe you better come into my office."

Frank accepted the less-than-gracious invitation and followed him back. Bruno closed the door behind them, although Frank figured the flimsy walls provided little true privacy.

"Have a seat, Mr. Malloy." Bruno moved a chair that had been sitting against the wall to a spot closer to his desk.

Frank sat and, with a practiced glance, took in the room. Bruno had been in this office a long time. He hadn't bothered to make it more comfortable, but the amount of papers piled on every surface said that he had made the dairy his life's work. Bruno waited until he was sitting, too—in the chair behind his desk so that Frank had to gaze at him over the mounds of paper that made him significant—before breaking the news.

"Harvey Pritchard is dead."

"Dead?" This time Frank feigned confusion. "Oh, not the father. I'm looking for Harvey, the son."

"And Harvey the son is dead, too. We found him this morning."

"Found him where?"

Bruno shifted uneasily. "In his office."

"You found him dead in his office," Frank repeated as if trying to absorb it. "What happened? Was it some kind of accident?"

Bruno flinched ever so slightly. "The police say he was murdered."

"How?"

"Strangled, they said."

"Like his father."

Bruno shifted uncomfortably in his chair. "Not . . . exactly. They said someone choked him with their bare hands."

No, not exactly. "So if it happened in his office, you must have seen who did it."

"What do you mean?" Bruno asked in apparent surprise.

"I mean if somebody went into his office and strangled him, there's a whole room full of men who would have seen who it was."

"Oh, I see. No. I mean, it happened . . . Nobody was here when it happened. He'd been dead for hours when I . . . He didn't come in this morning, you see. Nobody thought anything of it. He's the boss now. He can come in when he likes. But I went into his office to get something and I found him. He was on the floor behind his desk, so nobody had noticed him before then."

"When was the last time anybody saw him?"

"How should I know?"

Fair question. "All right, when did you see him last?"

Bruno frowned, as if he might refuse to answer, but he said, "Yesterday around five o'clock, when he left the office."

"He didn't come in last night? To oversee the, uh, other activities?"

"We didn't have any *other activities* last night," he said with what sounded like bitterness.

"Why not?"

"Not that it's any of your business, but Harvey put a stop to it. He said it was too dangerous with you snooping around."

Bruno said that with some satisfaction, and Frank winced at a pang of guilt. Could stopping the nighttime deliveries have gotten Harvey killed? According to Jack Robinson, Harvey was involved with some very dangerous people, so it was entirely possible.

"Did you send for the police when you found Harvey's body?"

"Of course." Bruno seemed offended by the question.

"And are they going to investigate?"

"I don't know. They asked a few questions and then they left. You'll have to ask them."

Frank intended to.

Detective Sergeant O'Connor wasn't very happy to see Frank. "It's not even my case."

Frank had managed to catch O'Connor as he was leaving Police Headquarters, so he hadn't had to go through the formalities of asking for the detective at the desk and being sent upstairs. "I just want to know if they're going to drop it like they did his father's murder."

"How should I know? Ask Devery," he added with an evil grin.

"I'll do that, and I'll be sure to tell him you sent me."

That wiped the grin off O'Connor's homely face. "All right. What do you want?"

"You know what I want."

"And I told you, I don't know. It depends on who wanted the old man's death covered up and if they're the same one who did in the son."

"And who wanted the old man's death covered up?"

"How should I know?" O'Connor said in exasperation.

"Because you hear the gossip just like everybody else. What are they saying?"

"About the old man?"

Frank gave him his best glare. He responded by spitting on the sidewalk.

"Nobody will ever know who told me," Frank tried.

"I can't tell you what I don't know."

"But you can guess."

O'Connor glanced around to see if anyone was

paying any attention to them. No one was, of course, but he still whispered it. "I heard it was Lawson."

"Lou Lawson?"

"Shhh!" O'Connor said, glancing around frantically this time.

Frank managed not to sigh. Why did everything lead back to Lawson? Sarah wasn't going to like this at all.

Sarah had been able to get Mrs. Ellsworth to lie down on the chaise in her own parlor and after a few more sips of brandy, she'd dozed off. After instructing the maid to send for her if Mrs. Ellsworth needed her, she returned home.

Knowing she'd have to get Catherine at school if Maeve wasn't back from the clinic in time, she had no choice but to wait. Fortunately, Maeve and Gino got back just in time for Maeve to go after Catherine. Sarah told Gino what little they knew about Harvey Pritchard's death, and just as she finished, someone rang the doorbell.

Sarah went herself, thinking it must be Mrs. Ellsworth's maid come to fetch her, but it was a telegram being delivered instead. She tore it open before she even closed the front door, remembering Mr. Robinson's caution to Malloy about confronting dangerous people on his own. If he had gone to see Lawson without telling her . . .

"What is it?" Gino asked from the parlor doorway.

Fortunately, it was not a message about Malloy being injured. "It's from Mrs. Pritchard. She would like to see us—Malloy and me—as soon as possible."

"She's changed her tune," Gino marveled.

"She certainly has. That poor woman. So much tragedy."

"I don't think she considered her husband's death much of a tragedy," Gino said.

"No, but her son's is horrible."

"And this probably means she wasn't involved in her husband's murder. She might have had a good reason to want her husband dead, but probably not her son."

"You're assuming the same person killed both of them," she chastened him. "I don't think we know enough about Harvey's death to be sure of anything yet."

"You're right. Mr. Malloy would probably have said the same thing, although it's hard to believe two people in the same family would be murdered by two different people."

"Yes, it is, so I'm very anxious to hear what Mrs. Pritchard has to say. She seemed almost reluctant to find out who killed her husband, but now . . . Well, I guess we're making another assumption as well."

"What's that?"

"That she's sent for us to ask for help finding Harvey's killer. Maybe she just wants to make sure we don't look into his death at all."

"I guess anything is possible. Theda will want you to investigate, though. More than ever, in fact."

"You're right, and her mother probably won't be able to discourage her, if that's her plan."

"I think I need to drive you and Mr. Malloy to this appointment in the motorcar, so I don't have to wait to find out what Mrs. Pritchard wants."

The winter sun had already sunk low enough so the tall buildings obscured it with their false horizon by the time Frank returned and they set out for the Pritchard house. On the way he told them about his visit to the dairy and Police Headquarters.

"I don't like this at all," Sarah said. She was pinching her lips together, which told Frank she was being totally serious and would brook no arguments from him. "If this Lawson character is as dangerous as he sounds, there's no reason you have to risk your life to solve this case, Malloy."

"I'm not planning to," he said.

"And Mr. Robinson said he'd go with you to make sure nothing happened, didn't he?" Gino said, earning a glare from Frank that he didn't even see because he was paying too much attention to his driving. Of course, Frank appreciated that, but still.

"Besides, I'm no threat to Lawson," Frank said. "I'm not with the police, so I'm not going to charge him with a crime. All I want to find out is if he's behind these murders. If he is, I can't do anything about it. The law won't go after him and he knows that. The best I can do is give Theda a reason why her father and brother died."

"And what if he's so insulted by your questions that he decides to kill you on general principles?" Sarah asked.

"I don't think gangsters have general principles."

"Malloy, this isn't funny."

"I'm not laughing. At least wait until we've talked to Mrs. Pritchard. We may not need to talk to Lawson at all."

Except Frank was pretty sure he'd end up there eventually. Lawson's name had come up too many times already.

Mrs. Pritchard's maid let them in and invited Gino to warm himself in the kitchen while he waited for the Malloys to finish their business with Mrs. Pritchard. Obviously, the boy had made an impression when he'd been here questioning the servants last week. Gino readily accepted the invitation, giving Frank a wink to let him know he'd see what the servants might have overheard. The maid then escorted Frank and Sarah into the parlor to see Mrs. Pritchard.

She was sitting on a sofa with Theda. They had obviously been weeping earlier but had settled into their grief now and were calm. Frank also wasn't surprised to see Otto Bergman with them, although he wondered why Bergman hadn't talked Mrs. Pritchard out of sending for them. He rose to greet Frank and Sarah.

While Sarah went straight to Mrs. Pritchard and Theda to express her condolences, Bergman said to Frank, "Thank you for coming so quickly. I . . . I'm afraid I owe you an apology for my conduct yesterday."

"Yes, you do." Frank was delighted to see the color rise in Bergman's face.

"I hope you won't let your feelings for me affect the way you deal with Mrs. Pritchard."

"I'll try not to. Whose idea was it to send for us?"

"Ilsa's. Theda suggested it immediately, but she didn't have to work very hard to convince Ilsa."

"And you allowed it?"

"I have no control over Ilsa, but I didn't even try to stop her. It's obvious we need help to find out who has done this."

"It must have been quite a shock."

"Worse than a shock," he said grimly. "I'm not sure Ilsa will ever recover."

"Do they have any idea what happened?"

"The policeman who came here didn't tell us much. I went down to the dairy right away, but all they could tell me was that he must have been killed sometime last evening or during the night.

Someone strangled him. I gathered Amelio Bruno found him in his office late this morning."

So they didn't know anything more than Frank had been able to find out this afternoon. "Did they give you any idea if they were going to investigate?"

"The young man who came was just sent to deliver the news. He didn't know anything else. We can offer a reward, of course, but I don't have much confidence in them now."

Frank nodded and went to pay his respects to Mrs. Pritchard, whose eyes reflected the agonizing shock of sudden loss. He'd seen that expression on too many women during his years with the police. Far too often he'd also had little to offer in the way of justice to help alleviate their suffering, but he hoped this time would be different.

"Thank you for coming, Mr. Malloy," Mrs. Pritchard was saying. "I'm afraid I was extremely rude to Mrs. Malloy at our last meeting, and now I must beg her forgiveness and yours and hope you will be kind enough to continue your investigation in spite of my ingratitude."

"Of course, Mrs. Pritchard," Frank said. "We understand. We're used to dealing with families who are upset." He glanced at Bergman, who had the grace to flush again.

"Besides, I was the one who hired them, Mother," Theda said.

"And I must be grateful you did, darling. If

we had to rely on the police, I don't know what would become of us. Please, won't you both sit down? I have so many questions for you."

Frank and Sarah sat down in the chairs opposite the sofa where Mrs. Pritchard and Theda were sitting. Bergman wandered over to the fireplace and leaned against the wall, as if he wanted to be ready in case called upon to do whatever service Mrs. Pritchard considered necessary.

"First of all, I must explain that when I called on you yesterday, Mrs. Malloy, I was concerned because . . ." Her voice broke and she pressed her black-bordered handkerchief to her lips for a moment. Theda instantly slipped an arm around her shoulders, and Bergman took a step forward, ready to assist, but she recovered quickly and held up her hand to stop him. "I'm sorry. It's so difficult when I remember what I was thinking then and how very unfair I was. You see, I imagined—I know, it seems ridiculous now, but it made perfect sense then—that Harvey might have had something to do with . . . with Clarence's death."

"Mother, how could you have thought such a thing?" Theda cried.

"I know, but if you'd been here these past weeks . . . Your father was so angry with Harvey. They hardly exchanged a civil word to each other. Your father was never an easy man, Theda, but lately he'd become impossible. Nothing I said would placate him. I feared he was going to drive Harvey completely out of the house. The poor boy never had a moment's peace, so when your father was murdered . . ."

"I think mothers often imagine the very worst possible things," Sarah said. "We can't seem to help ourselves."

"Yes, that's it," Mrs. Pritchard said. "I've always been like that. I didn't think Harvey would hurt his father on purpose, of course, but I could easily imagine Clarence driving him to violence. Now I feel foolish and so very guilty. How could I ever think Harvey capable of such a thing?"

"Oh, Mother, Harvey could be impetuous," Theda said. "So I guess I can understand why you could fear his emotion might have overcome his reason."

"But now that I know how wrong I was, we need to find the real killer," Mrs. Pritchard said.

"Mrs. Pritchard, we don't know for certain that the police will fail to investigate Harvey's death," Frank said gently.

"I'm afraid I've completely lost confidence in the police, Mr. Malloy. If they'd done their job and found my husband's killer, my son would still be alive."

Frank had been working for almost two weeks and hadn't found the killer yet. He doubted the police could have done any better, but he didn't bother pointing that out to Mrs. Pritchard.

"Have you made any progress, Mr. Malloy?"

Bergman asked. His expression was blank, but his voice held a note of challenge.

Frank wanted to grind his teeth, but he said, "We've learned a lot about Mr. Pritchard's life, and we've identified several people who might have borne him a grudge."

"Including me, I suppose."

"Otto, really," Mrs. Pritchard chided him.

"Yes, really, Uncle Otto," Theda said. "Why on earth would you want to kill Father?"

So she really had no idea about her mother's true relationship with Bergman.

Bergman smiled benevolently at the young woman. "I know you adored your father, Theda, but he could have been kinder to your mother."

"But that's hardly a reason to murder someone," Theda argued.

"You'd be surprised," Frank said. "I've seen murder committed for far less of a reason than that, and in a case like this, we have to consider everyone close to the victim."

"Even their loved ones?" Theda protested.

"The people closest to us often cause us the most pain," Sarah said.

"And people hardly ever kill strangers. The killer is usually a friend or a family member," Frank added.

"Really? I guess I never actually thought about it," Theda said.

"And why should you, darling?" her mother

said quickly. "In any case, Harvey's death does effectively clear him from the accusation, which is some tiny bit of consolation, I suppose."

"But only a tiny one," Theda said, dabbing at her eyes, "because I never believed for one moment that he'd killed Father."

"And I certainly didn't do it," Mrs. Pritchard said. "So it must have been a stranger, as unlikely as that may be."

Frank glanced at Bergman, who still managed to appear unmoved. "We have discovered some odd things going on at the dairy."

"The dairy?" Mrs. Pritchard echoed.

"What kind of odd things?" Bergman asked, no longer unmoved.

"We're not exactly sure," Frank hedged, "but we think Mr. Pritchard may have been involved in something illegal."

"Impossible," Theda said. "My father would never have broken the law."

"Theda is right," Mrs. Pritchard said. "Mr. Pritchard had his faults, but he was scrupulously honest and demanded the same from everyone with whom he did business."

"I don't think he was a willing participant, but we know someone at the dairy was."

"Who?" Theda demanded.

"We suspected Harvey," Frank said.

No one sprang to Harvey's defense, Frank noticed.

"Do you still suspect him?" Bergman said with just a trace of sarcasm.

"We think he was somehow involved, but others must have been as well."

"What will you do now?" Mrs. Pritchard asked.

"Now we have to rethink everything we already know."

"And you *will* do that, won't you?" Mrs. Pritchard said. "You won't let my boy's killer get away."

"We will do all we can," Frank assured her. "Maybe you can help us a bit. When was the last time you saw Harvey?"

"I . . ." Mrs. Pritchard frowned. "I'm trying to remember. He didn't come home last night, or at least not before I retired, but that wasn't unusual. He was often out late with his friends."

Gambling, Frank thought, but he said, "And you wouldn't have seen him this morning, of course. Did you see him yesterday morning?"

"Yes, he was at breakfast. Then he went to the dairy, I believe. At least, that's what he said he was going to do."

"Did he seem worried? Upset?"

"He's been very quiet since his father died, not himself at all," Mrs. Pritchard said, "but I thought he was just grieving."

"Did he mention anything that was bothering him?"

"No, nothing, but he wouldn't tell me, would he? He wouldn't want to worry me."

281

He also wouldn't want her to know what was going on. Frank looked up at Bergman and then at Theda. "Did either of you see him recently?"

"No," Theda said. "I've seen Mother, but not Harvey."

Bergman simply said, "No."

"That's not much help, is it?" Mrs. Pritchard asked.

"Don't worry," Frank said. "We'll figure it out."

Gino found the cook in the midst of preparing supper, but she greeted him with a sad smile. "Mr. Donatelli, what brings you back here?" Apparently, she'd forgotten how his last visit had ended.

"Hello, Mrs. Young. I drove my boss and his wife here in his motorcar. Mrs. Pritchard wanted to see him."

"Oh yes, about poor Mr. Harvey's death. It's a sad day, Mr. Donatelli. That poor young man. He had his faults, you understand, but I've known him since he was a baby, and I'll be mourning him till the day I die." She used the back of her hand to wipe away a stray tear.

"Who are you talking to? Oh, Mr. Donatelli," Mr. Zachary said, coming in from the butler's pantry. "I hope you've come because you're going to find out who killed poor Mr. Harvey."

"I believe that's why Mrs. Pritchard sent for my boss."

"Sit down and I'll pour you some coffee to warm you up," Mrs. Young said.

Gino thanked them and took a seat at the kitchen table while Mrs. Young got a cup and filled it from a pot on the stove. The maid Daisy came in and gave Gino another smile.

"He's going to find out who killed Mr. Harvey," Mrs. Young told her.

"Maybe you can help us," Gino said, accepting the cup of coffee from Mrs. Young.

"I don't know how we could," Mr. Zachary said with a worried frown.

"Remember I told you my boss said the servants always know everything? You may not realize it, but you probably know something that can help."

To Gino's surprise, they all exchanged a guilty look.

"What is it? You do know something, don't you?"

"Well, I do, at least," Zachary said, refusing to meet Gino's gaze.

"About Harvey?"

"When you were here before, you were asking about the goings-on at the dairy."

"And you said you didn't know anything about that."

"And we don't . . . except for what we hear, like you said."

Gino tried not to betray his excitement. "Did you hear something in particular?"

Zachary glanced at Mrs. Young again. She said, "When you were here before, you said there was gossip about Mr. Harvey. We knew he'd gotten himself in trouble at school and Mr. Pritchard was right put out with him, but we didn't want to say anything about that. We didn't want you thinking badly of him, because we knew he'd never kill his own father. That's why we got so mad."

"But now we're pretty sure he didn't," Gino said, "so anything you can tell me could help us find out who did."

Zachary shook his head. "I don't know about that, but I do know Mr. Harvey got himself in bad trouble here in the city, too."

"That's why Mr. Pritchard was so mad," Daisy said, earning a sharp look from Mrs. Young. "Well, it was!"

"I guess you heard them arguing about it," Gino said.

Zachary nodded. "Oh yes."

"Because of his gambling?"

"You knew about that, did you?" Zachary said. He dropped his gaze, as if ashamed.

"We discovered that he was in debt to a very dangerous man. We wondered why Mr. Pritchard didn't just pay the debts," Gino said, to see what they'd say.

Zachary looked up instantly. "He tried!"

Gino blinked in confusion. "He did?"

"Of course he did. He was mad as a wet hen, but he couldn't let some gangster threaten Mr. Harvey."

"But you said he only *tried* to pay the debts."

"That's right. Mr. Pritchard went to see him, but he wouldn't take the money. He said Mr. Harvey had already taken care of it."

This time Gino blinked in surprise. "If Harvey had paid the debt, then why—?"

"He didn't *pay* it," Zachary said. "He *took care of it*. Mr. Harvey had made some kind of deal with the man."

"And it somehow involved the dairy and the milk wagons," Mrs. Young added.

"Which is why Mr. Pritchard was so mad," Daisy added, earning another black look from Mrs. Young, which she ignored.

Now everything was starting to make sense. "But Mr. Pritchard wouldn't have liked having his dairy involved in something illegal," Gino mused.

"No, he would not," Zachary confirmed heartily. "Mr. Pritchard, he didn't put up with anything the least bit shady, so he wasn't going to have a criminal using his wagons."

"But how could he stop it?" Gino asked, not really expecting an answer.

Zachary had one anyway. "He was going to go to the police."

"He was? Did he say that?"

"Oh yes. That night, New Year's Eve, he and

Mr. Harvey were arguing again. Mr. Harvey said Mr. Pritchard should be grateful because once his debts were settled, this man was going to pay them to keep doing whatever it was. They'd make a fortune."

"But Mr. Pritchard couldn't stand the thought of it," Mrs. Young added. "He might've shut his eyes for a little while to get Harvey out of trouble, but he wasn't going to do something illegal for profit."

"He told Mr. Harvey he was going to the police right after the holiday," Zachary said. "So Mr. Harvey stormed out of the house."

To do what?

Gino could think of several things, any one of which could have led to Clarence Pritchard's death.

# XII

Maeve had already put the children to bed by the time Frank, Sarah, and Gino returned home from the visit to the Pritchard house. Gino had told Frank and Sarah what he had learned from the servants, and all the way home they had been discussing that and their reactions to Mrs. Pritchard's summons. Maeve and Mrs. Malloy were waiting for them in the parlor.

"Come along to the kitchen," Mother Malloy told them. "Velvet put supper by for you. I'll heat it up."

They gathered at the kitchen table while Mother Malloy bustled around, clanging pots and pulling dishes from the cabinet. By the time they'd finished telling Maeve what they'd learned, their plates were full.

"So now what do you do?" Maeve asked.

"I think we need to find out exactly what's going on at the dairy," Malloy said. "That means we need to talk to somebody besides Bruno, who obviously doesn't want us to find out anything."

"Do you want to go there tonight? We could follow one of the wagons. Maybe the driver would talk to us," Gino said. "Somebody might have seen something last night, too."

"Bruno said they didn't take the wagons out last night, which is convenient," Malloy said.

"But he might be lying," Sarah pointed out.

"Or maybe whoever killed Harvey knew nobody would be there last night so it would be a good time to kill him."

"But if nothing was going on, why was Harvey at the dairy last night?" Gino asked.

"And why kill Harvey at all?" Maeve asked. "He wasn't as honest as his father, and he didn't strike me as the type to turn down an opportunity to make more money."

"The last time I spoke with him, Harvey was surprised when I asked him about the milk wagons going out in the evening," Malloy said. "He seemed to think that had stopped."

That made no sense. "Why would it have stopped? With Mr. Pritchard dead, there was no reason to," Sarah pointed out.

"That's true," Gino said.

"But if Harvey thought it had stopped and it hadn't, who was keeping it going?" Maeve asked.

"That's easy. Amelio Bruno," Malloy said. "I think we need to visit the dairy tonight. And stop frowning, Sarah, my girl. We can take care of ourselves."

"I certainly hope so."

Gino and Frank parked the motorcar out of sight of the dairy and walked over, but they saw no signs of activity inside. They were peering into one of the windows when a voice called out.

"What are you doing there?"

Frank jumped guiltily and Gino instinctively ducked. When they saw a shadowy figure that was obviously not a policeman, Frank felt more than a little foolish. "We're looking for Amelio Bruno," Frank said with what he hoped sounded like confidence.

"Nobody's here now. The dairy is closed," the voice said.

"Who's that?" Gino called. "Don't I know you?"

The figure emerged from the shadows. He was an older man, wearing a uniform that marked him as one of the dairy's employees. He had a club of some kind, but it was dangling from a strap around his wrist, so he obviously didn't consider either of them any more of a threat than they considered him. "I remember you," he said to Gino. "You've been nosing around here before."

"Yes, I have. Mr. Malloy, this fine gentleman spoke to me the first time we visited the dairy. He's worked here for many years," Gino said.

"Is that so?" Frank said.

"Yes, it is, and he also told me not to ask questions, but now Mr. Pritchard and his son are both dead, and Mrs. Pritchard has hired us to find out who killed them."

"Did she, now?" the man said.

"Yes, she did," Frank said. "So we can probably

ask whatever we want. But meanwhile, what are you doing here?"

"I'm the night watchman," he said a little indignantly. "It's my job to be here."

"And were you here last night when Harvey Pritchard was killed?"

"Was he killed last night?" the man said in dismay. "Nobody told me when it happened."

"That's what the police think. Did you know he was here?"

"Nobody was here last night," the man said.

"Harvey was," Gino said.

"And his killer was," Frank said.

"So maybe you killed him," Gino said.

"What? No, I never . . . I wasn't even here!" he cried.

"I thought it was your job to be here," Frank said.

The man's frightened gaze darted back and forth between Frank and Gino. "They . . . they told me to go home."

"Who did?"

"Uh, Mr. White."

"So somebody was here. Why did you lie to us?" Frank asked.

"I didn't . . . I mean, they . . . They always send me home when they're using the wagons."

"Why do they send you home?"

"I don't know. They say they don't need a night watchman if there's other people working here."

"Or maybe they just don't want you to see what they're doing," Frank said.

"Everybody knows what they're doing," the watchman said with contempt.

"Even Mr. Pritchard?" Frank asked.

The man glanced around, as if making sure no one was nearby to overhear. "He knew. He knew everything."

"And I guess Harvey did, too."

"Of course he did. He set it up, didn't he? Poor Mr. Pritchard didn't know a thing about it until it was too late, though."

"And did Mr. Pritchard know you weren't doing your job?" Gino asked.

"I did what they told me to do! Mr. Bruno, he's my boss and he tells me when to work and when to go home. And he paid me even when I didn't work, so what was I supposed to do?"

"Nothing," Frank said quickly, hoping to calm him. "You did what you were told. That's all any of us can do. But tell me about last night. You didn't see Harvey, but White and Bruno were here?"

"Well, Mr. White was. I didn't really see Mr. Bruno, but when Mr. White is here, he tells everyone what to do."

"And were there other people here, too? To take the wagons out?"

"No, not last night."

"Didn't you think that was funny?"

"I . . . It was still early. I thought maybe they'd be in later."

"And did they come later?" Frank asked.

"No."

"How can you be sure?" Gino asked.

"I know. Everybody knows. They see the wagons were disturbed and some of the horses are wore out. They never clean the wagons right either. Makes more work for everybody."

"I guess there was a lot of talk, then," Frank said.

"Not a lot, no. Just complaining about the extra work. Nobody wanted to lose their job. This is a good place to work, or at least it was when Mr. Pritchard was alive. Now . . . Well, I guess we was all worried about working for Mr. Harvey, but we don't have to worry about that anymore, do we?"

"No, you don't."

"Who's going to take over now, though?" the watchman asked.

"I'm sure they'll figure something out," Frank said. "So the only person you saw last night was White?"

"That's right."

Frank exchanged a glance with Gino, who looked as puzzled as he did. "Do you know where I can find this Mr. White?"

"No. He just shows up here on the nights when they take the wagons out. That's all I know and all I want to know."

"Do you have any idea why Mr. Harvey would have been here last night?"

"None at all, and no, I never saw him."

"What time did White send you home?" Gino asked.

"I guess around ten. Maybe a little after. I didn't pay particular attention. Look, you've got no business here, so you need to go."

"All right," Frank said. "We'll go, but first, did you tell the police all this?"

"The police?" he echoed in surprise.

"Yes, didn't they ask you any questions?" Gino said.

"No. I never even saw the police. They were gone by the time I came to work."

This time when Frank glanced at Gino, he saw his own amazement mirrored on Gino's face. If the police were investigating, they were doing a pretty poor job of it.

Frank pulled out one of his cards. "If you think of anything that would help us figure out who killed Harvey and Mr. Pritchard, here's where you can find us."

"I don't know," the watchman said, shaking his head and making no move to accept the card.

"What's your name?" Gino asked.

"Walter."

"Thank you for your help, Walter," Gino said. "I'm sure Mrs. Pritchard and her daughter will be very grateful."

"You won't tell Mr. Bruno, will you?"

"No, we won't tell anyone anything until we've figured out who killed these men," Frank said. "But whoever is in charge of the dairy when it's all over is going to be grateful."

Walter stared at the card Frank was still holding out to him for another few seconds and then he took it.

As Frank and Gino walked back to the car, Gino said, "Do you think he knows who killed Harvey?"

"I think he's afraid he does."

"Because White was the only one here."

"That does look suspicious. Why send him home if they aren't using the wagons that night?"

Gino nodded. "Yeah, unless you're going to do something you don't want any witnesses to see. So how are we going to find this Mr. White?"

Frank sighed wearily. "I'm afraid we're going to have to ask Amelio Bruno."

"Do you think he'll tell us?"

Frank smiled grimly. "I don't even think he knows."

"Of course I'll be happy to take the children on Saturday," Sarah's mother said. Elizabeth Decker was always happy to spend time with her grandchildren. "Although I'd love to attend the wedding, too. I'm sure I'll never see another like it." She had stopped by that morning on her way to her dressmaker's to tell Sarah how sorry she was to hear of Harvey Pritchard's death, and Sarah had asked her to take the children for the day on Saturday so Sarah wouldn't feel guilty about leaving them two Saturdays in a row.

"I'm afraid you aren't invited to the wedding," Sarah said with a smile, "because it isn't an actual wedding. It's really an elopement."

"I always think of elopements as exciting affairs with ladders leading up to bedroom windows and an irate father running down the street in his nightshirt, brandishing a shotgun."

"That's a little *too* exciting, don't you think?"

"Probably, but still . . . I don't suppose we could convince this Mr. Robinson to sneak his bride out of the clinic with a ladder, at least."

"Absolutely not. I just hope I'm doing the right thing."

"It's not like you forced either of them into this, although I have to admit, you were quite clever to have thought of it in the first place."

"Do you really think so, Mother?"

"It might be unorthodox, but it's a sensible arrangement for both parties. Arranged marriages were always the way it was done for centuries, and things worked pretty well."

"It didn't seem to work too well for the Pritchards."

"The Pritchards?" her mother echoed. "You mean the father and mother? Did they have an arranged marriage?"

"More or less. I'm not sure they call it that when the families involved aren't wealthy, and Mrs. Pritchard's family certainly wasn't, but Mrs. Pritchard was in love with someone else. Her parents pressured her to marry Mr. Pritchard instead because he was already a successful businessman."

"That's very sensible, I suppose. We all want the best for our children. Was the man she loved not as prosperous?"

"He was still very young at that time, but he became just as wealthy as Mr. Pritchard."

"How ironic."

"And sad. They're apparently still in love."

"Mrs. Pritchard and the other man? Oh my, this sounds like a novel."

"Not a romantic novel, I'm afraid. More like a potboiler."

"Then you don't think they'll come together now that Mr. Pritchard is dead?"

"It's certainly possible . . . unless one or both of them had something to do with Mr. Pritchard's death and ends up in jail."

"Oh dear, you did say it was a potboiler, didn't you?"

"Yes, I did."

"But surely neither of them would have wanted to kill the son. Especially his mother. Losing a child . . . You never get over it."

Sarah took her mother's hand as they both

remembered Sarah's sister, gone far too long now. "No, I'm sure Mrs. Pritchard couldn't have done it, but who knows about the other man?"

Her mother considered that for a moment. "I don't know. Would he want to hurt her that way? No matter how much he might want to be rid of the son?"

"I don't know him well enough to judge. But if he was willing to do that, I don't see how they could ever be happy together, even if she never knew."

"I think you're probably right. He wouldn't be the man she thought he was."

"Maybe her parents were right not to let her marry him," Sarah said with a sigh. "So this is another good argument for my arranged marriage."

"I'm not saying arranged marriages work all the time, mind you, but whenever you have both parties providing something of importance to the union, I think your chances for success are greatly increased."

"And in this case, they are providing each other with something they couldn't provide for themselves, so that's even better. Thank you, Mother. I feel better."

"I'm happy to help. And be sure to let me know when the Pritchard funeral will be, too. I'll be happy to take the children that day as well."

"Mrs. Ellsworth just sent me word that it's going to be tomorrow."

"Then I'll pick them both up from school. Mrs. Malloy will want to attend the funeral to support Mrs. Ellsworth, so that way she won't have to be worried about Brian."

"Have I told you how grateful I am that you've taken such an interest in Brian?"

"And why should we not? If he's your son, he's our grandson. Besides," she added with a tiny grin, "just between us, I think your father enjoys having a boy to fuss over. Did you know he's been secretly practicing signing?"

"He has?" Sarah could not have been more surprised if her mother had said her father was learning to speak Chinese.

"Oh yes. He said what was the use of having a grandson if he couldn't speak to him? I had to agree."

Sarah had to blink furiously to keep from tearing up. Her mother pretended not to notice. She said, "But poor Theda. She must be devastated over losing her brother, too."

"She is, of course, and I know just how she feels. I only hope we can bring them some peace by finding the killer and seeing that he's punished."

"Does Frank have any idea who did it?"

Sarah sighed. "He went out to the dairy again this morning. We've discovered that some gangster had forced Mr. Pritchard to let him use the milk wagons to transport stolen merchandise around the city."

"My goodness, how clever," her mother said. "Nobody would look twice at a milk wagon. How did they convince him to do this?"

"It seems Harvey had run up some rather large gambling debts, and this was a way of working them off."

"Why didn't Mr. Pritchard just pay the debts?"

"We heard that he tried, but the gangster refused to accept payment. He liked the arrangement and he even wanted to continue it after Harvey's debts were paid."

"But why would Mr. Pritchard continue to allow it?"

"Apparently, the gangster was going to pay and thought that would be incentive enough."

"Pay whom? Mr. Pritchard?"

"I suppose, but Mr. Pritchard wasn't going to let him. He told Harvey the night he died that he was going to the police."

"Oh dear."

"Yes, oh dear. So we think that's why Mr. Pritchard was murdered."

"But why kill his son?"

"We aren't sure, but we suspect Harvey may have tried to back out of the deal, too."

Her mother frowned, not at all happy with that logic. "Even if he did, why kill him?"

"Because . . ." Sarah realized she couldn't come up with a logical reason. "I think we just assumed the gangster killed Mr. Pritchard because he believed Harvey would continue the arrangement, and when Harvey refused . . .”

“They killed him, too, but who’s to say the next person in charge would agree? They might end up killing a dozen people and still not get one who would go along with their scheme.”

“You’re absolutely right, Mother. So maybe we’re wrong about the gangster. But if we are, then we have no idea who might have killed those two men.”

Frank’s morning visit to the dairy had been a waste of time, and he already regretted sending Gino to the office. Amelio Bruno had actually refused to see Frank at all, sending him away without even hearing his questions. Maybe Gino would have had better luck, but it was too late. So now Frank was knocking on a familiar door, and a man with a familiar face answered it.

“Mr. Malloy, how nice to see you again,” the man dressed as a butler said as he ushered Frank into the well-appointed home.

“It’s nice to see you again, too, Tom. Mr. Robinson told me he had hired you and Marie.”

“Oh yes. We were thinking of retiring, but Mr. Robinson made us a good offer, so we decided we were too young to retire.”

“Do you like working for Mr. Robinson?”

“Indeed we do. He’s particularly grateful for all we do, and Marie was very happy to hear he’s taking himself a bride. But then you know all about that."

"Yes, I do. My wife and I are looking forward to the wedding. I'm hoping to finally get to taste Marie's meat pie."

"Oh, she wouldn't serve that at a wedding. Not fancy enough. But wait until you see the cake. Now, I suppose you're wanting to see Mr. Robinson."

"Yes, I am. Is he in?"

"He's in, but he's not receiving visitors yet. He keeps late hours, you know."

"I do know, but I'll be glad to wait while he makes himself presentable. He told me to call on him if I ever needed help, and that's why I'm here." Sarah wouldn't like it, but by the time she found out, it would all be over.

"He's probably feeling generous because of what you and your wife are doing, so I'll go tell him you're here. Meanwhile, why don't you go say hello to Marie? She'll be glad to see you."

Tom escorted Frank to the kitchen.

"Look who's come calling," Tom said as he held the kitchen door open for Frank before going to find Jack Robinson.

Frank braced himself for Marie's sharp tongue, but to his surprise, she greeted him with a warm smile. "I hear you're coming to the wedding on Saturday, Mr. Malloy."

"Yes. I'm the best man, it appears."

"Oh, I think Mr. Robinson is the *best* man," she told him with a grin. "He's the one getting married, after all. So what's the bride like? Mr. Robinson has been singing her praises, but we think he might be a bit prejudiced."

"She has a lot of potential, I think," Frank said. "And I'm sure she'll benefit from your guidance."

"She'll get that, all right. Of course, I wish he was marrying our girl, but . . ."

To Frank's surprise, she had to stop and use the corner of her apron to wipe away a tear.

"Yes, I'm sure he wishes that, too," Frank said.

Marie lifted her chin determinedly. "But he can't, so if this girl can give him some comfort and a little happiness, we'll be grateful."

"Yes, we will. Now, where's this cake I've heard so much about?"

Marie, of course, would not allow anyone to see the cake, but while they waited for Tom to return she did manage to find out everything Frank knew about Miss Jocelyn Vane.

Robinson received Frank in the dining room. He was still in his dressing gown. Tom served them both coffee and, a few minutes later, brought Robinson a hastily prepared breakfast.

"I've seen this White around," Robinson said when Frank had told him what they knew. "But I wouldn't know where to find him. Men like him don't have offices."

"What about Lou Lawson? Does he have an office?"

Robinson rubbed his unshaved chin. "I think I mentioned that Lawson is something of a recluse."

"Did you? I thought you just didn't know him very well."

"*No one* knows him very well. In fact, hardly anyone has ever seen him."

Frank frowned as he tried to remember what he'd heard about the man during his years on the police force. "Now that you say it, I know I've never seen him, but I'd never seen you before either."

"And that's the way I like it. I pay off the top people at the police and the courts and no one bothers me. In the old days, I had to do a lot of the work myself, but now . . ." He shrugged. Frank knew Robinson had many people working for him, managing and operating his businesses. They were the ones who got arrested if the police decided they needed to stage a raid to give the public the idea they were doing something about crime. Nobody would bother Jack Robinson, though, no matter how loudly the public clamored about law and order.

"Are you saying I won't be able to find Lawson?"

"I'm saying you won't be able to find him on your own. I can, though. Is that what you want?"

"I can't say I *want* to find him, but it doesn't look like we're going to get to the bottom of this without at least talking to him."

"He's a dangerous man, Malloy. Are you sure about this?"

"Now you sound like my wife."

"And I'm thinking about what I'd say to her if anything happened to you."

Frank sighed in exasperation. "Nothing is going to happen to me. I'm not planning to accuse him of anything. I just want to know about his arrangement with Pritchard and find out if he knew Pritchard had decided to go to the police."

"And of course you also want to know if he had Pritchard and his son killed," Robinson reminded him.

"I wouldn't expect him to admit it, even if I asked him, and I have no intention of asking him."

Robinson popped the last bite of toast into his mouth and chewed thoughtfully. "And what if he admits it?"

Frank hadn't even considered that. "Do you think he would?"

"To intimidate you, maybe."

"Why would he want to do that? I'm just a private detective. I can't arrest him."

"You can cause him trouble."

"How? The police have already been paid off—probably by him—so they aren't going to pay any attention to anything I accuse him of."

"You could go to the newspapers. Or to the reformers who would go to the newspapers. This would be a great story—evil gangster blackmails honest businessman into helping him steal from honest merchants. And the honest businessman sells milk, of all things! What could be more wholesome? Suddenly, everybody knows about Lou Lawson and everybody wants his scalp."

"That's actually a good plan," Frank said with a grin. "I could threaten him with it, at least."

"Not if you wanted to walk out of the meeting under your own power," Robinson said grimly.

He had a point. "I guess I won't mention it, then."

"Lawson will think of it, though. You have to be smart to be successful, and he's more successful than most. That means he's always looking ahead, figuring out what could go wrong and planning for it."

Frank considered this for a moment. "If he's that careful, why didn't he think about how this could go wrong for him before he started it? No matter how wild Harvey was, everybody knew Pritchard was painfully honest, and that he wouldn't go along with anything illegal."

"Are you sure *everybody* knew?"

"I can't speak for Lawson, but everybody who knew Pritchard did. I even had a dairy owner out in Brooklyn tell me that."

"I wonder if Pritchard would have been clever

305

enough to go to the newspapers when the police ignored his complaints, which of course they would have."

"He probably would've made a fuss of some kind. The newspapers would have caught wind of it sooner or later."

Robinson nodded. "You're right, that does sound foolish of Lawson not to have thought of possible consequences. It's almost as if . . ."

"As if what?" Frank asked when Robinson got lost in thought. Or maybe he was still not fully awake.

"As if he was more interested in aggravating Pritchard than anything else."

Did that even make sense? "Do men like Lawson even care about things like that?"

"Men like Lawson are still men," Robinson said with a shrug. "We're all petty creatures."

"But why would he even care about Clarence Pritchard?"

"I have no idea. Maybe Clarence delivered sour milk to his house one day."

"I don't think Clarence actually delivered milk to anyone."

"Well, his dairy's wagon did. I don't know, and you can't expect me to be clever at this hour of the morning."

"It's almost eleven o'clock."

Robinson glared at him before pouring himself another cup of coffee. "Or maybe I'm just being imaginative and Lawson simply made a mistake. But still . . ."

"Still?" Frank said encouragingly.

"It seems like a small operation for Lawson. I mean, how much can a few milk wagons carry?"

"My wife pointed out that they may have been carrying small things that are very valuable, like jewelry."

"She could be right, of course. Since I don't move stolen goods around the city, I can't really be sure."

"So that's another thing we can ask Mr. Lawson."

Robinson winced, but he said, "I'll need some time to set up a meeting."

"Send me a telegram. To my office," Frank added a little sheepishly.

Robinson's eyebrows rose. "Am I going to be as afraid of my wife as you are of yours?"

"I hope so."

Robinson didn't need as much time as Frank had expected. He received the telegram a few hours later. He and Gino had been reviewing the case in the privacy of their offices and trying to decide what Frank should ask Lawson and what he actually *could* ask Lawson without giving too much offense. Unfortunately, they hadn't reached any good conclusions. Robinson's instructions were to meet him at the corner of Madison Avenue and 66th Street. It was a familiar area, not too far from Robinson's house and close to the Pritchards' and even to Bergman's house. How odd they all lived in the same neighborhood.

"Mr. Donatelli," Robinson said with some amusement when Gino and Frank found him sitting in his carriage at the appointed meeting spot. "Are you Malloy's bodyguard?"

"That's what I'm going to tell Mrs. Malloy," Gino replied, equally amused.

"No, you aren't, because I don't think we're going to tell her anything at all about this," Frank said.

Neither man seemed to believe him. Robinson climbed down from his carriage and said, "It's that building."

"We were just there the other day," Gino said.

"Not seeing Mr. Lawson, I assume," Robinson said.

"No, someone else connected with the Pritchards," Frank said.

"But not the killer?" Robinson asked, leading the way across the street.

"Unfortunately, no."

Robinson didn't bother checking the building directory but led them straight to the elevator. The operator took them to the fourth floor.

"Gino, you wait in the hall," Frank said. "We don't want Mr. Lawson to think we're ganging up on him," Frank said.

Gino nodded and stepped back when Robinson

stopped in front of an unmarked door. "This is it."

"You've been here before?" Frank asked.

Robinson just smiled and opened the door.

"Good afternoon, Mr. Robinson," a woman's voice said. "Mr. Lawson is expecting you."

She was a lot friendlier than the last time Frank had encountered her, but when she saw Frank come in behind Robinson, her smile vanished, and Miss Kathleen Denson actually gasped.

"Miss Denson, how nice to see you again," Frank said, equally surprised.

She rose from her chair, her disbelieving gaze locked on Frank. "You didn't say you were bringing anyone with you," she said to Robinson.

"I'm sure I did," Robinson lied.

Before Kathleen Denson could think of a suitable reply, the door to the adjoining office opened and Otto Bergman stepped out.

"Jack, how are you?"

But that was as far as he got before he saw Frank, who was trying to come to terms with the knowledge that Otto Bergman was really Lou Lawson.

# XIII

"Malloy," Bergman said through gritted teeth. "What are you doing here?"

A rather large man who had been sitting unobtrusively in the corner, suddenly stopped being unobtrusive and rose in a threatening manner. His crooked nose and cauliflower ear marked him as someone who could handle himself in a fight. "Boss?" he asked, his gimlet gaze fixed on Frank.

Bergman gestured impatiently. "It's all right, George. Mr. Malloy is not a threat."

Frank deeply resented that dismissal, although he had to admit, he was grateful not to have to deal with George. He felt sure he could handle him, but an encounter would leave bruises he would have to explain to Sarah.

"I see Mr. Malloy needs no introduction," Robinson said, obviously amused and bewildered in equal measure.

"No, but he does need an explanation," Bergman said. "Come into my office and you can give it to me."

Frank followed Robinson into an office that was much more elaborately furnished than the one he'd visited with Gino one floor below this one. Directly below, Frank realized. Bergman

311

probably had a private staircase to easily move between his two identities.

"Have a seat, gentlemen," Bergman said, gesturing to the two leather, wingback chairs that sat in front of his massive mahogany desk.

"Do I need to apologize, Lou?" Robinson asked, although he didn't sound very sorry. "Mr. Malloy asked me to introduce you to him because he needed your help, and since I owed him a favor, I saw no harm in bringing him over."

Bergman didn't even glance at Robinson. He just continued to glare at Frank. This was a very different man from the one Frank had spoken with downstairs. This was a man who knew his power and how to wield it. He didn't need to make threats because his very name—the one he used in this world—was threat enough.

"And what exactly did you need my help with?" Bergman asked.

Frank took a minute to reply. He spent that minute by leaning back in his chair and folding his hands across his stomach as he waited for all the pieces to fall into place and everything to make some kind of sense. "I think you know, Mr. *Lawson*." Frank glanced meaningfully at Robinson, silently letting Bergman know he wouldn't reveal Bergman's other identity. "But now I have some more questions that I think you might prefer to discuss in private."

Bergman finally glanced at Robinson, but only

for an instant. "What makes you think I'll answer any of your questions, privately or not?"

"The last time I saw you, you indicated you wanted Harvey Pritchard's murder solved. People you care about want that, too."

"I can't help you with that."

"I think you can, but we won't find out which of us is right until I ask my new questions."

Jack Robinson rose from his chair, still both amused and bewildered. "I can see I am no longer needed here. I will leave you gentlemen to your private business."

Finally, Bergman fully acknowledged Robinson's presence. "We'll discuss this later, Jack."

"Of course." If Jack had any apprehension about that discussion, he gave no sign of it.

Both men waited until the door had closed behind Robinson. Even then, Frank held his tongue, knowing how uncomfortable silence made most people, so uncomfortable that they had to fill it. He wanted to see what Bergman would say to him.

Bergman didn't last even a minute. "All right, you've discovered my secret. What do you want?"

"I just want some answers."

"White told me you'd been snooping around the dairy after hours."

"Did he tell you I wanted to see you?"

"You must understand by now why that wasn't possible."

"Yeah, it's all perfectly clear now, but it raises all kinds of new questions."

"Which I don't need to answer."

"No, and I can't make you, but unless you're planning to have George out there throw me into the East River—and I wouldn't advise it because then you'd have to deal with the wrath of my wife—then I could reveal your secret. Killing me seems a drastic step when simply answering a few questions would buy my silence."

Bergman sighed in obvious frustration. "I don't have people murdered, Mr. Malloy. It's very bad for business, because dead men can never make good on their debts. Usually just the sight of someone like George is enough to persuade people. I'm not saying I haven't had the odd associate who offended the wrong person and ended up with fatal injuries, but it wasn't by my orders."

"Then tell me what happened with Harvey."

Bergman rubbed the bridge of his nose as if his head was beginning to ache. "Harvey had a gambling problem."

"I know. It got him kicked out of school."

"Out of college, yes. He'd run up debts and the school felt he was a bad influence on the other students. His parents believed him when he promised not to gamble anymore, but I know his type. I make my living off of men like that. He wouldn't be able to stop, so I made sure he only gambled at places I own."

"Did Mrs. Pritchard know?"

"Of course not. She doesn't know anything about Lou Lawson. She thinks I own a lot of tailor shops."

No wonder Frank hadn't been able to find any of them. "Is that why you created Lawson? So she wouldn't know about your . . . activities?"

Bergman's scowl told Frank how much he hated admitting all this. "Her parents wouldn't let us marry because I didn't have any money, so I decided to make some as fast as I could. I started working for . . . Well, for men who knew how to make a lot of money fast. I was smart and ambitious, but by the time I was rich enough, Ilsa was married to Pritchard. I thought she'd leave him for me, but it wasn't that easy."

"Pritchard wouldn't divorce her, I guess."

"She was expecting Theda by then, and even if he'd agreed to a divorce, he'd never let her keep the baby. Then Harvey made it twice as hard for her to leave."

So they'd settled for seeing each other secretly, although Frank saw no reason to annoy him by mentioning that. "What I don't understand is why you wouldn't let Pritchard just pay off Harvey's debts."

"Who told you that?" he asked, furious all over again.

Frank shrugged. "Harvey and his father argued about it in front of the servants."

Bergman rubbed the bridge of his nose again. "It was White's idea. He's always getting ideas. Nobody looks twice at a milk wagon, he said. We could move things around the city at will, he said."

"And he was right, but I'm surprised you agreed to it, knowing how scrupulously honest Pritchard was."

To Frank's surprise, Bergman smiled. It was a mirthless smile, grim and full of anger, and it sent chills up Frank's spine. "That was how White convinced me. Pritchard was so damn honest, and we would be forcing him to break the law to protect his son."

"So you saw it as revenge."

"I like to think of it as retribution."

Frank thought of it quite differently. Bergman certainly had reason to be jealous of Pritchard and to hate him for taking the woman he loved, but had Pritchard deliberately set out to ruin Bergman's life? Frank doubted it. The fact that Bergman was considered a dear family friend meant that Pritchard had no idea how deeply he had injured Bergman, much less that Bergman was still in love with Ilsa and having an affair with her after all these years.

"Retribution, then. So White convinced Harvey and somebody told Amelio Bruno to go along, and suddenly all of Harvey's debts disappeared."

"It seemed fair to me," Bergman said, showing

no remorse. "Pritchard should have been relieved that he didn't have to pay them."

"Instead he was infuriated because his wagons were being used for something illegal."

"Which was the whole point."

So it was *petty* revenge or retribution. Robinson was right—men were petty creatures. "And you were going to keep using them, even after Harvey had worked off his debt."

"I actually didn't expect Harvey to ever work off his debt. He promised his parents again that he wouldn't gamble anymore, but I knew that sooner or later, he'd be back at it, especially if he knew how easy it was to pay off the debts."

"But then Pritchard decided to go to the police."

Bergman stiffened. "What?"

"He decided to go to the police. He told Harvey on New Year's Eve, the night he was murdered."

"Who told you that?"

Frank sighed wearily. "Someone who heard him say it. And you found out and—"

*"No!"* Bergman almost shouted.

The door burst open and George was there, chest puffed out, fists clenched, eyes scanning the room for threats.

"It's all right, George. Mr. Malloy startled me, that's all."

George scanned the room once more, then nodded and withdrew.

Frank managed not to sigh with relief.

"No," Bergman repeated as if they had not been interrupted. "I did not do anything because I did not know Clarence had threatened to go to the police."

"I used to be a police detective, Mr. Bergman, so forgive me for saying this, but any detective worth his salt would put it together like this: Pritchard tells his son he's going to tell the police that some gangster is using his milk wagons to move stolen merchandise. Harvey storms out of the house, probably to warn that gangster or at least his people that trouble is coming. Later that same night, someone the gangster sent finds Pritchard in the crowd at Trinity Church and strangles him."

"Except that Harvey never told me Pritchard was going to the police."

"How could he? He had no idea that you are Lou Lawson. But he might have told your man White."

"White would have come to me."

"Are you sure?"

"Positive."

"Does White know about your special relationship with the Pritchard family?"

Bergman's face colored, but he said, "He knows we are friends. Nobody knows the rest of it."

"And you don't think White could have decided to take care of Pritchard without bothering you?"

That at least made Bergman stop and think. "I don't believe he'd take a chance of angering me that much. He knows how I feel about outright murder."

"Maybe you need to make sure, because if he took it upon himself to kill Pritchard and then killed Harvey to cover it up . . ."

"I would never forgive him for killing Harvey. I don't think Ilsa will ever . . ." His voice broke, and he had to take a moment to recover himself. "You must believe me, Malloy. I might have hated Pritchard, but I would never have harmed that boy."

Frank did believe him, which didn't help a thing, because he was running out of suspects. Maybe White had gone renegade and defied a boss most people feared crossing, but that seemed doubtful. If the notorious Lou Lawson and his crew hadn't killed the Pritchards, then who had and why?

"If you wouldn't mind," Frank said, "I'd like to talk to White once you've finished with him."

Bergman's expression gave Frank chills. "Assuming I'm satisfied that he didn't kill them without my knowledge, because if he did, you won't have to trouble yourself with him at all."

Frank figured that went without saying. He rose from the comfortable wingback chair and then remembered one more thing he needed to ask. "By the way, are you the one who paid off Devery not to investigate Pritchard's death?"

Bergman hesitated just a moment as he rose

from his own chair, and some emotion flickered across his face, too quickly for Frank to identify it. "I did."

"You know that makes you look guilty, don't you?"

"Does it? That's funny, because the reason I paid him off was because I was sure Harvey had done it. I couldn't let them arrest him."

Which made perfect sense. "I'm sure Mrs. Pritchard would be grateful if she knew."

Bergman frowned. "You won't tell Ilsa and Theda, will you? About me being Lawson, I mean," he asked. For the first time, he actually looked uncertain.

"No, I won't, although I'd advise you to. If they ever find out some other way, it will be much worse than if you tell them yourself."

His expression hardened. "But it's much better if they never know at all."

Frank had no answer for that. "Let me know when I can talk to White."

"I will."

Bergman escorted him to the door and opened it for him. George was instantly on his feet, but Bergman gave him some kind of signal that caused him to relax. Miss Denson's expression told him how little she appreciated his unexpected visit. Just to annoy her, he pulled one of his calling cards from his pocket and laid it on her desk. "In case you need to get in touch with me."

The look she gave him would have drawn blood on a leather boot.

George opened the outer door for him and closed it behind him with a little more force than necessary.

Frank found Gino waiting in the hallway, just where he'd left him.

"Was that Miss Denson? Bergman's girl secretary?" Gino asked in an excited whisper.

Frank nodded and started walking to the elevator.

"Does she work for Lawson, too?"

"I'll explain when we get downstairs. What did Robinson say?"

"That he'd wait for us in his carriage."

"Good."

As soon as they reached the first floor and exited the elevator where the operator might have overheard them, Gino grabbed Frank's arm and stopped him in his tracks. "Now, tell me why Miss Denson also works for Lou Lawson."

"Because Lou Lawson is also Otto Bergman."

Gino's expression made Frank smile, in spite of everything, and Frank had to take Gino's arm to get him to move again. "Let's see if we can find Robinson's carriage."

That was no problem, since it was sitting right where they'd left it. When they'd climbed in, he asked, "Would you like me to take you somewhere?"

"Our office," Frank said, not wanting to have

to explain to Sarah how they'd met up with Robinson.

Robinson instructed his driver, and the carriage pulled out into traffic.

"So how do you know Lawson?" Robinson asked with great interest.

"Through a client, although I knew him by another name, and don't bother asking what it was, because I'm not going to annoy Mr. Lawson by telling his secrets." Frank gave Gino a warning look that he could not misinterpret. "He did convince me he didn't personally murder either of the Pritchards, though, and he promised to let me talk to one of his men who might know more about all this."

"Then you found this to be a profitable encounter," Robinson guessed.

In many ways, but Frank only said, "Yes."

"Do I now need to hire a bodyguard to protect me from George?" Robinson asked with the ghost of a smile.

"I don't think so. Lawson has his own reasons for wanting these murders solved, so if we can do that, I don't think he'll even care that you brought me to him."

"And *can* you solve them?" Robinson asked.

Frank exchanged a look with Gino. "We're certainly going to try."

"Oh, Mrs. Malloy, I don't know how we're going to get through this," Mrs. Ellsworth said as she and Sarah sat in Mrs. Ellsworth's kitchen, waiting for the water to boil for tea.

Sarah had brought over some food for their supper tonight. With the funeral tomorrow, Sarah didn't think they would feel much like cooking. Or eating, either, but at least they'd have something available if they did.

Mrs. Ellsworth shook her head in despair. "Theda can hardly go half an hour without crying, and with the funeral tomorrow . . ."

"Is she resting?" Sarah asked, having seen no sight of Mrs. Ellsworth's daughter-in-law.

"She's gone to visit her mother, although I don't think that will help anything. Mrs. Pritchard is suffering just as much, I'm sure, but they needed to discuss the funeral plans for tomorrow."

"I know it's distressing, seeing her like that, but I don't think her reaction is unusual. She lost two people whom she loved dearly."

"You're right, I know, but still, they were such violent deaths and so sudden."

"And so close together. I think it would be a wonder if she *wasn't* shattered. But at least she has Nelson."

Mrs. Ellsworth dabbed at her eyes. Sarah noticed her handkerchief had a black border, which meant she was sharing in Theda's mourning. "Poor boy, I know he feels helpless. I certainly do."

"What Theda needs now is someone to love

her, and I'm sure you're both doing a beautiful job of that."

"We're trying. I hope once the funeral is over, she can at least start to recover."

"She'll need some time, I'm sure."

The doorbell rang, and Mrs. Ellsworth's maid went to answer it while Mrs. Ellsworth got up to pour the boiling water into the teapot.

The maid came back looking a little puzzled. "There's a gentleman here. Says he wants to see Mrs. Nelson."

"Didn't you tell him she's out?" Mrs. Ellsworth asked.

"I did, but he said he'd wait."

Sarah and Mrs. Ellsworth exchanged a puzzled glance.

"Did he give his name?" Mrs. Ellsworth asked.

"Mr. Bruno, he said."

Mrs. Ellsworth frowned in confusion.

"He works at the dairy," Sarah said. "I think he worked directly under Mr. Pritchard, in fact." Sarah also remembered he'd once been in love with Theda and had spoken to her at her father's funeral. How interesting.

"Why would he be calling on Theda, though?"

"Probably just to pay his respects," Sarah said, deciding not to distress Mrs. Ellsworth by reminding her of Bruno's history with Theda. "I believe he was the one who found Harvey."

"Then we definitely don't want him talking to

Theda. People always think the bereaved want to know every detail of their loved one's death, but that isn't always true."

"No, it isn't." Sarah also remembered how distressed Theda had been when Bruno spoke to her at her father's funeral. She'd have to ask Theda about it. "I think the best thing would be to send Mr. Bruno on his way."

"Oh dear," Mrs. Ellsworth said, wringing her hands. "What if he refuses to leave?"

"I'll go with you. Surely, he won't dare defy both of us," Sarah said with forced enthusiasm.

"You're so kind to me, Mrs. Malloy."

Sarah followed Mrs. Ellsworth out to where Amelio Bruno stood in the foyer. He was holding a bouquet of flowers, of all things. His head jerked up expectantly when he heard their approach, but his expression grew grim when he realized neither of them was Theda.

"Mr. Bruno, is it?" Mrs. Ellsworth said. "I understand you're here to pay your respects to my daughter-in-law, but I'm afraid she isn't home just now."

"I told that girl I'd wait," he said. For some reason he seemed angry.

"That's very kind of you," Mrs. Ellsworth said, "but she has gone to visit her mother, and she'll probably be gone for hours. I would be happy to tell her you called and . . . are those flowers for her?"

He glanced at the bouquet as if he'd forgotten

he had it. The flowers were wrapped in a paper cone, the way florists wrapped them, and they looked a little the worse for wear for having been carried through the streets on a January afternoon. "I . . . I wanted to give them to her myself."

"Then you could bring them to the funeral tomorrow, but they might not keep well," Mrs. Ellsworth said practically. "If you leave them, I can put them right in some water. I'll make sure she sees them first thing."

"And you'll tell her I brought them?" he asked with another doubtful glance at the flowers.

"Of course."

Plainly, he hated the idea of leaving without seeing Theda, but Mrs. Ellsworth had skillfully left him with no other choice. "Can you tell her . . . ?"

"Tell her what, Mr. Bruno?" Mrs. Ellsworth asked when he seemed unable to continue.

"Tell her I'll see her tomorrow, at the funeral."

"I would be happy to."

He looked at the flowers again, obviously loathe to turn them over, but after another moment's hesitation, he thrust them in Mrs. Ellsworth's direction. She took them awkwardly, almost dropping them, but Bruno didn't seem to notice. He turned abruptly, opened the front door himself, and hurried down the front stoop, leaving it to them to close the door behind him.

"What an odd young man," Mrs. Ellsworth said as Sarah hurried to shut the door.

"I think he just isn't used to dealing with things like this."

Mrs. Ellsworth smirked. "You mean he doesn't know how to behave in polite company."

"I'm sure that's what my mother would have said."

Mrs. Ellsworth eyed the flowers suspiciously. "I suppose I better put these in water, although it looks like some of them are actually frozen."

"Theda will appreciate the thought, I'm sure."

"I'm not sure at all. I just realized that's the young man who once tried to court her."

So much for sparing Mrs. Ellsworth. "Now that you say it, I remember Theda mentioned him. It never came to anything, though."

"Oh yes, it did." Mrs. Ellsworth turned and headed back to the kitchen, leaving Sarah to follow. "She told me about it after you left. He made rather a nuisance of himself, too, I understand."

"I did see him speaking to Theda after her father's funeral. Nelson had to come to her rescue."

"I don't think she really required a *rescue,* but Theda did feel uncomfortable with his attentions. She didn't want to speak to him, but she also didn't want to have to worry about someone else's feelings when she was grieving her father."

They'd reached the kitchen, and Mrs. Ellsworth

laid the flowers on the table while she searched for a vase.

"Why would she have to worry about his feelings?" Sarah asked, sitting down at the table again.

"He's apparently still a little tender about being denied the opportunity to win her, although he couldn't have imagined for a moment that Mr. Pritchard would let his daughter marry one of his employees."

"But I gathered Mr. Bruno held an important position at the dairy."

"Maybe he does. I have no idea. I only know what Theda said." Mrs. Ellsworth had filled the vase with water. She set it on the table and began to unwrap the flowers and arrange them in the vase, discarding the ones she judged to be beyond saving.

"What exactly did Theda say about him?"

Mrs. Ellsworth's nose wrinkled as she tried to recall. "As a matter of fact, she tried to make it sound like her mother's ill-fated childhood romance with Mr. Bergman. Mr. Pritchard didn't consider Bruno a suitable husband for Theda and advised her to marry someone else."

"Are you saying Theda was really in love with Bruno and only married Nelson because her father insisted?" Sarah asked in surprise.

"Oh no!" Mrs. Ellsworth assured her. "It wasn't like that at all, even though Theda compared it to her mother's situation. Theda assured me she had no feelings whatsoever for Mr. Bruno. In fact, she had hardly even noticed him before he came calling one Sunday afternoon."

"And she gave him no encouragement?"

"I'm sure she wouldn't have—Theda is too kind for that—but I don't think she even had the opportunity to discourage him. Her father sent him packing immediately, with orders never to try something like that again."

"So he might be excused for imagining she returned his regard."

But Mrs. Ellsworth was shaking her head. "Perhaps at first, but certainly not after she married Nelson."

"No, not after that," Sarah said, but she couldn't help thinking that young men in love often delude themselves. Mr. Bruno's gesture indicated he still had feelings for Theda. Did he know the story of the Pritchards' marriage? Unlikely, but even still, maybe he imagined that Mr. Pritchard had forced Theda to marry Nelson when she might have chosen him if she'd been free to do so. How sad. Someone should tell him he was making a fool of himself, but even Sarah couldn't think who that should be. Bruno would hardly take Nelson's word for it. The most logical ones would be Mr. Pritchard or Harvey, but with them dead . . . A shiver crawled up Sarah's spine and she told herself to stop worrying about it. She'd seen obsessive love before, but surely Bruno wasn't afflicted with it. He also wasn't the first young man to be disappointed in love, and he was no business of hers.

"I can't believe you went to see Lou Lawson without telling me," Sarah said, not sure whether to be furious or terrified.

Malloy had waited until after supper, when Maeve had put the children to bed and he and Sarah had retired to their private parlor, before telling her about his visit with Lawson. He had obviously been expecting her to be furious.

"Jack Robinson was with me, and Gino," he reminded her.

"And I suppose you think the fact that nothing happened to you makes it all right that you didn't even mention it to me." She'd decided to be furious since the time for terror had clearly passed.

She was sitting on the love seat they had placed comfortably close to the fireplace in their private parlor, but she had her arms crossed in a very unwelcoming way. No one had ever accused Malloy of lacking courage, however, and he gingerly sat down beside her. "I was pretty sure Lawson wouldn't murder me right in his office."

"Don't joke. Nothing about this is funny."

"I'm perfectly serious. And besides, it turns out Lou Lawson is actually Otto Bergman."

Nothing about that sentence made any sense at all. *"What?"*

He tried a little grin, but she was having none of it, so he sobered instantly. "It seems that when Ilsa Pritchard's parents refused to allow them to marry, Otto Bergman decided he needed to find a way to make a lot of money very fast. He took up with some men who showed him the ropes, and before he knew it, he was rich. But he also figured Ilsa's parents wouldn't approve of a gangster, so he made up Lou Lawson to be the gangster, and Otto Bergman went on pretending to be a tailor."

Sarah couldn't even think of a response to such an amazing story. "He . . . he told you all this?"

"He had to give me some kind of explanation when I walked in and recognized him."

"What did Mr. Robinson have to say about it?"

"Nothing. He could see Bergman and I knew each other, so I had to tell him I knew Lawson through a client, but I didn't tell him anything else."

"Not even Bergman's real name?"

Malloy had the grace to wince at her tone. "Especially not Bergman's real name. And Robinson had the good sense to excuse himself when he realized Bergman and I knew each other."

"You see, even Jack Robinson is afraid of this Lawson."

Malloy chose not to comment on that. "At least

331

now we know that Lawson is just as interested in solving the murders as Otto Bergman."

"I thought we'd decided Lawson was the one who had both men killed, and now that we know he's also Bergman, he's got even more reasons to want Mr. Pritchard dead."

"But not Harvey."

"Are we sure about that?"

"I don't know how he personally felt about Harvey, but he really does care for Ilsa, and I don't think he would have killed her son. In fact, he pointed out that in spite of his reputation, he doesn't resort to murder, since it's very bad for business."

"*Bad for business?* Did he actually say that?" Sarah scoffed.

"Yes, he did. Dead men can't pay their gambling debts, apparently. So you see, I was never in any danger."

"Since you don't have any gambling debts, I don't think you can assume that."

Malloy sighed in defeat. "You're right, Sarah. I should have told you I was going to see Lawson. I just didn't want you to worry."

"Oh no, far better for me to be surprised when they find your body."

"Well, they didn't find my body, and I'm very sorry I didn't consult you. How long are you going to be mad at me for this?"

"I don't know exactly, but it will be a while.

Meanwhile, now that you've exonerated Lou Lawson, who is left who could have killed the Pritchards?"

"I have no idea. I was hoping you'd have some."

"None at all. I did learn a few new things today, but I don't see how any of them relate to the murders."

"Let me be the judge. What did you learn?"

"My mother came by this morning. She'd seen the notice of Harvey Pritchard's death in the newspaper, and she wanted to express her condolences."

"Did she think you'd be grieving Harvey Pritchard?"

"No, but Theda had lost her sibling, so she knew I'd be thinking about my own sister."

"Oh. I'm sorry. I should have realized that myself." He slipped his arm around her shoulders, and even though she still didn't feel like she should uncross her arms, she did allow him to pull her close as she blinked at the sting of tears.

"Anyway, Mother had some interesting observations about the case."

"You know I have great respect for your mother's observations."

She somehow managed not to smile at that because she was still angry at him, but she said, "Mother pointed out that it didn't make a lot of sense for the gangster who was using the milk wagons to kill Mr. Pritchard and Harvey."

"I wish she'd told you this sooner. I wouldn't have had to go see Lawson at all."

She did smile at that, but only a little and very grudgingly.

"Maybe you'll tell me her reasoning," Malloy said.

"She could see that the gangster would be angry if Mr. Pritchard threatened to go to the police. If the gangster could be sure Harvey would take over the dairy with Mr. Pritchard dead, then killing the father made some sense, but what if Harvey didn't want to go along with the scheme either?"

"And it looks like he might not have, which would explain why he was also killed."

"Except who is going to run the dairy now that Harvey is dead?"

She was gratified to see that Malloy had no answer. "I hadn't thought about it."

"I'm sure no one else has either, certainly not *before* Harvey was killed. So if no one knows for sure—and Mrs. Pritchard might even sell the dairy—how could the gangster be certain whoever took charge would go along with his scheme?"

"I see, so killing Harvey and even Mr. Pritchard was no guarantee that the scheme would continue."

"Exactly."

"Bergman said he was going to let me question his man White."

Sarah didn't like the sound of that. "Why? I thought you were convinced Lawson or Bergman or whoever he is didn't kill the Pritchards."

"I'm not positive one of his men didn't, though. Somebody may have decided it would help and did it without Lawson's permission."

"So you're going to meet with a man you think committed the murders," she said, not bothering to hide her dismay.

"But this time I'm telling you about it ahead of time." He went on before she could object. "You said you'd learned a *few* things today. Was there something else?"

She gave him a glare to let him know how displeased she was, but she said, "Amelio Bruno tried to call on Theda today."

"Bruno? What for?"

"He wanted to give her some flowers."

"That's a little strange."

"Especially when you remember that he once fancied himself in love with Theda, and apparently his feelings haven't changed very much even though she's married now."

"He was talking to her at her father's funeral," Malloy remembered.

"Yes, and she didn't seem very happy about it."

Before Malloy could reply, they heard the doorbell ring.

"Who could that be at this hour?" Sarah asked.

"I don't know, but I'll go."

He hurried out and Sarah followed, stopping at the top of the stairs, where she could hear what was said without being noticed.

Malloy had sent their maid, Hattie, back to her room, and he opened the door.

"I'm sorry to bother you so late, Mr. Malloy, but Mr. Lawson said I needed to see you right away."

# XIV

Frank didn't like the way White stood there with his hands in his pockets, where he could be hiding anything, but maybe he was just cold. He also didn't want to invite White in, but he couldn't have a conversation with him standing on the stoop.

With a quick glance out to the street, Frank determined the man had arrived alone. "You better come inside, then."

White stepped in, and Frank closed the door after checking the street again. White pulled his hands out of his pockets, and when Frank saw they were empty, he said, "Can I take your coat?"

White gave it up without hesitation, making Frank feel a little easier.

"Come inside and I'll get you a drink."

"I'd appreciate it." He rubbed some warmth back into his hands as they moved into the parlor. Frank turned on a few of the electric lamps. He hadn't intended the gesture to impress his visitor, but he could see that it did. The room really did look nice.

He invited White to sit in one of the overstuffed chairs while he poured each of them a glass of whiskey. White accepted his gratefully and took a swallow while Frank sat down in the chair beside his.

"I didn't expect to see you so soon," Frank said.

"Mr. Lawson told me to find you right away so I could set you straight." White grinned mirthlessly. "He doesn't like being suspected of murder, I guess."

"I was willing to believe he didn't know anything about it, but I thought maybe you'd decided to take matters into your own hands."

"And go against Mr. Lawson?" White asked without the slightest trace of irony. "No man with good sense would even consider that, Mr. Malloy."

"Can I assume you've got good sense?"

"I wouldn't have lived this long if I didn't. Only a fool crosses Mr. Lawson."

So much for Lawson's claim that he didn't like to use violence. "Did Lawson tell you to answer my questions?"

White winced. "He did."

"I can understand that you don't like this, Mr. White, but I'm trying to solve two murders."

"I don't know anything about them, I swear."

"You probably know something, though. Let's start with New Year's Eve."

White took another sip of his drink, apparently in fortification. "All right."

"Did you take the milk wagons out that night?"

"No. We decided too many people would be out because they'd be celebrating."

"But you were at the dairy anyway."

338

"How did you know that?"

Frank had no intention of admitting he'd guessed. "And young Harvey came to see you, all upset because his father was going to tell the police what you were doing with the wagons."

White nodded, albeit grudgingly. "I don't think Harvey ever really understood very much about how we run our business. We already pay the cops to look the other way, so it probably wouldn't have made any difference if the old man had gone to them, but you never know, and Harvey certainly didn't know that, so naturally he was upset."

"If his debts were already paid off, why should he care if his father put a stop to it?"

"Who told you they were paid off?" White asked with some amusement.

"They weren't?"

"I don't know what he told you, but Harvey wasn't ever going to get square because he could never stop gambling. I told him when he'd worked off his debts, we'd start paying to use the milk wagons, but we knew he'd never stop, so we'd never have to actually pay."

"But Harvey did come to the dairy to warn you."

"Yes."

"Why were you there that night if you weren't going to take the wagons out?"

White shrugged. "To make sure nobody got the

idea to use the wagons on their own. Some of our men are ambitious, and I didn't want to explain it to Mr. Lawson if one of them went off on his own and got caught."

"Who else was there?"

"Harvey, like I told you."

"And . . . ?"

"Bruno was working late, I guess. He was there when I arrived."

"Did he see Harvey?"

"Sure. He . . ." White had obviously remembered something important.

"He what?"

"He told Harvey not to worry. He said he'd convince the old man not to go to the cops."

Wasn't that interesting? "What made him think he could do that?"

"I don't know. I figured he was just saying that to calm Harvey down. The old man was pretty straight, and he hated what we were doing, so I didn't think anybody could talk him out of going to the cops if that's what he'd decided to do, but if Bruno wanted to try, more power to him."

"Did Harvey believe he could do it?"

"It's funny, but he did, I think. He calmed down, at least. In the end, Harvey arranged to meet Bruno later for a drink to celebrate the New Year."

"What was Harvey going to do until then?"

"He said he was going to try to find his father

and get him home before he got himself in trouble. Something about arguing with people about the New Year. It didn't make much sense to me, but he seemed real worried about the old man."

"Did Bruno go with him?"

"No. In fact, he kept trying to convince Harvey not to go himself, but he couldn't. Harvey had been drinking, and you know how the Germans are, head like a rock when they get an idea in it."

Frank didn't think that trait was reserved only for Germans, but he didn't bother to argue. "What did Bruno do?"

"After Harvey left, he said he had some things to do himself and he left, too."

"How soon after Harvey?"

"A few minutes. He went back upstairs and turned out the lights and got his coat and hat. Not long."

"So he might've followed Harvey."

"He wouldn't have to follow him. Harvey said the old man was going down to Trinity Church, so all Bruno had to do was head down there if he wanted to catch up with Harvey."

"That's true. When the old man died, what kind of a deal did you make with Harvey?"

White frowned. "What does that mean?"

"That means, did you change anything?"

Plainly, White didn't want to answer that, but he said, "We never got the chance."

"What do you mean?"

"I mean, after the old man died, Mr. Lawson said we should lay off for a while."

"But you didn't lay off. You came to Pritchard's funeral."

"That was just to keep an eye on Harvey, in case he got drunk and started saying things he shouldn't. Mr. Lawson was worried about him. But Mr. Lawson didn't want us to use the wagons for a while, at least."

"But I saw the wagons going out just a few days later."

"Because Bruno told us it was all right to start up again."

"Bruno? Did you take your orders from him?"

"He was running the place."

"But I saw Harvey in the office."

White gave him a pitying look and tried to take another sip of his drink, but his glass was empty. Frank got up and filled it again. When White had taken a healthy swig, he said, "Harvey may have come into the office, but Bruno was running the place. He told us we could start the runs again, so we did."

"Did you do them every night?"

White grinned at that. "No, not every night. Even Lou Lawson doesn't steal that much stuff."

"So you didn't use them the night Harvey was murdered."

"Tuesday night, you mean? No, we didn't use them that night, but not because we didn't need them. It was because Harvey and Bruno had an argument about it."

"When was this?"

"The night before. Harvey showed up at the dairy that night, and he was hopping mad when he saw us taking the wagons out. Seems like Harvey hadn't really given Bruno permission to start up the runs again. In fact, he'd asked Bruno about it that afternoon, and Bruno had sworn it had stopped."

Monday was the day Frank had gone to Harvey's office to ask him about the late-night runs. Harvey had insisted they weren't happening anymore. Frank had thought he was lying, but what if he simply hadn't known? Would Bruno really have gone behind Harvey's back? "Why would Bruno tell you to use the wagons without telling Harvey?"

"You'll have to ask him. I just do what I'm told."

"Were you paying Bruno something on top of taking care of Harvey's debts?" White shifted uneasily in his chair, and Frank realized he was onto something. "You were, weren't you? But why did you have to pay him?"

"He said the regular drivers were complaining. They'd come in and find the wagons were dirty or the horses weren't groomed or some other thing. It was extra work for them, so he needed to give them something extra, too, he said. He didn't want much, so I slipped it to him without Harvey or the old man knowing. We didn't want some driver complaining to the wrong people, did we?"

"And did you come in at all on Tuesday night?" Frank already knew the night watchman had seen him there.

"Yeah, but just to make sure nobody showed up for a run by mistake."

"Did you see anybody while you were there?"

"You mean did I see somebody kill Harvey? No, I didn't even go upstairs. Why should I?"

"I don't know, maybe to see Bruno."

"Why would I need to see him?"

"Because he tells you when you can use the wagons."

That shut him up. Frank let him stew for a minute, waiting to see what he'd say to fill the uncomfortable silence.

"All right, I did see Bruno. He told me he'd calm Harvey down and let me know when it was safe to start up again. He said he had to do everything now that the old man was dead, because Harvey didn't know how to do anything. But I didn't see Harvey."

"What about the night watchman?"

"Oh yeah, I forgot about him."

Frank doubted that, but he said, "Did you talk to him?"

"I . . . I guess I did. Bruno said to send him home."

"Then you *were* going to take the wagons out that night."

"No, I told you . . . Come to think of it, that's strange, isn't it? We usually only sent him home on the nights we used the wagons. I wonder . . ."

"What do you wonder?"

"Maybe Bruno had something of his own going on. He's a sly one."

"So he sent you and the night watchman home so he could do something of his own?"

White shrugged again, and Frank remembered his conversation with the night watchman. He'd been disturbed about something. Gino had wondered if the watchman knew who had killed Harvey, and Frank had theorized that he was afraid that he did. Now Frank knew—if White was telling the truth—that the only person left at the dairy the night Harvey was murdered there was Amelio Bruno.

Sarah stayed hidden until Malloy had closed the door behind White. When she stepped out of the shadows in the hallway, he said, "Did you hear?"

"Yes. Most of it, anyway. But why would Bruno have killed the Pritchards?"

"I've been trying to figure that out. White admits he was paying him off, so maybe . . ."

"Yes, but he wasn't paying him much, and he had to give at least some of that to the drivers who were complaining."

"He might have been lying about that and keeping the payments for himself. And maybe he thought if he ran the dairy and without Harvey's gambling debts to settle, they'd pay him a lot more."

"Maybe." Sarah took his arm and led him up the stairs. "But with both the Pritchards dead, how could he be sure he'd be the one to take over for them? Mrs. Pritchard might have decided to sell the whole thing and there's no guarantee he'd still even have a job there."

"But she wouldn't have sold with just Pritchard dead because she'd probably expect Harvey to take over, and Harvey obviously didn't know how to run the place, so Bruno would really be in charge."

"But Harvey would still be gambling, so how much money could Bruno really expect?"

"Not enough to tempt most people, I'd think, so killing Harvey doesn't make sense at all."

"Maybe he just got angry and killed him without thinking," Sarah said.

"Or maybe we're missing something," Malloy said.

"You mean we might have overlooked the fact that Bruno seems to still be in love with Theda?"

"That seems a little drastic. Even a gangster like Lou Lawson didn't *kill* Ilsa's family, and Bruno is no gangster."

"You're right, and killing her family hardly

seems likely to endear him to poor Theda either."

"I really need to talk to Bruno again."

"The funeral is tomorrow. Maybe you'll get a chance then." Although she thought that very unlikely.

Clarence Pritchard's funeral service had been a sad affair, with his daughter sobbing and his many friends lamenting his tragic loss. Harvey Pritchard's funeral less than a week later was more pathetic than sad. Harvey didn't have many friends to recall his great contributions to the dairy industry. Harvey also hadn't made any such contributions. In fact, he hadn't done much of anything worth recalling. One scrawny young man who had apparently known Harvey since childhood got up and mumbled how much he would miss Harvey, but otherwise, the minister was left with the task of eulogizing the young man. Even he had little to say.

Poor Theda was sobbing just as hard at this funeral, and this time her mother was, too. Ilsa might not have cared much for her husband, but she'd obviously loved her son and felt his loss to the depth of her soul. She might have been annoyed by his gambling and his having been sent home from college, but he was still her beloved boy.

Frank noted that Otto Bergman was no longer being discreet. He walked with Ilsa down the aisle behind the coffin and sat beside her in the family pew, offering what comfort he could. At least that helped ease the burden on Nelson, who had to comfort only Theda.

They had scheduled the service for the afternoon so the dairy employees could attend. Only a few of them hitched rides in the rented carriages for the trip to the gravesite afterward, though. Most dispersed to their own pursuits. So much for loyalty to the boss's son.

Although Frank would have greatly preferred riding in a carriage himself, he'd had Gino drive them in the motorcar. His mother had refused to go with them, judging the motorcar to be far too dangerous, and had chosen instead to ride in the carriage that picked up Nelson, Theda, and Mrs. Ellsworth, so Maeve had gone with them in the motorcar, too. Mrs. Decker was going to look after the children, so Frank would have four people watching to see how Amelio Bruno behaved.

"Did you see?" Gino asked when they were bundled into their dusters and lap robes for the trip to the cemetery. "Bruno drove one of the milk wagons."

"To a funeral?" Maeve marveled.

"See, there it is," Gino said as the wagon came lumbering by. "He's got it all decked out in mourning."

Indeed, he'd hung a black wreath on the back doors and draped the rest of the wagon with black crepe. Even the horses sported black plumes, like the horses pulling the hearse.

"I notice no other dairy employees are riding with him," Sarah said.

"They're probably too embarrassed," Maeve said. "Who is he trying to impress?"

"I hope it's not Theda," Sarah said.

No one had a response to that.

Gino cranked the engine and got them on their way. He'd hung back to join in at the end of the funeral procession, since some horses still shied or bolted when confronted with a motorcar, and he didn't want to cause a catastrophe. As a result, the trip to the cemetery was much slower than it would have been if he could have simply driven straight there. By the time they arrived and had walked to the gravesite, the coffin had been lowered into the freshly dug hole beside the still-raw earth of Harvey's father's grave.

Theda and her mother appeared to have exhausted themselves and stared dry-eyed down into the opening as the minister quoted scriptures meant to comfort them. How much tragedy could people stand? Frank knew the pain of losing a loved one, and while he didn't know the answer to that question, he did know Theda and her mother were near the breaking point.

Sarah clung to his arm as they listened to the minister's words, and he automatically glanced over the crowd of mourners to see who had made the trip. He found Amelio Bruno, his handsome face grim. Frank noted he had found a spot immediately behind the family, almost as if he were insinuating himself into that select group. He looked pretty harmless standing there, but in Frank's experience, few murderers looked the part.

At last the minister concluded his remarks, and the mourners stood back so the family could make their way to the lead coach. Frank watched Bruno, but he made no effort to follow or to speak to them. Like everyone else, he waited and then walked slowly on cold-numbed feet back to the ridiculously decked-out milk wagon.

Would he try to speak to Theda again, the way he had at her father's funeral? This time Frank wouldn't let Nelson be the one to interfere.

The scene at the Pritchard house was all too familiar, with the buffet in the dining room and mourners taking turns speaking to the surviving family members in the parlor. Sarah knew Malloy had assigned Gino and Maeve to watch Amelio Bruno and alert them if he did anything suspicious, but he seemed to be intent on behaving completely normally instead.

He greeted the handful of dairy employees who had come to the house, but they didn't seem particularly happy to see him, and they didn't stand around chatting with him either. Sarah couldn't spend the afternoon staring at him, so she found Mrs. Ellsworth and her own mother-in-law in a corner where they were unlikely to be noticed and joined them.

"It was a lovely service," she said because it was what people always said after a funeral.

"I wish they hadn't let that boy give the eulogy," Mrs. Ellsworth said. "I don't think he even knew Harvey very well."

Sarah thought his current associates would have been even less appropriate, but she didn't say so. "I've just remembered that Mr. Bruno spoke to Theda after her father's funeral and she seemed upset. I hope he's not going to upset her again."

"I do, too," Mrs. Ellsworth said. "I already warned Nelson. He wasn't at all pleased when he saw those flowers."

"What flowers?" Mother Malloy asked.

Mrs. Ellsworth explained.

"What kind of man brings flowers to another man's wife?" Mother Malloy asked when she'd finished.

"That's what Nelson wanted to know," Mrs. Ellsworth said, "although he didn't say that to Theda. She wasn't any happier about it than he was, I can tell you."

"Do you happen to know what he said at Mr. Pritchard's funeral that upset her?"

Mrs. Ellsworth frowned. "I asked her, and she couldn't remember exactly, but something about how she was free now that her father was dead and could do whatever she liked, so she should be happy. She didn't know what he was talking about, and she certainly wasn't a bit freer or happier now that her father was dead."

"What an awful thing to say," Mother Malloy said.

But it confirmed Sarah's worst suspicions about Amelio Bruno. She needed to find Malloy. She excused herself, but before she could escape, she had to pass Theda, who was, for the moment, alone. She reached out her hand, and Sarah could not ignore her silent request for company.

"How are you doing?" Sarah asked, taking a seat beside her on the sofa.

"I don't really know. When I'm not overcome with grief, I just feel numb. I keep thinking Harvey will come through the door and say something to make me mad. I used to think he was so annoying, but now I'd give anything to have him here to annoy me again."

"I know. I lost my sister a number of years ago, and I still think of things I'd like to tell her."

"Oh, Mrs. Malloy, I had no idea. How sad for you. But tell me, does it ever get easier?"

"I don't know if *easier* is the right word. You never stop missing them, I imagine, but you do eventually get used to not having them with you anymore."

"Does it help having new people to love?"

"I think it must."

Theda nodded. "I'm so lucky to have Nelson. He's been so kind to me these past weeks. I don't know what I would have done without him."

"He's a good man."

Theda looked around the room. "I wonder what's become of him. He went to get me some tea, but he's been gone for a long time."

"Someone probably stopped him to talk. People do that at events like this, and Nelson is too well mannered to ignore them, I'm afraid."

"You're probably right, but . . . I'm just being foolish, I suppose, but after everything else, I just don't want him out of my sight."

"I'd be glad to go find him for you, if you like."

"Would you?" she asked hopefully.

"Of course," Sarah said because she had just realized that two of the three most important men in Theda's life had been murdered and the last remaining one might be in mortal danger.

Frank was trying to decide which dessert to choose from the heavily laden buffet table when Maeve came pushing her way unceremoniously through the crowd. Oblivious of the nasty looks being cast her way, she squeezed in between two matrons and whispered in Frank's ear.

"Gino says to get your coat and get out to the motorcar as fast as you can."

"Why—?"

"Just go!"

Frank had no idea where his coat was, so he had to find a maid and she had to show him where she had piled them. He was sorting through them when Sarah found him.

"What are you doing?" she asked.

"Trying to find my coat. Maeve told me Gino wants me to meet him outside."

She started looking, too. "Have you seen Nelson?"

"Nelson? No." He'd found his coat and began to pull it on.

"I can't find him either. He's nowhere in the house." She grabbed Frank's arm when he would have hurried out. "Malloy, listen to me. I just realized that the man who stopped Amelio Bruno from courting Theda is dead, and Bruno actually told her that with her father dead, she'd finally be free. Now with Harvey dead, she's even freer, and that only leaves her husband."

Suddenly, Frank had a very good idea of why Gino needed him. "Dear God. Gino must have seen Bruno do something to Nelson."

"So now we know for sure why he killed them."

"And why he still needs to kill Nelson."

By the time Frank got outside, still buttoning his coat, Gino had started the motorcar and pulled it up to the front door to meet him.

"What's going on?" Frank asked as he climbed into the front seat.

Gino barely gave him time to get seated before pulling away. "I think Bruno kidnapped Nelson Ellsworth."

For a full minute, Frank was too busy trying not to fall out of the motorcar to even register what Gino had said. When he finally felt secure enough, he said, *"Kidnapped?"* Not as bad as he'd feared, but if he'd kidnapped Nelson, it very well might be.

"Yes. That milk wagon. I think I know why he brought it."

They were whipping through the streets now, or at least moving steadily. The frigid wind made it hard to keep his eyes open until Gino passed him a pair of goggles. When he'd managed to get them on, he turned back to Gino. "What happened?"

"I was watching Bruno, like you told me to. He went up to Nelson and said something. I was expecting trouble, but Nelson didn't seem alarmed or mad or anything. He just nodded and followed Bruno out of the room."

"And you followed them?"

"Of course." Gino took a corner a little too fast and Frank had to grab on to his seat to keep from being flung out of it.

"And they went outside?"

"I think Bruno must've told Nelson there was something in the milk wagon he needed help with. Nelson didn't seem to think anything was wrong, and they both went to the back of the wagon and opened the doors. I was still inside, peeking out the window, so I couldn't see exactly what happened, but after a minute or two, Bruno closed the doors, hopped into the front seat, and drove away."

"Where was Nelson?"

"That's just it—I didn't see him. I ran outside to see if he was standing there or even lying in the street or something, but there was no sign of him. So I ran inside and told Maeve to find you."

"So he must have somehow gotten Nelson into the wagon and locked him in."

"That's what I think. I didn't see any blood, and he didn't have much time, so maybe Nelson is still all right, at least for now."

"Please God, I hope so. How do you know where they went?"

"I made sure to watch which way he turned. I don't think he's going to the dairy because that's the other direction."

Frank craned his neck to see as far ahead as possible. The January sun had dropped below the city's horizon, casting the streets into shadows, and the streetlights weren't lit yet. "I don't see him anywhere."

"No, but it shouldn't be too hard to find him." Gino slowed down at the next corner, where a cop was busy holding up the building. "Excuse me, sir! Did you see a milk wagon go by here, all draped in black crepe?"

The cop blinked in surprise. For a second Frank wondered if he should claim to be a brother police officer, but he didn't need to. "Yeah, it just went by a few minutes ago."

"Did you notice if he turned off?"

"Yeah, right at the second corner. Why was it all draped in black?"

"Funeral. Thanks!"

Gino gave the engine some juice and they took off again, sending pedestrians scattering. The cop yelled something, but they couldn't hear it, so they paid him no mind.

"I see what you mean about not having any trouble following it," Frank said.

"Even if he hadn't put all that crepe on it, there aren't usually any milk wagons on the street this time of day." They'd reached the second corner, and Gino turned right. "You look down the side streets on your side and I'll look on this side," Gino shouted.

Gino was taking years off Frank's life by zigzagging in between the carriages, passing whenever the opportunity afforded and often when it really didn't, and the rapidly fading light made it harder and harder to see.

"There," Frank shouted when he caught a glimpse of the wagon several blocks down the side street.

Even Gino couldn't make the left turn that quickly, so he turned at the next street, inspiring a string of profanity from a cab driver whose horse almost reared when they turned only inches in front of him.

"Where could he be going?" Gino asked.

"He's heading toward the river."

This time Gino was the one who swore. "Do you think he's going to throw Nelson in?"

"That might be his plan. I'm pretty sure he wants to make Theda a widow."

# XV

Sarah made a point of not returning to the parlor. She didn't want to frighten Theda by telling her she hadn't found Nelson. Better that she just be a little worried because he hadn't returned yet. She found Maeve instead, and they compared what they knew, realizing neither of them knew very much.

"Gino and I were watching Bruno, like Mr. Malloy told us to," Maeve said when Sarah had told her what she suspected about Bruno. "Bruno was talking to Nelson, and the two of them went outside. Bruno drove away in the milk wagon and Nelson never came back inside."

"What do you mean Nelson never came back inside?" Mrs. Ellsworth asked in alarm, having managed to approach without their noticing. "Where would he have gone?"

Sarah and Maeve exchanged a desperate glance, and Sarah decided she needed to tell her the truth, as far as she knew it. "Gino saw Nelson go outside to the milk wagon with Amelio Bruno."

"The milk wagon? Why on earth did he bring that to a funeral, for heaven's sake? Oh, never mind. But why did Nelson go outside?"

"We don't know, but we do know he never came

back inside and Bruno drove off in the wagon."

Poor Mrs. Ellsworth was terribly confused. "Did Nelson go with him?"

"We think so."

"But . . . Nelson wouldn't just leave his brother-in-law's funeral."

Sarah took her hand. "We know. That's why Gino and Malloy have gone after them in the motor-car."

Suddenly, Mrs. Ellsworth understood. "Dear heaven, is Bruno . . . ? But why . . . ? Oh dear, does he intend to . . . ?" Tears filled her eyes and Sarah took her arm when she swayed.

"We don't know anything for sure," Sarah said, "but the important thing is that Malloy and Gino have gone after them. They won't let anything happen to Nelson."

Mrs. Ellsworth nodded, but her eyes were still filled with terror when Sarah managed to ease her down into a chair.


Amelio Bruno had timed his departure well. Twilight in the city muted colors and blended everything into shadows. Frank had begun to think his eyes had deceived him as they rumbled around corners to backtrack to the street where he'd seen the milk wagon, only to find no trace of it there.

Gino pulled up again, this time beside a group of young men who must have just finished their workday and were deciding how to spend their evening. "Say, did any of you happen to see a milk wagon go by here in the past few minutes? It was all draped in black crepe."

The young men had indeed seen it and they had found it hilarious, but they needed to argue for a minute or two before they could decide which way it had turned. Consensus finally put Gino and Frank back on the trail, and a right turn sent them closer to the river.

"What if we don't find him in time?" Gino shouted.

Frank didn't even want to think of that. "There, is that it?" he called, pointing.

Gino strained to see, but the darkness was closing in now, and the gas lamps in this neighborhood hadn't been lit yet. At least traffic was lighter as they neared the edge of Manhattan island. Work at the docks required daylight, so things were quiet here now.

But that also meant fewer people to help them track the milk wagon.

They slowed at every intersection but saw no sign of it.

"What should we do?" Gino asked.

"Keep heading to the water. That's probably what he'll do. We'll be able to see farther when we get away from the buildings."

So Gino gave the motorcar more juice and they sped forward, with Frank clinging to the frame and leaning as far forward as he dared, hoping for a glimpse of their quarry. When they finally cleared the last street, the vastness of the docks loomed before them. Enormous ships sat at anchor, dark and silent, but not every berth was filled. Like a mouth with missing teeth, black vacancies loomed here and there, and they would provide the easiest access to the water.

Gino stopped the motorcar with a jerk, and both he and Frank stood up, peering into the darkness. Frank scrambled up to the tonneau for a better view, and that's when he saw the milk wagon rumbling back toward the city.

Were they too late?

"What's the matter? What's going on?" Theda demanded when she came out into the hallway and saw Sarah and Maeve fussing over a distraught Mrs. Ellsworth. "It's Nelson, isn't it? What's happened to him?"

"Nothing," Maeve said quickly, moving to slip a comforting arm around Theda.

"Where is he, then?" Theda demanded, not fooled at all.

"Mr. Bruno has taken him," Mrs. Ellsworth said baldly.

Sarah managed not to snap at her for being so tactless.

"Taken him where?" Theda cried.

"We aren't sure of anything," Sarah told her,

using her most reasonable voice. Her mother would be so proud. "All we know is that Mr. Bruno apparently asked Nelson for assistance with something outside. Then Mr. Donatelli saw Mr. Bruno drive away in the milk wagon, and we can't find Nelson anywhere."

Theda raised a trembling hand to her lips as she absorbed this information. "You think . . . He's the one, isn't he? The one who killed Father and Harvey?"

Gino juiced the motorcar again, racing after the milk wagon at speeds Frank was sure exceeded twenty miles per hour. Frank somehow managed not to be thrown over the backseat and completely out of the motorcar, and he held on for dear life as Gino expertly cut across the horse's path and set it rearing in terror.

As soon as the motorcar stopped, Frank clambered down. He could clearly see no one was in the milk wagon's driver's seat. The horse must have been frightened into running, and when Frank reached the back, he saw the doors hanging open, the wreath gone, and the rear section of the wagon completely empty.

"They're not here," Frank shouted, running back and jumping into the front passenger seat. He pointed in the direction from which the wagon had come, and Gino jerked the tiller toward it, accelerating the vehicle like a madman.

● ● ●

"Theda, what's wrong?" her mother demanded. She'd been drawn by the sound of Theda's distressed cry when she'd realized what had become of her husband. Otto Bergman was at Mrs. Pritchard's heels, also demanding to know what was going on.

"Amelio Bruno is the one who killed Father and Harvey!" Theda cried. "And now he's got Nelson."

"What do you mean he's got Nelson?" her mother asked.

Sarah explained as briefly and as tactfully as she could. The need to protect Theda from the truth was gone now.

"How did Malloy know where they were going?" Bergman asked, and Sarah heard a tone in his voice she had never heard him use before. This was Lou Lawson, she knew.

"I think they were trying to follow the milk wagon. I imagine it wasn't too difficult to keep it in sight."

"But Bruno would have gotten a good head start. Where are those people from the dairy?" Bergman moved to the dining room door and scanned the remaining crowd. Within moments he had informed them of the crisis and sent them off to search the dairy and to find Bruno's lodgings and search them as well.

Sarah doubted Bruno would go to either place,

but she recognized Bergman's need to do something and the employees' need to help and left them to it.

The remaining mourners either offered to help with the search or simply slipped away, instinctively recognizing that the Pritchard family's new tragedy did not require an audience. Mrs. Pritchard and Mother Malloy took charge of Mrs. Ellsworth and Theda, making them as comfortable as possible under the circumstances, while Maeve and Sarah tried to answer everyone's questions, even though they had no more idea of what was going on than anyone else did.

Otto Bergman had the most questions, and when he was satisfied he'd gotten every fact that Maeve and Sarah actually knew, he'd telephoned someone—Sarah strongly suspected it was his "girl secretary," as Malloy had called her—and instructed her to spread the word to his men that he was offering a reward for the safe return of Nelson Ellsworth.

Sarah doubted the reward would be claimed. When she checked the clock on the mantel, she realized how much time had passed since Nelson had disappeared. If Bruno had intended to murder him, he'd certainly had ample time to do so unless Malloy had managed to catch up to him first. What chance would anyone else have of happening upon Bruno and Nelson in time?

Mother Malloy had just directed the maids to

fix everyone some strong, hot coffee when the telephone rang, its insistent shrill cutting the air like a knife. Everyone turned toward the sound, but for a long moment no one moved. It could be heralding good news, but it could also mean disaster. When no one made a move toward it after the second ring, Sarah rose.

"I'll get it."

It rang a third time before Sarah could reach the place of honor where it sat in the front hall. She picked it up, holding the mouthpiece close to her lips, and snatched the earpiece from its holder. "Hello, Pritchard residence."

"Sarah, is that you?" Malloy's voice crackled through the line.

"Yes! Where are you?"

"Police Headquarters."

Frank craned his neck, searching frantically in every direction, seeking signs of life in every shadow and finding nothing time after time. Gino was searching, too, moving the tiller back and forth as he swerved this way and that, hoping for a better view.

Then they saw them.

Two figures so closely locked in struggle that at first they seemed to be one enormous beast thrashing in the darkness.

"There!" Frank shouted, but Gino had already steered straight toward them.

Frank leaped from the motorcar before Gino even managed to stop it, and he raced toward the two men. One figure loomed over the other, hands around his throat, forcing the other to his knees.

"Bruno!" Frank shouted, and the figure jolted in surprise.

But before Frank could reach them, the figure on his knees delivered a roundhouse punch to his attacker's head, sending him sprawling.

Which was which? Frank realized it didn't matter. He ran to the sprawled figure while Gino went to the other. Frank recognized Bruno as he scrambled to his feet again, but this time Frank stopped him cold with a solid punch to the stomach, just the way he'd learned to handle rowdy drunks when he'd been a patrolman. A follow-up sock to the jaw sent Bruno down in a heap that didn't move again.

Frank turned to see Gino helping Nelson Ellsworth to his feet. He was rubbing his neck and coughing. "Are you all right, Nelson?"

"I think so," he managed. "He was going to kill me."

"We finally figured that out."

"He wanted to marry Theda," Nelson said in amazement. "He thought she wanted to marry him, too."

"I think we'll find that Mr. Bruno is a little crazy," Gino said.

Bruno groaned.

"Or more than a little," Frank said.

"Police Headquarters?" Sarah echoed, aware that everyone else had followed her out and now stood eavesdropping.

"Yes. Tell Theda that Nelson is fine."

"Nelson is fine," she announced to sighs and cries and cheers. "Why are you at Police Headquarters?"

"We delivered Bruno to O'Connor. He was very grateful after I told him Lou Lawson would most likely give him a reward."

Sarah glanced at Otto Bergman, who was watching her very closely. "I'm sure he will."

Malloy told her they would take Nelson home to his own house as soon as he'd given his statement, and she let Frank go back to finishing up his business.

"What did he say?" Theda asked, tears of joy running down her face.

"He said they're going to take Nelson home, but he has to tell the police what happened to him first."

"I'll send you and Mrs. Ellsworth home in my carriage to meet him," Bergman said.

In the end, Sarah joined them, along with Mother Malloy and Maeve. Bergman had decided to remain behind with Mrs. Pritchard, who refused Theda's invitation to join them. "I'm sure

Nelson won't feel like company, and besides, I'm exhausted. I'll come over tomorrow to hear all about it."

The men had not yet returned when Bergman's carriage delivered the women to Bank Street, but Sarah and her crew refused the invitation to wait at the Ellsworth house. They agreed with Mrs. Pritchard that Nelson wouldn't be in any condition for company and would appreciate being ministered to only by his wife and mother.

They heard the motorcar when the men finally arrived home and waited patiently while Malloy and Gino delivered Nelson to his loved ones and put the motorcar away. When the men came in, they all gathered around the kitchen table while Mother Malloy scrambled some eggs and made toast for the weary rescuers, who entertained them with the story of their adventure.

"Nelson was holding his own," Gino said when Malloy had finished. "But he was very glad to see us, all the same."

"Bruno didn't say it, but it was pretty obvious he intended to strangle Nelson and throw his body in the river," Malloy added.

"How on earth did he get Nelson into the wagon in the first place?" Maeve asked.

"He told him he'd brought something for the family, something from the dairy employees, I think he said," Malloy said.

"So Nelson went to help him carry it in," Gino

continued. "Once they were at the wagon, Bruno opened the doors and punched Nelson."

"While he was stunned, Bruno pushed him into the back of the wagon and shut the doors," Malloy added.

"I couldn't see any of that from the house, so I didn't realize what had happened until Bruno drove away and Nelson was gone," Gino said.

"But how did he hope to get away with it?" Sarah asked in amazement.

"The same way he'd gotten away with killing Pritchard and Harvey," Malloy said. "He had no idea we'd finally figured out that he was the killer, so he was feeling pretty confident, I guess."

"And he'd made sure there were no witnesses to any of the murders," Gino said. "Even this time, he didn't know we were watching him, and if anybody saw Nelson go outside with him, he could just say he was leaving and didn't know what had happened to Nelson."

"As far as anybody knew, he didn't have a reason to kill any of them, either," Malloy said.

"So Theda really was the reason?" Maeve asked.

"Yes," Malloy said. "He'd been stewing for months over Mr. Pritchard telling him he had no business courting Theda."

"Didn't he at least have the sense to give up on the poor girl when she married Nelson?" Mother Malloy asked as she went around the table refilling coffee cups.

"As a matter of fact, he convinced himself that Pritchard had forced her to marry Nelson and that she really wanted him," Malloy said.

"Why did he wait so long to get his revenge, then?" Maeve asked.

"I think the business with Harvey's gambling and using the milk wagons to move stolen goods gave him the idea of how to get away with it," Malloy said. "When Harvey came to the dairy on New Year's Eve, he told White and Bruno that his father was going to tell the police what was going on. Bruno didn't care one way or the other, but he realized that would be a good reason for White or his men to kill Pritchard."

"I see," Sarah said. "So he followed Harvey down to the church."

"Or just went there on his own, since Harvey had told them where Pritchard would be," Gino said.

"Harvey said he never found his father, but Bruno obviously did," Malloy said.

"Did he admit it?" Maeve asked in wonder.

"He was actually bragging about it by the time O'Connor got finished with him," Gino reported gleefully.

Mother Malloy muttered something disapproving.

"But why kill Harvey?" Maeve asked.

"White told me last night that Harvey and Bruno had an argument on Monday night. Harvey thought Lou Lawson had stopped using the milk wagons, and he was angry that Bruno had lied to him. According to Bruno, Harvey even threatened to fire him, and he certainly wasn't going to welcome Bruno as a suitor for his sister, so Bruno taunted Harvey on Tuesday about using the wagons again, and Harvey came back that night to make sure nothing was going on."

"But White knew he'd left Bruno and Harvey alone at the dairy that night," Maeve said. "He was a witness."

"Mr. White is not the sort of man who volunteers to testify in murder trials," Sarah said. "I'm sure Mr. Bruno wasn't worried about him coming forward."

"Not at all," Malloy confirmed. "And with Harvey and Pritchard out of the way, all he had to do was remove Nelson, and Theda would be his."

"Didn't Theda have anything to say about that?" Maeve asked in outrage.

"Don't forget, Bruno believed she was secretly in love with him."

"How could he believe a thing like that?" Mother Malloy asked. She'd taken a seat at the table, too.

Maeve smiled sweetly at Gino. "Young men are often delusional where romance is concerned."

"I'm so nervous," Jocelyn Vane said, placing a hand over her stomach. "What if he's changed his mind?"

372

They were tucked into the motorcar and wending their way through the streets to Jack Robinson's house. Gino was driving, but he was only a chauffeur today and wasn't going to stay for the ceremony.

"I'm sure Mr. Robinson is just as nervous and wondering if you've changed your mind, too," Sarah said.

"Even if he did change his mind, one look at you today and he'll change it back again," Gino shouted up from the front.

Jocelyn's mouth dropped open, so it was lucky Gino hadn't turned around to take a look at her himself. Sarah had to cover a smile. "You do look lovely," she said.

"I had to let this dress out. I'm getting fat. Do you think the judge will know?"

Sarah was sure the judge would have already guessed the reason for this hasty ceremony, but she said, "You still look fine."

"Am I doing the right thing, Mrs. Malloy?"

"That's a question only you can answer. We can take you back to the clinic if you like."

But Jocelyn didn't like that idea at all. She just shook her head and set her chin at a determined angle and stared straight forward until they reached their destination.

"Here is your new home," Sarah told her when Gino had stopped the motorcar.

"It's very nice," Jocelyn said in surprise.

"Yes, it is," Sarah said.

Malloy helped them both down from the tonneau, and Sarah allowed Jocelyn to hold her arm while they walked the short distance to the front stoop after they'd removed their goggles and dusters.

Tom O'Day opened the door and greeted them warmly. He wore his formal butler's outfit and looked very grand. "It's good to see you again, Mrs. Malloy," he added.

"Tom is an old friend," Sarah told Jocelyn.

"We're very pleased to welcome you, miss," Tom said with a small bow. "Everything is ready in the parlor, but Mr. Robinson thought you might want to freshen up after the ride in the motorcar. I'm told they're awfully windy."

"That's very thoughtful of Mr. Robinson," Jocelyn said, and Sarah smiled at the change in her. Suddenly, she'd transformed into the lady of the house, assuming the authority she would have here. If she was still nervous, it no longer showed.

"Callie will take you ladies upstairs," Tom said with an approving smile, indicating the maid waiting at the bottom of the stairs. "Mr. Malloy, Mr. Robinson asks if you will join him and the judge in the parlor."

Malloy was only too glad to make his escape, and the girl showed Sarah and Jocelyn to a bedroom that had been furnished with feminine touches but had the echoing emptiness of a room that was never used. "Do you suppose he intends this room to be mine?" Jocelyn asked, checking the wardrobe and finding it empty.

"I'm sure he hopes you'll be sharing his room, but this is a pleasant room all the same," Sarah said.

The two of them made repairs to their hair and when they were ready, Sarah opened the door to find the maid waiting with a small bouquet. "Mr. Robinson thought you'd like to carry this, miss," she said, dropping a tiny curtsy.

From Jocelyn's expression, she would like it very much.

Frank found Robinson and the judge in the parlor. The judge sat calmly on a sofa while Robinson paced nervously. "Is everything all right?" he asked the instant Frank stepped into the room.

"Perfectly fine. The ladies have gone to do whatever they do to make themselves more beautiful."

Robinson introduced Frank to the judge, but Frank well remembered him from his own days as a police detective.

"Did your visit with Lou Lawson have any repercussions?" Robinson asked when Frank and the judge had finished reminiscing.

"Lou Lawson?" the judge echoed in amazement. "What business did you have with him?"

"A case I was working on, and you'll be glad to know Mr. Lawson is very happy with the outcome. We found the murderer and Lawson wasn't involved at all."

"So I shouldn't worry that he'll bear me a grudge?" Robinson asked with mock concern.

"Not at all. In fact, if you need any favors from him, this might be a good time to ask."

The men were still chuckling over that outrageous statement when the parlor door opened and Jocelyn Vane made her entrance.

The maid escorted Sarah and Jocelyn downstairs and opened the parlor door for them. The men had been laughing about something, but they ceased the instant the door opened. Sarah stood back so Jocelyn could enter first. She wore a pale rose gown with darker pink roses and bright green leaves embroidered around the edges. Her hair was intricately knotted, thanks to Maeve's skill, and she wore a hat with a small veil over her eyes. The color suited her perfectly, and brought out the natural roses in her cheeks.

Jack's smile told Sarah—and hopefully Jocelyn—that he was far from changing his mind. In fact, he looked very happy with his choice at this moment. He came forward to greet them and lifted Jocelyn's hand to his lips as he had once before. The gesture had the desired effect of enchanting her once again.

"You look lovely, my dear."

"Thank you," she said, and her eyes said she thought he looked pretty good himself.

"Judge Willoughby, may I present my bride, Miss Vane?"

An older man with snow-white hair and a small, pointed beard came forward to acknowledge the introduction. "I can certainly see why you've chosen to give up your bachelor ways, Jack. How very nice to meet you, Miss Vane." He only shook the hand she offered, but she favored him with a smile as well.

"Shall we get on with it, then?" Jack said. "Mrs. O'Day, my cook, has a wonderful meal waiting for us, and she's warned me not to take too long or it will be ruined."

Jack offered his arm and escorted Jocelyn to the fireplace, where the judge had taken his place. Frank and Sarah stood to either side while the judge pulled a small book from his pocket, opened it to the proper page, and began the familiar ceremony.

Sarah remembered the day she and Malloy were married. It had taken two ceremonies to tie the knot for them, but they hadn't minded a bit. When she glanced over at him, he was watching her with a look that told her he was remembering, too.

When the judge called for the ring, Sarah knew a moment of dismay, wondering if Jack had even thought of that, but he reached into his pocket and pulled one out. Sarah had to blink at tears when he slipped it onto Jocelyn's finger.

A few moments later, the judge proclaimed them man and wife and told Jack he could kiss the bride. He turned to Jocelyn, gently cupped her face in both his hands, and kissed her tenderly. The roses in her cheeks bloomed and her eyes shone suspiciously bright, but she laughed in delight and the rest of them joined in.

After Frank and Sarah and the judge took their turns congratulating the couple, Marie O'Day came bustling in with a tray of glasses filled with champagne. Marie wore a neat black dress with a stiffly starched, snow-white apron, and she looked very pleased with herself.

When she'd served everyone, she took a moment to study the bride with a critical eye. If Jocelyn minded, she gave no indication. In fact, she studied Marie in turn. "Mr. Robinson says you have a marvelous meal in store for us. I can hardly wait."

"I hope it meets with your satisfaction, Mrs. Robinson," Marie said with a twinkle, making Jocelyn blush all over again at the use of her new name.

"If my husband is satisfied, I'm sure I will be, too."

And that was the moment when she won Marie.

Malloy came up beside Sarah and said, for her ears alone, "We're only two weeks into the New

Year and already you've saved one woman from becoming a widow and made another a bride."

"I can't take much credit for saving Nelson, but I'll happily claim the bride. Now, I think the best man should make a toast to the happy couple."

Malloy raised his glass. "Attention, everyone." When he had it, he said, "Best wishes to you, Mr. and Mrs. Robinson. May your troubles be less, and your blessings be more, and nothing but happiness come through your door."

Sarah thought that was a good wish for anyone.

# AUTHOR'S NOTE

I hope you enjoyed reading this book as much as I enjoyed writing it. I'm indebted to my friend, author Susanna Calkins, who suggested my victim could own a dairy when I was brainstorming with a few of my author friends. Neither of us knew about the history of milk in New York City, so imagine how excited I was when I read about the "milk wars," which happened a few years before this story and resulted in outlawing swill milk and saved countless young lives. Sarah is absolutely correct when she says that in the mid-1800s, half of all children in New York City died before the age of five. Contaminated milk was a leading cause of those deaths, and other diseases claimed those already weakened from the bad milk. Even after the milk laws were passed, some dairies still sold doctored swill milk for a period of time. We've come a long way in food purity since then.

The Checkered Game of Life was a real game, invented by a young draftsman named Milton Bradley in 1860. *Checkered* referred both to the board, which was patterned like a checkerboard, and also to the checkered way life sometimes goes. No dice were included because of their connection to gambling and because many people would not allow dice in their home, so

Bradley created an awkward cardboard device called a teetotum that spun like a top for players to use to determine how many spaces they could move. The game was played as I described, and even today it sounds like fun. One hundred years later, in 1960, the Milton Bradley company produced an updated version and called it simply the Game of Life, which you've probably played at least once. The new version is different from the original one, but the similarities are still very clear.

Fan favorite Black Jack Robinson originally appeared in *Murder in the Bowery*, so if you missed his story, you'll want to pick that one up, too.

Please let me know how you liked this book. You can contact me through my website, victoria thompson.com, or follow me on Facebook, Victoria.Thompson.Author, or on Twitter @gaslightvt.

Books are
produced in the
United States
using U.S.-based
materials

Books are printed
using a revolutionary
new process called
THINKtech™ that
lowers energy usage
by 70% and increases
overall quality

Books are
durable and
flexible
because of
Smyth-sewing

Paper is
sourced using
environmentally
responsible
foresting methods
and the
paper is acid-free

**Center Point Large Print**
600 Brooks Road / PO Box 1
Thorndike, ME 04986-0001 USA

**(207) 568-3717**

**US & Canada:**
**1 800 929-9108**
www.centerpointlargeprint.com